With This Heart

R.S. Grey

With This Heart

Published: R.S. Grey 2013

authorrsgrey@gmail.com

Editing: Taylor K's Editing Service

Cover Design: R.S. Grey

Cover Photos: Shutterstock ®

ISBN: 1497455642

ISBN-13: **978-1497455641**

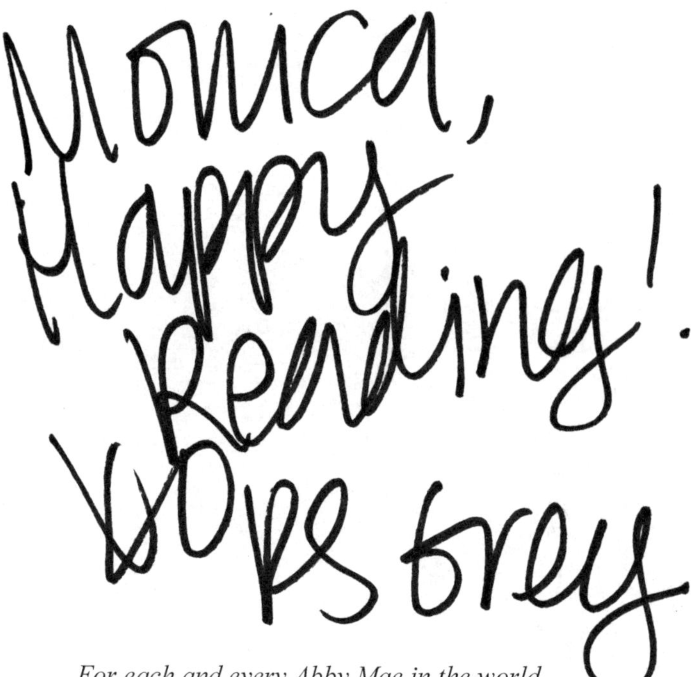

For each and every Abby Mae in the world.

CHAPTER ONE

On a rather insignificant Saturday afternoon, I stood in a funeral home searching through rows of urns as if I was browsing down the aisles of a super market. There were quite a few options to choose from. That fact surprised me. I thought there was a standard issue size and color, but no. They'd become a product of our economy long ago. Not to mention the guilt. Why would you want your loved one stuffed into a black, ceramic eyesore, when instead you could opt for a more personalized touch? They had it all: camo-print in the shape of a deer head, bedazzled hearts, and the ever-patriotic American flag emblazoned beneath a bald eagle.

Anyway, that's where I was standing, ogling all of the ridiculous choices, when he walked in.

The little bell on the door chimed merrily, which I thought was a strange touch for a funeral home, but I didn't turn around. Funeral homes are depressing and I had one mission: to pick out an urn and get out as quickly as possible. The echo of footsteps sounded behind me until a figure came to stand in my peripheral vision.

I froze.

Out of every aisle, this person needed to browse directly next to me? Wasn't this sort of a personal process? Does anyone have any decency anymore?

I didn't bother moving my gaze from the urns lined out before me, but he didn't let that deter him.

"I would definitely pick that one. Nothing says 'these are the remains of my loved one' quite like red and white polka dots," offered a gravelly voice.

It was that voice that convinced me to lose focus.

My gaze shifted to the left just enough to make out a guy with his hands tucked into his jean pockets and a navy baseball cap sitting on top of unruly brown hair.

His wry smile hinted at the fact that he was teasing me. In a funeral home.

I narrowed my eyes, trying to assess his motives, but I came up empty.

"I'll be sure to count your vote," I muttered flatly, and then turned to walk down another aisle. He didn't follow me right away, and I thought perhaps my curt response had offended him.

I was dragging my finger pad on the ledge of a shelf, letting it pick up dust, when an employee rounded the front desk. I hadn't noticed him before, but now he was impossible to miss. The grizzly looking man was a blob of black. He was trying in vain to fit into a cheap suit that might have fit him about ten years ago, perhaps when he could still see what his toes looked like.

"Hello. Welcome to Al's Funeral Parlor. Can I help you find anything today during your time of need?"

The spiel was obviously rehearsed, yet I still felt a pang of disappointment that his voice was bored and expressionless. Obviously the last thing he wanted to do was help me purchase an urn.

I didn't get the chance to answer.

"Yes. Al, is it?" said Gravelly Voice from behind me. I hadn't realized he'd followed me down the new aisle.

The employee shifted his thick eyebrows into a furrow. "No. I'm his grandson, Fred."

I didn't turn around, but I could feel the stranger stepping closer behind me. "Fred. What a great name. I do believe this young lady needs help. She looks sort of lost."

My head whipped around and I'm sure I was staring daggers at him. He said 'young lady' as if he wasn't a year or two older than me.

"What the hell. I'm not lost," I argued with a sharp stare.

His goofy smile never faltered. Who the hell was this guy?

My eyes swept down to his soft black t-shirt that read: "don't do school, eat your drugs, stay in vegetables". Then I glanced back up at his shadowed eyes. I could barely make out the color with his hat covering them, but everything else was there: the chiseled cheek bones, the straight nose, the sensual lips, the long lashes, and the strong eyebrows. If I wasn't standing in a funeral home, and if he wasn't borderline harassing me, I might have wondered if he traded his soul to look the way he did.

"Ma'am?" Fred asked, reminding me of the task at hand.

"Yeah, actually I'm looking for a simple black urn. Do you have any of those?" I gestured to encompass the parlor's entire stock. "It looks like I can get a black one if I also want it to have glitter, but that's about it…"

Fred did a poor job of hiding his eye roll before shifting his hefty weight and turning toward the door to the side of the front desk. "I'll check in the back." He grumbled like I was asking for the moon.

My eyes followed the man for a moment, and then I glanced up toward a sign hanging over the desk that read: "Our prices are *six feet* under the competition".

Tasteful.

"Well then," Gravelly Voice guy offered, rocking back on his heels and narrowing his eyes on me.

"I'm sorry, are you here to pick out an urn or…?" I asked, looking around for clues to his strange, albeit interesting, behavior.

"No," he answered simply.

"No?"

He shrugged his shoulders innocently. "I like coming in and checking out the latest models. Never know when you'll need one."

I gaped. "Are you serious?"

Cue a sexy smile. Damn. "No. I was getting a slurpee across the street and I saw you walk in, so I followed you on a whim."

I narrowed my eyes in confusion. Of course. He's too hot to be normal.

"So you're a stalker?" I asked with a hard stare.

He smirked, a knees-turning-to-jelly kind of smirk. "I prefer gravitationally linked by your presence."

Oh c'mon. I'd be lying if I said his answer didn't take me by surprise. I had to recover quickly and stay on task.

"Right. Uh, well you've successfully annoyed me so you can go about your day now." I was being harsh, but his entire demeanor felt like a threat to my rock-solid plan.

We stood there, locked in an awkward moment, and neither one of us made a point to end it. Most people I'd met in life were satisfied with surface content and meaningless pleasantries. Like the fact that everyone's default answer to "How are you?" is always "Good." But this guy was the exact opposite. He seemed curious, stubborn, and persistent, yet I didn't know him at all.

"What's the urn for?" he asked with brazen curiosity.

What?

"What? Who actually asks something like that? Don't you have a filter?" I could feel my eyebrows tugging together to form a judgmental scowl.

He slowly nodded his head once and I could tell he didn't want to drop the subject, yet he still backed off. "You're right. I'm sorry."

"It's for my dog." I crossed my arms and cocked my head to the side with a hint of attitude. There, now go away.

He licked his lips, trying to hide his grin. Shouldn't he feel terrible about bringing up my dead dog? Well, my fake dead dog, but he didn't know that.

"Ah, I'm so sorry to hear that. What was its name?"

He sounded sympathetic, but his eyes were narrowed on me as if he didn't quite believe me. It felt like he could see right through me.

"Sparky," then to truly seal my fate, I added, "he's real." Don't ask me why I felt like I had to justify my lie to him or why I chose to sound like a four-year-old when I said it.

He nodded thoughtfully. "Where are you going to keep his ashes?"

I could have lied, but something stopped me; instead, I found myself telling him, a complete stranger, about the secret adventure I'd been planning for the last month.

"I'm spreading them on a road trip." I said it with a shrug and a soft voice.

Without missing a beat, his smile unpeeled an inch wider. I couldn't strip my gaze away.

"I'll save you the trouble of asking. Of course I'll come with you."

I stared at him in utter bafflement. Every pre-set pathway in my brain was thrown for a loop by this guy, leaving me gaping in silence. He was the most arrogant person I'd ever met, but there was something hidden beneath his jokes. I think he actually wanted to go on the road trip with me even though he didn't know me at all.

Just as a retort formed on my lips, Fred stepped back through the storage room door. I paused and took in the stranger for one last moment before turning toward Fred.

A black urn was cradled in his puffy hands. Bingo.

"It's the only one we have, but it's got a chip on the corner," he muttered.

"Will you sell it to me for a discount?" I asked. It didn't need to be perfect for the plan.

"You can just have it," he shrugged, reaching out to hand it to me.

"Oh, okay, thanks. It's for my dog," I told him, letting the lie multiply and take root.

"Okay," he answered dead-pan. "Anything else?"

A whiff of sexy cologne brought my attention back to Gravelly Voice.

"I think this guy is looking for a casket," I offered, pointing behind me.

His throaty laugh followed me as I took flight toward the exit. My hands pushed against the thin metal handle of the door and soon the Texas heat greeted me with a vengeance. Oh, July, must you be so cruel?

"Hey, wait!"

The hairs on the back of my neck stood up on end. I tried to assess the situation as quickly as I could: It was the middle of a Saturday in a suburb of Dallas. People were milling about on the sidewalk. Cars zoomed by, making the hot asphalt seem even more extreme. This guy couldn't do me any harm in broad daylight. Though, if he did, we would definitely end up on the five o'clock news. *Talk about living on the edge.*

With that thought, I decided I could spare him a few more minutes.

"What's your name?" he asked the moment my ballet flats spun me around to face him.

His eyes were a light hazel with a bit of swirly green madness. I could see them perfectly now that we were in the sun.

"Abby."

He smiled like I'd just told him he'd won the lottery. It split his face in two, and instinctively I felt the corners of my mouth lift in response.

"Abby," he repeated. It sounded better coming from his lips than it ever had from mine.

"Yup." I tapped my foot.

"I'm Beck," he answered, pressing his hand over his heart. It seemed endearing even though I hadn't decided what to make of him yet.

"Like the band?" I asked, squinting my eyes and holding a hand at my brow line to shield the sun.

"Literally."

I smiled then because I couldn't help it anymore. It's hard fighting relentlessly quirky charm.

"I want to go on your road trip," he said again so confidently that I had to wonder if he'd ever been rejected before.

I cocked my head, and then shook it back and forth. "*My* road trip isn't accepting any new passengers, but I'm sure there are plenty of other road trips occurring throughout the world at the same time that mine is taking place."

He thought I was funny. He smiled at my comment, but I could see it more in his eyes. They were pinned on me, scrunched at the corners as he contemplated my rejection.

"I'm sure," he began, "but something tells me that *yours* is one I don't want to miss."

I rolled my eyes and took a step back for reasons I later realized were my body's last attempt at staying away from someone like Beck.

"How long will you be gone?" he asked. Maybe he had short-term memory loss. Either that or he was really good at sports as a kid. No one had beaten the fight out of him yet.

"Two weeks… but I'm not sure why you're asking since I would never go on a road trip with a stranger unless I wanted to end up joining a cult and drinking the Kool-Aid."

He thought my rambling was funny enough for another smirk. "Not everyone drank the Kool-Aid," he clarified. "Some people were sleeping or deaf, and they missed the call. Besides, it was Flavor Aid."

My mouth hung open. Then I studied him with narrowed eyes. "You're the strangest person I've ever met."

He didn't fight that comment. He reached into his back pocket and pulled out what looked to be a beat-up business card and a pen. With a flick, he flipped it over and wrote something down quickly.

"Let me know if you change your mind about the additional passenger." He smiled one last time and handed me the card. I took it even though I knew I wouldn't be changing my plans.

He didn't say bye or anything. He turned on his heel and jogged across the street like the last thirty minutes had never happened. I stood there, frozen, long enough to see him walk inside the gas station's store. When he emerged a minute later, he had a blue slurpee in hand and a pair of wayfarer sunglasses masking his greenish hazel eyes. *Maybe he hadn't been feeding me a line about the slurpee.*

His gaze lifted to me, and when I squinted I could see his wide grin across the expanse of suburban asphalt. No amount of sprawl could keep his charm from reaching me. He sidled over to an old blue Ford truck, hopped in, and pulled away without a second glance.

CHAPTER TWO

"Where are you keeping your spices?" Mom asked.

"What spices?" I asked, shifting my eyes around my counters.

"Like rosemary and thyme…those sorts of things."

"I have salt and pepper."

My mother's tight-lipped smile did a poor job of hiding her worry. As if by not having spices, I could therefore not provide for myself in other areas of life. Did she wonder how I even brushed my teeth on my own?

"We'll go grocery shopping again sometime this week and pick up the basics," she answered while nodding. She was nodding because my answer didn't matter. She had said a statement and then nodded to *herself* in agreement.

I ground my molars together, wondering if pieces of the calcium could chip off and get lodged in my throat.

What a strange way to go.

"You don't have to do that. I can go by myself." I tried to keep my tone calm and collected.

My father turned away from the stove where he was preparing egg whites and a vegetarian version of bacon. "Pumpkin, why don't you let your mother help you?" His hard stare told me to pick my battles carefully. What he didn't realize was that maybe I'd been storing up past battles in my head for too long and soon all the battles were going to break through the surface and turn me into a maniac.

But who was I to deny my mom her thrills in life: keeping me alive, and now apparently making sure my food was flavorful.

"Sounds fun. I guess I could use some spices," I relented, feeling a wave of fatigue hit me out of nowhere. I shuffled back toward the table and sat, trying to ignore the worried glances from my parents.

"I've been on my feet all day, decorating the apartment and shopping with you guys. Don't look at me like that." My stamina still wasn't where it should have been for a healthy nineteen-year-old, but I was getting there. Having them look at me like I was a baby bird wasn't helping.

"So are you enjoying your apartment?" Mom asked, trying to change the subject.

I had moved into my own place a little over a month ago. It had taken a lot of lobbying, and even a well thought out power-point presentation, before my parents even considered the idea. We ended up compromising. I was allowed to get my own place if it was down the street from their house. So, there I was, sitting in my one bedroom crap-apartment two minutes from my childhood home, and

I loved it. It was freedom. That chipping paint was mine; the creaky floorboards were my home.

"I really like it."

"Have you met any of your neighbors?" my dad asked, flipping the eggs.

I considered lying to them, just to put their minds at ease, but instead I decided to withhold the truth. There's a difference. I didn't want to tell them I had met my neighbors to the left: an old gay couple, one part blind man, one part disabled veteran. It was quite an interesting amalgam until the blind man hammered drunkenly on my door the other night. Literally hammered, with a hammer. He was demanding that I give him back the thirteen dollars I'd apparently stolen from him. I had no clue what he was talking about. I never answered the door and he had eventually wandered back to his apartment.

"No, not yet, but I haven't left the apartment much," I lied.

"Hmm, I'm sure you'll meet some nice people soon," my father promised as he slid the eggs and faux bacon onto a large serving plate and brought it over to my kitchen table/desk/collector of random items. Currently, a distressed owl candle holder and a pile of medical pamphlets served as a centerpiece for our breakfast.

My mother's brown eyes caught mine as she took the seat opposite me and I wondered for the millionth time where the hell my features had come from. They both had brown hair and brown eyes. Yet, I had light strawberry blonde hair and sage green eyes. My mother always told me that my hair color skipped a generation; according to my mom, when my Nanna was young she had wild golden hair, too. I had to take her word for it since none of my grandparents were still alive.

We ate in silence for a few minutes until my parent's nervous fretting made my skin crawl.

"What are you guys planning to do for the rest of the day?" I asked, pleading with the gods that they had plans that took them far, far away.

"We were going to stay here to help you finish unpacking," my mother answered, offering me a smile.

Pick your battles, pick your battles, pick your battles. In a few days, I'd be gone, away from them, for two weeks. Happiness-coated-in-guilt settled in my stomach and I forced a nod. "Thanks. That'd be great."

• • •

Privacy was obviously a rare occurrence in my life and I made sure to soak up as much of it as I could as I tromped around my apartment, picking up things and putting them in spots I deemed to be their new home. My parents had left a little over an hour ago, after they were sure that I was well fed, showered, and in my pajamas. Apparently, I was a toddler.

I had no plans, even though it was a Sunday night and I had nothing to do the next day except meander around my apartment. I'm sure Mom would stop by at some point, but that didn't feel like enough anymore. For so long I had gotten away with watching TV and escaping into books because that's all that I could physically handle, but now what?

I was given this heart and at every turn I felt that sharp pang of guilt that I wasn't using it how other people, better people, would have.

Beck had flitted through my thoughts roughly one

trillion times since the day before. The moment I'd closed my car door I had flipped his business card over. On one side it read: "Daniel Prescott, CEO Prescott Publishing" with a phone and fax number. On the back there was Beck's name and number, scribbled in handwriting so messy that I'd have assumed it was written by an infant had I not witnessed it being done with my own eyes.

When he'd handed the card to me, I'd had no intentions of doing anything with it. But now, as I tried to decide if I wanted to watch reruns of the Real Housewives of Whatever City, or you know, throw myself out of my second story window, I decided there wasn't much left to do other than see what sort of weirdness Beck could add to my life. And yes, to be honest, I couldn't stop thinking about how good-looking he was. There. Are you happy?

I pushed myself up off the kitchen chair and grabbed my phone from the counter. For one wild minute I considered calling him, but then I remembered that I hadn't actually spoken with a guy on the phone before. Well, other than my dad, but he hardly counted. What if I sounded really strange on the phone? You know how when you hear yourself speak and you think Holy God, how do people even stand listening to my voice? So, I texted him instead.

Abby: Why do you want to go on my road trip?

My heart puttered wildly in my chest, and for one quick second I thought that it might decide right then to fail on me and stop beating. I smoothed the pad of my finger over the rough scar a few inches below my collar bone. Luckily for my heart, Beck texted me back quickly.

Beck: Abby?

I was excited to see his name flash across the screen, but then I thought, *what kind of desperate person actually texts back right away*? I'd learned enough from *Gossip Girl*, and other accurate pop culture aids, that the cool thing to do was to act as if you were too busy to text back quickly. So instead of responding, I slid across my apartment's old hardwood floors on my fuzzy socks a few times, pretending I was ice-skating. When enough time had passed, I hit send.

Abby: You answered my question with a question.

Beck: I don't like cliffhangers.

He had texted back quickly again, and in that moment I decided that *Gossip Girl* wasn't actually all that accurate considering they had cast thirty-year-olds to play high schoolers. So, instead of being cool, I responded.

Abby: You answered my question with a non sequitur. You're getting worse.

Beck: No, trust me, it's a sequitur. I don't like cliffhangers. Enter- girl buying an urn. She clearly lies about what it's for and then takes off into the sunset? I have to know how it ends. Murder suicide?

Abby: Don't you have a life?

Beck: I'm living it right now.

Abby: I mean work or a family. Oh god, are you a dad?

Beck: Do I look that old?

Abby: Maybe.

Beck: I'll take that as a compliment, and I'm

not leaving anything behind that can't be put on pause for two weeks.

I thought about how much that statement translated to my life as well. My stomach churned until I pushed the thought away so I could type out another text.

Abby: What percentage of you wants to rape and murder me on the side of the highway?

I had to ask. I could have probably been more suave about it, but there was no point. He wasn't actually going to come on my road trip anyway.

Beck: Are you crazy? The side of a highway is a terrible place for a murder. There are witnesses driving by. I don't know how long it'd take me to find a dump site. And Lord knows, you wouldn't be compliant. Plus, I'd never get past the cliffhanger you've thrown at me.

Abby: Sarcasm doesn't translate very well over text, so I'm going to assume you're serious and not text you anymore.

I didn't put my phone away. I knew he was kidding, and even if he wasn't kidding, his greenish swirly eyes were almost worth taking the chance on him being a serial killer.

Beck: Not texting me is a sure fire way to get to the top of my murder list… You'd be leap-frogging the guy in Chipotle earlier who skimped on my rice.

Abby: La la la… This is me not responding.

Beck: Okay, hold on. We just met and I've made two murder jokes...

Abby: Stay on topic...

Beck: Sometimes you have to trust people.

I snorted. Yeah, right.

Abby: You just answered my question with a cliché.

My phone dropped on the table and I left it there as I wandered around my apartment. I went to my refrigerator and browsed the bleak contents. I strolled through my room, rearranging things that I'd just placed thirty minutes earlier.

But the only thing I *actually* did was consider Beck's comment and the way it had burrowed into my consciousness.

An hour later, I replied again with two simply words.

Abby: I know.

I said "I know", but I couldn't think of a single person I had been forced to trust like that. For the rest of the night as I laid in my bed, I tried to imagine Beck and I living like the gay, one part blind couple next door. They seemed really happy, albeit suffering from an alcohol addiction. They had a few cats and sometimes through the walls I could hear them playing music and laughing. That seemed like love to me.

• • •

The next morning, I woke up to a text.

Beck: When do we leave?

I didn't answer. It was one thing to consider taking him on my road trip in the middle of the night when I was nearing unconsciousness and feeling lonely in my tiny apartment. In the light of day, clarity sank back in and I shoved my phone into my purse without a response.

I started that day like I did every day since the transplant; I took my temperature and then swallowed each of my anti-rejection drugs in one big gulp. I'd learned that trick early on. I would say I was pretty talented at being sick.

Once a week I had an appointment with my doctor to make sure my body wasn't attacking my shiny, new heart. That's where I was heading with my mom that day. I was staring out the window, letting my eyes lose focus on the homes flashing by, when I considered for the first time that I *wanted* Beck to go on the road trip with me. In fact, I didn't want to go on the road trip *without* Beck anymore. I squashed the thought by turning the stereo up louder, but Mom quickly turned it back down.

"You don't listen to music that loud when you drive, do you?"

"Um, no, not really," I lied. The louder, the better. How can you feel the music if it's not blocking out every other sound?

"Abby, you can't be distracted when you drive. It's important to focus on the road and to drive defensively."

You might be wondering why my mother was repeating all of this even though I was nineteen and should have been driving for three years already. Well, it turns out that when you have congenital heart failure, your heart can crap out on you at any moment and you'll pass out, and you know, take out quite a few people heading south on highway - 71. So even though I had my license, I didn't start driving until after the transplant two months ago.

"We're just doing lab tests today, right?" I asked, trying to turn her focus toward my health. It was her favorite distraction, and I was actually quite thankful to have her help 99% of time.

"Yes, and then I think Dr. Pierce will do a quick physical like usual."

• • •

I pulled my sleeve back down after they drew a few tubes of blood. I hated wearing a long-sleeved shirt in summer, but I always had to wear layers to Dr. Pierce's office. I'd lost so much weight in the last few years, and even though the new heart was helping me put some of it back on, I still felt chilled to the bone most of the time. Good thing I lived in Texas. At least I'd warm up when we walked outside.

"You're all done. I think your mom is waiting out in the lobby for you," the medical assistant offered politely, finally making eye contact. She was always the one to take my blood. The first time I went in, she couldn't find my vein despite me being ten shades beyond pale. After that incident, she just took my blood and we averted eye contact until the very end. Humans are weird.

"Oh, actually, is Alyssa here?" I asked, shuffling my feet awkwardly.

The medical assistant eyed me skeptically and then

nodded. "Yeah, she's on break though…"

She really wanted to add, *so go away and don't interrupt her fifteen minutes of peace.*

Too bad, lady.

"It's just a really quick something, and I promise she likes me. She told me once that I was her favorite patient." I couldn't actually recall Alyssa ever saying that. She had a straight forward, cut-the-crap attitude. I actually don't recall her ever paying me a compliment, but it worked. The medical assistant turned toward the break room to retrieve Alyssa.

CHAPTER THREE

"'My favorite patient'?" Alyssa repeated with a smirk as she stepped closer. Her brown gaze shifted above my head, most likely to confirm that the coast was clear. I turned with her gaze to see my mom immersed in a conversation with Dr. Pierce out in the hallway. I swear the two women had become best friends considering the amount of time they'd spent together. I imagined them talking about the singular interest that brought them together: me and my ol', well new, heart.

"Are you sure you want to talk about this right now?" Alyssa asked with a warning tone.

"Yeah, it's sorta urgent."

"Sort of?" she mocked.

I scrunched my nose in protest. "I'm nineteen, remember? I'm allowed to use words like 'like' and 'sorta.'"

Alyssa laughed and gently tugged my arm so she could pull us into the closest exam room.

"You realize you're putting not only my job, but this practice and the hospital, in jeopardy by asking what you're asking." Every feature of her face was stern, which only added to the seriousness of her warning.

"Alyssa, I realize there are ramifications for my actions. They sound really terrible, and I promise I won't use the information recklessly."

She rolled her eyes and then narrowed them on me, as if judging how worthy I was. I hoped in that moment that my makeup-less face portrayed me as innocently as possible. For good measure, I widened my sage green eyes and flashed her a pleading smile. I gave her the full on sick-kid face, and I knew she was putty in my hands. I'm sorry that you have to know about that. I wish I could say that I never used my sickness for selfish reasons, but I thought of it like this: life had dealt me a really shitty hand. Other people were pretty or smart, and they used those qualities to their advantage in life. Why couldn't I, ONLY once or twice, use my sickness to my advantage? I mean, I didn't even get a Wish. This was my Wish. Alyssa was my quasi-Make-A-Wish Genie in that moment.

Maybe I should have told her.

Anyway, she pulled out a piece of paper from one of the like twelve dozen pockets on her scrubs and shoved it into my hand like she was dealing drugs and wanted to get the paraphernalia out of her hands, lest the police roll up soon.

"That's their name and address. You DO NOT know me and you DO NOT say the true reason you're there, ever."

My hand shook a little bit when she gave me that

speech. The whole idea felt serious in that moment, like the road trip might actually happen after all. Beck's handsome features materialized in my thoughts.

"How long are you planning on being gone?" she asked with a flash of concern.

"Two weeks," I whispered, fearing her reprimand.

"So you're going to miss two weekly check-ups?" Her voice was harsh. I wanted to scream, *YES. I'm going to miss two appointments so I can LIVE my life! What's the point of getting a new heart if all it's good for is watching reality TV and picking out spices with my mom?!*

I wanted to say that so badly, but out of respect I offered only a nod.

"Yes, but I'll be fine. I'll take all of my medications and take my temperature every day."

I knew that wasn't enough. There were so many things that could go wrong.

She mashed her lips together in deliberation before she tugged the piece of paper away from my still-trembling hand. "Here, let me write my cell number on the back so you can call me if anything comes up."

• • •

Mom didn't leave me alone until late on Monday night and I told myself I was too tired to worry about the fact that I hadn't heard from Beck all day. I mean, he had texted me that morning and I never responded, but what kind of determination was that? One text and he gave up? I thought romance was supposed to be desperate and wild.

Just as I began to ponder that fact, my phone buzzed next to me on the night stand and I shifted my weight to peek at who was calling. **CAROLINE** lit up the screen with her cheerful, steroid-y face. She was my best friend, besides my parents and obviously now the gay couple next door. Oh, I should have mentioned earlier that the blind man is not actually blind blind, just that strange kind of blind where you aren't sure if they're looking *at* you or straight *through* you. Earlier today I was taking my trash down to the dumpster and the blind man had stepped out of his apartment at the exact same moment.

"Is that Otis you have there?" he asked, eyeing the trash bag.

Otis?

"Uh…huh, it...Is…" My words sounded scraggly and half-hearted. I had no clue what else to say. What was I supposed to do? Admit to the poor guy that it was a trashbag full of yesterday's salmon smashed into the remnants of whatever organic/vegan/gluten-free dish I had consumed alongside it?

That's the sort of awkward I am. I would rather proceed with a ridiculous lie than make either one of us endure one of humanity's pained moments.

The phone buzzed once more in my hand and I swiped my finger to answer it. Oh, right.

"Hey Caroline."

"Hi Abby."

She sounded tired like she always did lately.

"How's life over at Methodist?" That was the hospital where most of the sick kids I knew received treatment. I met Caroline there when we were both suffering through an extended stay a few years ago. We were on the donor waiting list at the time. Obviously, I wasn't on that list anymore. Caroline still was. She needed a transplant because she had a rare form of liver cancer that had originated as intrahepatic bile duct cancer. She was on the donor list, but they don't give new livers to patients that still have cancer. There are too many people who need them that are cancer-free.

So Caroline was too sick to be cured and too sick to get a new liver. She was the biggest reason I had a problem with the whole fairness-of-life thing.

"Same ol', same ol'. My parents are both working to keep up with the bills, so it gets pretty boring during the day," she answered,

"Are you having to go to any groups?"

"I told my mother that they depressed me and she said I didn't have to go anymore."

I frowned, thinking back to how boring and sad those groups had been. "Yeah, I agree. I have a book I need to lend you. It has tons of steamy romance." I hopped off my bed to start a collection of books to take to her soon. There was already a bag sitting by my desk, so I picked up various books off my shelves and started stuffing them inside.

"Oh good," she answered. "I've been swapping between TV and books."

"Same."

"Did you finish getting your GED?"

Right before the transplant, when the prospect of me continuing to exist as a human looked pretty slim, my parents became lenient about school. As soon as I was healthy enough post-transplant, I started studying for the GED so I could start to become an actual member of society and not just a sick person. It's a strange concept, considering for so many years I tried to push thoughts of the future out of my mind. It was too painful to consider the possibilities of a future career when the odds of reaching my nineteenth birthday were less than likely.

"Yeah like a week or two ago. I should have invited you to my graduation."

She laughed, a sad little laugh. "You had a graduation?"

"My mom and dad made this giant deal of it. They ordered a cake. Oh, and they printed out my certificate and had it placed in this extravagant gold frame."

"Where is it now?"

"Behind my door in my bedroom. It's pretty ugly, but I told them I would hang it up soon."

A part of my brain warned me to walk on eggshells, that I was being insensitive to Caroline, complaining of things like ugly framed diplomas, when she would never get one of her own. However, a bigger part of me remembered that she was my best friend and if I couldn't be honest with her then we had nothing left.

"When do you get to come home, Caro?" I asked.

"Soon I hope. Maybe this week."

"That's awesome." I tried to have genuine hope in my voice, but it was hard when I knew that she was going home with cancer still in tow.

"My mom has me going to some career counselor tomorrow," I began, hoping the situation would make her laugh, "but I'll stop by after that and if you're out by Wednesday, let's get coffee somewhere. We've never done that before. Y'know, just sitting somewhere and chatting about real-life guys… not just movie stars."

I could hear her smile through the phone when she replied, "We'd have to actually meet them before we did that."

"I'm working on it..." I murmured.

"Alright, I'll see you then."

"Bye, Caroline."

• • •

Precisely thirty minutes before my counseling session, Mom picked me up in her fancy silver SUV. I slid onto the cool cream leather, and she gave me one of her isn't-life-grand smiles. My dad made enough at his job so that we never had to worry about medical bills, which in turn allowed my mom to devote every ounce of her spare time in the past nineteen years to making sure I was happy and healthy.

"Mom, thanks for picking me up and coming with me today."

A smile spread across her face and I knew it was the right thing to say. Sometimes I got so lost in the cynical side of life that remembering to feel extremely freaking lucky about certain things just slipped through the cracks.

Oh yeah, I should apologize in advance. If you're reading this because you thought I was inherently selfless, you might want to turn back now. Most of my worldly knowledge comes from quotes from famous books, minimally acclaimed documentaries, and Reddit.

We drove downtown to a shiny new medical complex. I'd never been to any sort of counseling, but I'd looked Dr. Lucas up last night and she seemed to know her stuff. The little plaque beneath her office read: "Dr. Patricia Lucas: Life Coach, Career Counselor".

I was still mulling over that bit of information when we strolled into the waiting room. Above the shiny granite check-in desk, there was a massive stenciled quote: "*Clear your mind of can't*". I tried to do just that, but nothing really happened. I shifted in my Keds awkwardly before taking a seat. I wasn't quite sure what it *really* meant, because it wasn't as if I had a dream to be an astronaut and I was sitting around thinking: "Now, Abby, you know you have to have perfect vision for that job and you only have 20/50…so you CAN'T be an astronaut". Having a career goal in life would have been a luxury for me. Every time I tried to think about the future, I felt an overwhelming pressure in my chest. How could I make a career decision when there were so many people depending on me to do something noble with my second chance at life?

But that's why I was at the life coach; I suppose she might illuminate it all for me.

"So, Abby, tell me a little bit about yourself," Dr. Lucas prodded with a gentle smile.

I wanted to be helpful, but nothing really came to mind other than pre-transplant information that I'm sure mom had already filled her in on. My hobby was being sick. My hobby was waiting. Waiting for the beeper to go off. There wasn't room for anything else.

"I'm not sure there's much to tell," I offered genuinely, no hint of teenage-attitude present.

Dr. Lucas dressed really well: J. Crew pencil skirt and slim-fitting blouse. Her outfit told me I could put my future in her hands. She wouldn't steer me wrong.

"I like your outfit," I offered, because I felt bad about my lack of personal details to divulge.

She laughed shyly and then scanned over my outfit. "Thanks, I like yours too, Abby."

She was trying to earn my trust and make me feel at ease. I looked down at my clothes. I never strayed from the basics most of the time: Jean cut-offs of various levels of distressing and pretty, summer tops. It was easy and I prided myself on taking 0.5 seconds to get ready in the morning. Brush hair, brush teeth, moisturizer, and hair in a messy bun or side braid— done. Makeup was for the birds (or you know, girls who were actually on guys' radars).

"Thanks…" I dragged it out awkwardly, not sure where the counseling session was going to go from there. Were we just going to compliment each other for 60 minutes?

"Your mother told me you earned your GED a few weeks ago?"

I nodded. "It wasn't so bad."

"Have you put any thought toward applying to college?" She broached the subject lightly, as if she didn't want to offend me.

Of course I had. Everyone thinks about going to college. I had read enough New Adult Romances to know that the moment I stepped on campus, I would surely be noticed by the mysterious loner jock or hot nerd that didn't get noticed in high school, or maybe the off-limits TA.

"Yes. I've put some thought into it," I offered plainly.

"And?"

"And that's all. I've thought about it."

She nodded for what felt like an eternity after that, scanning my face and acting as if she was reading between the lines. Could she discern something in my sage green eyes that had eluded me in the mirror that morning? Maybe my future career path was tattooed around my irises in plain view of everyone but me.

"Abby, I'm going to have you take a career aptitude

assessment. I always give this to individuals like yourself; those who find themselves unsure of what they would enjoy doing in life." She didn't wait for my response. She stood to retrieve the test and a pencil from her desk.

I blurted out, "Can anyone be a Life Coach? I've never heard of it before."

She cleared her throat, obviously surprised by my question. I didn't want to be disrespectful of her in her own office, but it just seemed silly to me in a way. Counseling is counseling and I'm sure people genuinely benefit from it, but life seemed to be quite a strange thing and to think that any of us knows enough to not only coach ourselves in it, but to coach others as well… it just made me think of that quote from Socrates that said: "true wisdom comes to each of us when we realize how little we understand about life, ourselves, and the world around us" or something.

Weren't we all just faking it anyway?

"There's no real regulation of it, but I also have a master's degree in family counseling and have had twenty years of experience in helping people meet their life goals."

She had me there. She had twenty years of experience and I had only been *alive* nineteen years, so surely she knew more about what I should do than I did.

CHAPTER FOUR

I was lying awake that Tuesday night, tossing and turning. Nothing seemed to lull me to sleep. I tried turning on white noise (it was supposed to sound like beluga whales under water, but it skewed more toward creepy and I turned it off), rereading a boring book, and suffocating my face a little bit with a pillow in hopes that I would pass out. I finally caved and texted Beck.

Abby: Are you awake?

I didn't think to check the time until after I sent the message. It was two-thirty in the morning. Whoops. My phone vibrated in my hand and I thought he had texted back, but when I looked down my eyes practically bulged out of my face. He was *calling* me, like a real person would do. I played with the idea of ignoring it, but curiosity won out.

"Hello?" I croaked, apparently my vocal cords weren't aware that they were still needed for the day.

"Abby." I could hear his smile through the phone. I had forgotten the way my name sounded on his lips.

"Hi," I chirped for lack of any better conversational skills.

"Hi."

"What are you doing up so late?" I asked.

He cleared his throat and then I heard rustling in the background. Was he on his bed? An image of him in boxers instantly flitted through my mind.

"Watching *The Walking Dead*."

Ten points for Beckindor. I loved that show. "Isn't it a little late for that?" I asked, trying to sound aloof.

"I usually have a hard time getting to sleep."

"Maybe it's because you're watching zombies," I suggested.

He chuckled. "Correction: people killing zombies."

"I used to watch that show, but the medical inaccuracies pissed me off." This aloof thing wasn't really working. I just sounded bitchy and constipated.

"Yeah, I watch zombie shows because of their strict adherence to reality, too."

Even I had to laugh at that.

"I get your point, but c'mon. Not even in a TV show can you have zombie guts spread all over your face and NOT get the virus. If someone coughs two apartments down from me, I catch a cold."

He laughed then, and I smiled wide into the darkness of my room. It felt important that he thought I was funny, or at least interesting. He seemed like the coolest person ever to grace my life and I didn't want to be a disappointment to him.

"Why are you awake, Abby?"

"For reasons unexplained. My brain doesn't want to shut off," I said.

"I wish I could help you," he said, and my heart leapt.

"You are…sort of," I admitted, only because his voice sounded so sincere.

"Did you know that no one knows why our bodies demand sleep?" he offered, and I sat up against my pillows.

"What? I thought that was decided ages ago?"

"Nope. There's a ton of stuff that happens while we sleep, but there's not one main reason."

"What if it's for some really strange reason?"

"Like what?" he asked with amusement.

Silence hung on the phone line, amplifying each of our shallow breaths until I finally cut it off.

"Like… I don't know." I tried really hard to come up with a reason, but I couldn't because I was already wondering about something else. "What if you could pick what would happen to you while you slept? Like if you had a really bad day, you could erase it. Or if you had cancer, you could ask your body to get rid of it. Or if you were really fat, you could wake up skinny."

Beck was quiet after that, and I thought for a moment he had fallen asleep.

"I don't think we should erase the bad days," he finally announced.

"Hmm."

"What if the only way it worked is if you transferred those things— your shitty day or cancer— to other people while you slept?" he asked.

"Conservation of energy. Or maybe collectivism in practice," I said.

"Exactly," he said.

I rolled over to face my window so I could look out into the wild nature surrounding me. No, that's not true. I stared outside and my view was cut off by the apartment building that sat three feet from mine. I could see a sloping brown roof and layers of white siding.

"When you point it out like that, I don't have an answer. But I do know that we do things everyday that affect people almost as implicitly as what you're suggesting. I've caused people to have bad days. I'm a bitchy teenager to my parents 50% of the time. Companies that make junk-food aid in America's quest to be the fattest-country-ever, while their CEOs stay skinny and rich." I was sort of rambling. The topic was interesting and Beck was easy to talk to.

"Nah, I bet they're fat, too," he laughed.

I smiled. "Me too."

"*Fat cats*," he quipped.

"*Fat cats*," I repeated for emphasis.

"So, what about when you cause people to have good days?" Beck mentioned.

I nodded into the darkness and thought about that idea for a little while.

"One time, when I was young, I was in the hospital for some check-up or something. I was walking down the hallway with a teddy bear in my arm that was pretty much my best friend and sole confidant at that age."

I made sure to leave out any details about my old disease while describing my visit.

"Seems like a respectable type of bear," he said.

"He was. The best kind," I said. "Anyway, I was in the hospital and a little girl was being carted down the hallway next to me on a hospital bed that swallowed her up— it was so big. I thought she was the same age as me because she looked about my size. I didn't know where they were taking her, but for this really long expanse of hallway, our eyes locked and we just stared at each other. I can't remember what I saw in her eyes, but even as a kid I knew she had it worse than I did. I was walking, holding onto my teddy bear and my mom's hand, and she was being carted by some nurse to god knows where."

"You gave her that bear didn't you?"

"Yes. Right before she was pushed into the elevator. I remember sort of half tossing, half tripping in my journey to get to her."

"Were you sad that you gave up your best friend? Or just happy that you made someone's day less worse?"

"Probably neither. I was too young to even realize what I was actually doing."

"I wonder what that bear is doing now..."

"He's probably a fat cat," I quipped.

He laughed a deep rumbling laugh that was too good for this earth.

"What's your full name, Abby?" he asked out of the blue.

"Abby Mae McAllister."

"Well Abby Mae… it's now 3:08 in the morning."

"That's late," I said.

"Early," he corrected.

"What's yours?"

"Beckham Dilan Prescott."

What a fancy name. Much better than Abby Mae.

"Well Beck*ham*, we should go to bed," I declared, because it seemed like he wanted to hang up. I could've talked for the rest of my life.

"You're right. Morning, Abby."

I smiled at his joke. "Morning, Beck."

After I'd hung up, I stared at the phone screen in a daze. *Beckham Dilan Prescott*, I repeated out loud.

• • •

Caroline was still in the hospital on Wednesday, which rendered our coffee shop idea null and void. Instead, I picked up two hot chocolates and a piece of lemon pound cake from Starbucks on my way to the hospital. It seemed like a shitty alternative, but at least it was *something*.

Caroline deserved a freaking normal Starbucks experience.

On a whim, I drove past the hospital and headed toward the mall to find one of those candle stores. I hadn't actually been to the mall in years, it always seemed like too much of an undertaking, but there I was, meandering through housewives and pushy sales people. *No, I don't want to try your hand cream or hair straightener, I just want to get my cancerific friend a candle.*

I could only find one candle that was even remotely close to the trademark coffee scent. It was called Donut Shop. Donut Shop actually smelled nothing like coffee, but I was betting on the fact that maybe Caroline was too hopped up on drugs to notice.

You should know that I also stopped to get her an actual donut after that. I realized that if she could in fact still smell, and I arrived with a donut candle sans donut, then it would make me the shittiest friend ever.

She didn't quite understand any of this by the time I got to the hospital and explained it to her.

"Thanks for the donut," she said smiling as I stuffed the candle back into my purse. Note to anyone that cares: they don't actually let you light candles in hospitals due to the whole fire hazard thing… not even if you promise to be really careful.

"How has life in prison been?"

"Can we not talk about it? Don't you have any juicy stories yet? You've been living on your own for a while now… I need to hear about something other than my illness for like five minutes. The other day you mentioned you were working on meeting guys? Any luck?"

I nodded and broke off a piece of the lemon pound cake. I hadn't actually told anyone about Beck yet. To be honest, at that point I still wondered if maybe I had a brain tumor like that doctor did on *Grey's Anatomy* and Beck wasn't actually real at all. Wait, was Denny real? I couldn't remember.

I went out on a limb and told her about Beck anyway.

"He just walked up to you at a funeral home?" she asked, thoroughly confused.

"Yeah, it was really weird."

The sunlight streaming in through the window highlighted her dark brown hair and hollowed cheekbones. I hadn't remembered her looking so pale the week before.

"But you said he was really hot?" She arched her eyebrows suspiciously.

"Yes, much too good-looking for normal girls."

"Maybe he's a prostitute," she offered.

“Maybe he’s a Russian spy,” I said, my eyes growing wide with wonder.

“Maybe he’s a neo-Nazi,” she replied with a grin.

“Oh! Maybe he’s the Zodiac killer,” I said, thinking I’d most likely nailed it.

She laughed and tipped back a sip of her hot chocolate. “I thought they caught that guy in like the 80’s.”

“No. The person they suspected it to be passed away and then the strange calls and killings stopped happening, so they just figured it was him.”

“I doubt Hot Guy is a crazy person. You should have faith in people.”

I rolled my eyes and shot her a you-know-better-than-that stare. “You sound like him.”

“Huh,” she smirked. “I like him already.”

“I’m thinking about letting him come on the road trip with me…” I all but whispered, scared of what her reaction would be. Ninety-nine percent of me assumed she would throw the rest of her donut at my head as an attempt to knock some sense into me.

“You should. If I weren’t about to freaking DIE, I would go on a road trip with a random hot guy. What do you possibly have to lose?”

I flashed her a pointed stare. “Uh, my life...my virginity…my freedom…my parent’s trust.”

“So nothing of importance?” she laughed, smoothing her hair back into a ponytail. Her arms were so small, skin and bone, if that.

I smiled at her and shook my head.

“It doesn’t matter. I’m not sure I should go at all anymore,” I muttered.

“Why!?”

I didn't answer because the reason was staring me in the face and she wouldn't take too kindly to my response.

"It better not be because of me!" she bellowed with a hard stare.

I blanched. "I can go on a road trip *anytime.* You're really sick, Caroline."

I thought I could see black plumes of smoke shooting out of her ears in that moment. "Abby. If you do not go on that road trip in a few days, I'll forbid the hospital from letting you in. I'll tell them that you mentioned bringing a bomb in and I'll make them put you on their watch list."

"Wow," I mouthed, trying to hold back my laughter. Caroline was so ridiculous, but I half believed her.

"Yeah, I'm that serious."

"Okay, psychopath. Jeez, I can't imagine what you would be like if you weren't strapped down by ten machines right now."

"A real force of nature," she replied proudly.

"Exactly."

"So you'll go?" she asked, hope dancing in her hollowed eyes.

"Yes," I answered, even though the guilt was hard to push through.

"With him?"

"We'll see..."

CHAPTER FIVE

On Thursday morning I headed to the drug store to fill my prescriptions and pick up a few travel-sized essentials.

My original plan was to leave for the road trip the next day, but I hadn't talked to Beck since earlier in the week. Was twenty-four hours enough notice? Was I really going to be insane enough to bring him along with me? I knew that any normal person wouldn't even consider it, but I just need you to be on my side. When that career counselor asked me to tell her about myself, I drew a giant BLANK. There was nothing— I had no reckless nights of sneaking out or drinking, going to parties, or any other normal teenage mischief. I needed something, at least one or two shenanigans, to cling onto when I was ninety. I could look back and shake my head at how careless I had been.

Just. This. Once.

So I did it. I was in that drug store, deciding between getting one or two mini-toothpastes, when I called Beck.

He picked up on the third ring. "Abby Mae."

I don't know if he was surprised to hear from me or if he always greeted people with a hint of cheerfulness.

"Good morning, Beck. It has come to my attention that I have an additional seat available for my road trip, which leaves tomorrow at eleven am sharp." I cut right to the chase.

"Which one?"

"Which one, what?" I asked, picking up three tubes of toothpaste, optimistic that Beck would want to come with me. Therefore, we would need a bit more than two tubes, but not quite four.

"Which road trip are you talking about? I've been invited on a few that leave tomorrow, so it's been hard to keep them all straight."

I covered my smile with my hand as if he could have seen it from his end of the line.

"Your attempt at humor is suddenly making me rethink the available seat."

I toyed with one of the toothpaste tubes.

He laughed and then asked, "Shouldn't we meet up and plan out the trip before tomorrow?"

My heart, *the* heart, leaped into action at the thought. He had a good point; I really had no plan at all, just one end goal.

"I have to go to R.E.I. this afternoon to grab a sleeping bag, want to meet there?"

"The one on Market Street?" he asked.

"Yeah, around four?" I held my breath, hoping he wouldn't laugh in my face.

"I'll see you then."

I dropped the phone back in my bag and then continued strolling down the aisles. I'd be lying if I said that having sex with Beck hadn't crossed my mind since meeting him. Sorry if that shocks you. Teenage hormones are real and scary. I'd had some crazy dreams the past few nights that involved Beck and sundae toppings.

But when I turned down *that* aisle and was forced to look directly at the condoms and the indiscrete bottles of lube, I suddenly felt supremely out of my league. I had no clue what the road trip would be like, but something told me I should be prepared in *every* area. Even if I didn't have sex with Beck, maybe we'd pick up a hitchhiker that just happened to be Orlando Bloom and he'd want to take my virginity. I pulled a box of regular sized condoms off the shelf and a box of magnum sized as well. I'd never actually seen a penis in real life, so I had no basis of knowledge for what the average size was.

I couldn't look the pharmacist in the eye when I picked up my prescriptions and paid for my Cosmo, toothpaste, and condoms. The Cosmo was mostly for *research*.

"Do you need me to explain any of these medications to you?" she asked, shuffling the pill bottles into the crinkly sack. I could feel the people behind me in line leering over my shoulder toward the counter. Did they need to print the word 'Magnum' in bold, bright red letters?

I shook my head, let out a strange grunt, and shoved all of the items into my over-sized bag before practically sprinting out of the store.

• • •

It was already four-fifteen by the time I found parking on Market Street. I tugged on the hem of my light yellow summer dress and practically jogged toward the entrance of R.E.I., hoping that Beck hadn't been waiting on me for too long.

When I pushed through the heavy double doors, I was greeted by that outdoorsy smell, which was strange considering I was stepping *out* of nature.

If you've never been inside one of these stores, I should tell you that they usually have these awesome campsite displays set up with a tent, chairs, and fake fire at the front end.

That's where Beck was standing when I walked in. He was just behind the fake fire with his arms crossed over his chest and a lazy grin dotting his features. Unlike last time, he wasn't wearing a baseball hat, so there was nothing to hide every ounce of his grade-A hotness. His hair was scruffy and perfectly tousled. His muscles stood out and his skin was tan and healthy, so different than mine.

Seeing him like that was easily the highlight of my week until I saw that he was talking to an equally gorgeous girl. She was wearing a pocketed vest and hiking boots. She was almost as tall as Beck, which was practically a foot taller than me. Damnit. I straightened my shoulders instinctively and took a few steps closer. That's when I saw Pretty Girl's employee name tag. It read: Bekah. As in Rebecca shortened to Becca then morphed to Bekah. Who did she think she was having a cool, quirky name like that?

"Abby!" Beck called, and my eyes shifted toward him again.

I sort of half-waved and muttered a "hi" as I reached them. Bekah offered me a smile, and then we all stood there awkwardly for a moment because in reality we were all pretty much strangers.

Beck was the one to finally break the silence. "Bekah here was just laughing about our names."

I scrunched my brows and then finally got it. Beck and Bekah. They were freaking meant to be.

"Wow. That's a *neat* coincidence," I nodded, and then fiddled with the strap on my purse. Beck gave me the widest grin I've ever seen and then placed an arm around my shoulders. His grip was warm on my bare skin and I felt a tingle run down my spine.

"Well, it was nice talking to you, Bekah," he said, already pushing us away from the campsite. I had to take twice as many steps as he did in order to keep up.

"Oh yeah sure, let me know if you need my help or anything!" she offered desperately, but she was pretty enough to where it just came off as being friendly. Damn girls like that.

The moment we walked out of earshot, Beck let go of my shoulders and turned to face me. His hazel eyes bore right into my green ones. I had to remind myself to breathe. "You should know that you have one of the most expressive faces I've ever seen. You're like an open book."

"What? What do you mean?" I asked, realizing my eyebrows were scrunched together and I was wearing a tight frown. I instantly relaxed my features. Okay, maybe he was right.

"You have to work on your poker face," he laughed. "'A neat coincidence?' You might as well have said 'that's the least interesting thing I've ever heard'."

I gaped up at him. "Excuse me! It was a cool coincidence. What are the *odds*? You guys should get married." Sarcasm was dripping from my mouth.

He replied instantaneously. "Nah, she probably

stopped watching *The Walking Dead* because of the 'medical inaccuracies'. We would never work out."

He was teasing me with a confident smirk across his face. I did everything I could to meet his hazel eyes, but in the end I just couldn't do it. I could feel how red my face had become and I busied myself with a display of water filters.

"Ha-Ha. Alright, you win. Now help me pick out a sleeping bag," I said, turning away from him and trying to regain an ounce of composure.

"So we're camping during this road trip?" Beck asked as we tested out various sleeping bags. There was a row of them hanging on a rack, new and plush. Each of the various models boasted of keeping humans warm at impossible temperatures or being capable of withstanding a bear attack. I'm not sure about the last part; I might have been too preoccupied pretending not to watch Beck to actually read the labels properly.

"I wasn't planning on it at first because I was going to be alone, but now I think we should camp at least a few nights."

"I agree. I love camping and I have a tent," he said, grabbing a thick, navy blue sleeping bag from the rack. With confidence, he turned and laid it out on the ground in the middle of the aisle. My mouth opened to protest, but no sound came out. Without a moment's hesitation, he bent down and snuggled into it like it was a completely normal thing to do. I'd never seen anyone do that in the store before. A sales assistant saw him from afar and started to head over, but the moment Beck smiled up at her, she suddenly didn't mind so much. *Hot guy perks.*

He was still laying there when he offered, "We should take my grandfather's car. It's an old VW Camper, but he used it to surf so there's no back seat. It's just a flat surface— so we could sleep there if we didn't want to stay in a hotel or camp."

I was planning on taking my car, but his idea did sound pretty good. I didn't want to be tied down to hotels or camp sites.

"It's big enough for two people?" I asked, not turning to face him. My face was bright red at the idea of sleeping in the back of a car with him. *Please don't let him be a crazy person. Please*. I turned at the sound of his voice.

"Oh, I just thought you'd be sleeping outside," he answered with a perfectly straight face.

I gave him a pointed stare and then pretended like I was going to step on him beneath the sleeping bag.

He barked out a laugh and then rolled to a sitting position. "Yes, there's enough room for two people. Try this bag out, I think it's a good one."

I did as he said. He held the top so I could slip my Keds through the opening. I had to hold my dress down so he wouldn't get a peak at my polka dot underwear.

He'd been laying in it for hardly three minutes, but the sleeping bag already smelled like him; the remnants of his cologne clung to the fabric. I decided I would get it for that reason alone.

"So do we have any destinations in mind?" he asked as we roamed through aisles, loading up on random items: water bottles, a lantern, and a mini camping kitchen set that stacked together nicely.

"A few," I answered, "but I'm also open to random stops. I just have to be in Odessa, Texas at some point."

"Sounds good. If I get to choose a stop, I want to go

to Marfa."

"Marfa?" I asked, shuffling items between my arms as we headed to the register. He stepped in front of me, halting my forward momentum with his hands on my shoulders. His fingers gripped my skin, hitting the thin string of my spaghetti strap. I gulped and stared at his shirt like it was the most interesting thing in the world. That didn't help because the cotton did a poor job of hiding his body beneath it.

The entire moment lasted less than a few seconds, but the feel of my stomach dropping and my heart speeding to keep up would forever remain with me.

"It's a small town way out in west Texas," he answered, coaxing me back into the land of the living.

I nodded, trying to think if I had ever heard of it. "Is there a reason why you want to go there?"

"It's a secret," he smirked as we moved to wait in line.

"That's where the cult is, isn't it?"

It was his turn to give me a pointed stare.

I was positioned first in line at the checkout, but when it came time for me to pay, Beck cut in. "Oh, I'm a member here. Let me pay with my card so I get the points. You can just pay me back."

It seemed reasonable, so I let him pay without thinking much of it, but as we walked out with our purchases, I flitted my eyes over to him. "I don't have enough cash on me, but I can run to an ATM really quick."

"Nah," he said, holding the door open for a woman entering behind us. "We're even."

I scoffed and shook my head. "Beck, that was really expensive and we aren't even friends. I can't accept this stuff."

"We'll figure it out on the road trip— don't worry. And yes, by the way, we are now officially friends, Abby Mae McAllister," he declared, holding out his hand for me to shake.

I grabbed it with an amused smile. "Is this our secret handshake?" His warm skin pressed against mine and his pointer finger hit my wrist directly over my pulse.

"Sometimes you just have to go back to basics," he quipped before dropping my hand. He was already starting to back up in the opposite direction, but I stood my ground, shaking my head incredulously.

"Tomorrow at eleven SHARP, we are leaving on a road trip of tremendous importance. I hope you're ready!" he exclaimed as he continued to back away from me. No one on the street really paid him much attention, but I did.

I couldn't look away.

• • •

That night was a complete cluster-fuck. My parents came over to cook me dinner and watch a movie. Every chance I got, I escaped to my room to pack what I could without them knowing. It was always part of the plan to hide the road trip from them because they would have nixed the idea immediately. But now that Beck was joining me, I had to keep it a mega-secret. I felt so shitty, lying to them like that, but I couldn't turn back. I just prayed they would understand my reasoning after everything was said and done.

I was stuffing all my bathroom essentials into a travel bag when my mother knocked on the door. I jumped and spun around to hide the bag in case she was about to barge in.

"Sweetie?" My mom's voice called from the other side of the bathroom door.

"Oh, I'll be right out," I answered with a shaky voice.

"Okay, I just wanted to make sure you were feeling alright." She sounded so sincere.

I sat down on the lid of the toilet and hid my head in my hands. *I'm a terrible person. I can't do this to her.*

"Yes, Mom, thanks. I'll come help with dinner in one second." I tried to smile so she would hear it in my voice. The second she walked away, I snuck into my room and into my closet so I could dial Caroline.

I didn't think she would answer. It rang half a dozen times and then I finally heard a cough.

"Sweet Caroline?" I asked hesitantly. Her cough sounded terrible and I wasn't sure it would stop. Another few seconds passed and then finally I heard raspy breathing.

"Hey Abby."

"Dude, you sound like you've got the black plague." It was hard to act normal and tease her in that moment. Her sickness scared me, but I couldn't turn into another person that walked on eggshells around her. She'd never forgive me.

"I liked you better when you had that old crappy heart. You had less energy to devote to sarcasm."

That was Caroline.

"Yeah, maybe this new heart is super evil."

"Ew, that's weird."

"I'm kidding, but hey, should I or should I not feel like a complete bitch for lying to my parents about this road trip?"

"You cannot be having second thoughts. He bought

you a freaking sleeping bag and stuff. That's practically an engagement ring."

I ignored her blatant hyperbole. "So they'll understand why I went?"

"Yes. You deserve to go, and they'll understand later. Like when you're fifty. I wouldn't mention it until then."

"Okay, that's what I needed to hear," I paused, letting the guilt sink in about leaving Caroline.

"Hey, I know you'll yell at me about it, but it's not too late for me to cancel the trip and stay. I really don't want to leave you." The more I talked about it, the more I felt like that was the right decision. I'd stay with Caroline and visit her in the hospital and do… I don't know what with the rest of my time. Get a job? Yeah. I needed a job. Just the thought brought back the sinking feeling in my stomach.

"I cannot believe you're even bringing that up again. Abby, I've told you a million times and now it's just annoying. I *want* you to go. I *want* you to have crazy campfire sex with this guy."

"Ew, like on the fire? What the hell are you into, Caro?"

"I'm serious, Abby. Please don't stay for me. You'll make me feel like crap." It was that sentence that sealed my fate. I didn't think Caroline was lying. I knew what it felt like to be a burden.

"Okay," I relented. "I've gotta go help my parents steam quinoa."

"That was the most boring sentence I've ever heard."

Boring? Fine.

"I bought condoms at the store today, did I tell you that?"

"You're dropping that bomb on me right before you

hang up?!" she exclaimed, causing a whole new coughing fit.

"Crap. Sorry, seriously heal up. I'll update you if we do the deed or anything."

She laughed wistfully. "Please do, I'm living vicariously through you."

"K. Love ya, C."

"Love ya, Abs."

CHAPTER SIX

I changed ten times Friday morning, finally settling on a short pair of faded denim cut-offs and a fitted t-shirt with my standard white Keds. Anything else felt like I was trying too hard, which I was. I tugged my hair into a loose braid and looked at my reflection in the mirror. Sage green eyes, even skin tone, standard eyebrows and eyelashes. I'd never thought I needed makeup before, but I suddenly felt self-conscious. I pinched my cheeks like they always do in Jane Austen books and then laughed out loud because I was acting insane. Beck knew what I look like and he seemed to like it so far, right?

I made myself some organic egg whites with a side of banana and peanut butter. Then I painted my nails a bright pink color, hated it, and swapped it out for a bright red.

After all that, it was still only ten thirty in the

morning.

Crap.

I clicked on the TV and flipped through day-time shows, not really concentrating on any of it. My finger kept clicking aimlessly until I looked up and saw that it was five minutes to eleven. Yesterday we'd arranged for Beck to pick me up at my apartment, so when I heard a loud BEEP-BEEP a second later, my heart rate leapt. I hopped off the couch and straightened my shirt.

I had three bags filled with my essentials, plus my sleeping bag and a grocery bag full of healthy snacks. My trusty black urn sat beside the pile, taped on all sides so it wouldn't spill open. That black urn was the most important thing I was taking on the trip. Well, other than my medications. I grabbed my first bag and opened my front door to find Beck standing a few feet outside. I took in his messy brown hair, white t-shirt, and dark jeans. Why did a white t-shirt look so good on him? Maybe because it was fitted enough to show off his toned body without being obnoxiously tight? I wasn't quite sure.

He didn't say anything at first. His hazel eyes scanned down my body, lingering a moment longer on my bare legs, and then he looked back up at me with a wide, perfectly straight smile.

"Is that all you're bringing?" he asked, pointing at the smallest of my three bags.

"Hah! Yeah right, I have like ten times more stuff."

He shook his head and narrowed his eyes on me playfully. "I like a girl with baggage, Abby Mae. Keeps things interesting."

His comment was too much; it stripped away my normal sarcastic responses. I was left with nothing but the bag in my hand, so I tossed it at him. He had to think fast and catch it before it fell to the ground at his feet.

"Good. Help me load it up then," I smirked, and then turned to collect the rest of my stuff.

"Don't forget to go to the bathroom! We aren't stopping until we're out of hell!" he called behind me.

"You mean Dallas?" I asked over my shoulder.

"Exactly!"

I was sitting in the passenger seat in Beck's old, yellow VW Camper. It had been renovated recently, so the inside was all new leather, but it still had a lot of the classic details.

Our stuff fit easily in the back and he wasn't kidding about there being space to sleep. We'd have to be really close, but there was definitely room. My face reddened at the thought.

I wedged the urn between my feet so that it wouldn't tip over, and then buckled my seat belt. When I looked up, Beck was watching me with a bemused smile. My hand instinctively slid over my side braid and my face. I didn't feel anything out of the ordinary.

"What?" I asked.

He shook his head, but his grin never faltered. "Nothing. Just trying to remember this moment."

I furrowed my brows in wonder and tilted my head. The sun shone through the windshield of the Camper, highlighting the green details in his eyes. Beck wasn't movie-star good-looking; he was boy-next-door good-looking— the kind of guy that might not know the full extent of his effect on the female population.

"Why?" I asked.

"Because our lives will never be the same."

A small dimple formed on the corner of his mouth before he turned toward the steering wheel and pulled out of my apartment complex.

That dimple was the first thing I told myself to remember about the road trip.

Just as we turned onto the entrance for the highway, I peered over at Beck. "Just so you know, my faith in humanity is dangling by a few threads. If you murder me, I'll pretty much lose all hope."

I couldn't keep the hint of a smile from my lips.

He nodded. "And if you murder me?"

I shrugged. "That would just be a good plot twist."

We watched the Dallas landscape disappear behind us to the tune of Vampire Weekend. Beck thumbed the steering wheel to the beat of the song and I propped my feet up on the dashboard. It felt like the first day of summer, too good to be true. It was like the world might say "just kidding" and I'd wake up in my bed back home with nothing to look forward to except visiting Caroline.

I snuck glances in his direction every now and then, wondering what he was thinking about as he steered us toward our first destination.

"There's a campsite about three hours from here. What if we stayed there tonight?" he asked as we weaved through the rolling hills of Central Texas.

"Sounds good."

"We just need to stop for food before we get there."

I thought about my organic peanut butter and jelly sitting in my bag. "I brought some food with me."

"Supplies for s'mores?" he asked with a dead-serious tone.

"No… Do we need those?"

He shot me a pitiful look. "Oh, sweet, naive, Abby. Camping without s'mores is not camping at all."

"What is it then?" I asked, peering over at him from the corner of my eye.

"Unadulterated torture," he offered deadpan.

I let out a soft laugh. "Wow. Alright, then we'll make s'mores."

• • •

Chocolate, graham crackers, and marshmallows, in quantities that could feed a small country, spilled out of my arms as we headed toward the camp ground. I'd assumed, you know, one package of each ingredient was enough, but Beck insisted we needed to stock up. *"We never know when we'll need s'mores during the trip."* I wondered if he planned on subsisting on them for the remainder of our travels.

"Do you think they'll still have campsites available?" I asked as we pulled into the state park.

"Hopefully. It's hot so I doubt there will be too many people."

He had a point. The sun was setting soon, but the temperature was still hovering in the nineties. He pulled up toward the ranger's cabin and a friendly redheaded woman poked her head out of the side window.

"Evening, you two."

I reached for my wallet to pay for half of the camping spot, but Beck beat me to it.

"Here you go, I have a Texas State Park Pass for the summer," he said, handing over the card to the woman. I thought about protesting, but I didn't want to annoy the Park Ranger. "Are there any good camping sites left?"

She nodded emphatically. "Oh yeah, there's hardly anyone in here today. It should pick up a bit tomorrow, though."

She handed over a park map. "You'll want to pick a spot near the lake. The temperature's a little cooler near the water and it's pretty during sunset." She gave me a suggestive smile and I wondered if she thought we were dating or something. *We aren't going to get it on in your park, lady.*

"Is it near a restroom?" I asked.

"Yes, there are a few restrooms placed sporadically throughout the park, but make sure to close the door when you go in so that wildlife doesn't sneak up on you."

I chewed on my lip, thinking about a bear following me into the restroom in the dead of night. *Are there bears in Texas?*

I was still mulling over that fear by the time we arrived at the campsite the ranger had circled on the map for us. The site was tucked in among tall cedars and pines and the lake she'd mentioned was only a few yards away. It was calm and quiet in the late evening. We positioned our tent so that the opening faced the lake. Actually, I should say Beck positioned our tent while I handed him the rods.

"Do you want to throw our pillows and stuff in the tent while I start to get a fire going?" he asked, stretching his arms out above his head so that a sliver of his torso peeked out beneath the bottom of his shirt. Toned with a hint of a tan. I ended up not really being able to form a coherent sentence after that, so I just nodded and started laying out our sleeping bags. The tent was a really tight fit, so I put our backpacks in one corner. Our sleeping bags ended up right next to each other.

Ten minutes later, Beck was adding bigger logs to the fire and I was arranging camping chairs a few feet back from the smoky flames.

"It's too hot to sit close."

He frowned. "Yeah. I'm about to swim in that lake if it doesn't cool off soon."

I hadn't even thought about swimming in the lake. It definitely looked deep enough, but the edge was rimmed with algae and leaves.

"Do you want a P and BJ?" I asked. The moment the letters slipped out of my mouth, I realized my slip up and all but convulsed on the spot. I stuttered and cleared my throat, anything to distract him. "I…I mean a PB and J… before you start eating s'mores?" I asked, plopping my grocery bag on top of the campsite's picnic table.

I knew I was beet-red. *I just asked Beck if he wanted a blow job. What a wonderful way to start our camping trip.* To his credit, he didn't make a joke out of it.

"Sure, thanks. Extra peanut butter, please," Beck said, maneuvering behind me. I thought he'd sit down and wait for me to bring a sandwich over to him, but instead he unpacked two plastic plates and went to work preparing the bread while I smeared peanut butter and jelly on each one. He grabbed our water bottles and met me by the camping chairs.

We made a good little team.

We were munching on the sandwiches when I finally asked him something I'd been wondering about. "How did you drop everything and come on this road trip? Aren't you in school or something?"

"It's summer," he noted, as if that explained everything.

"Yes…" I agreed, hinting that I wanted more details.

He shrugged. "I was in college up in Boston, but I'm not sure how it will work out."

I mashed my lips together, wondering if I had the right to ask why. I decided on an easier question. "What year are you?"

"I just finished my junior year."

"You only have one year left and you don't think it's going to work out?"

He narrowed his eyes out over the lake. "Yup."

"Hmm."

"Hmm, what?" he asked, glancing back toward me. He'd finished his sandwich and unwrapped a chocolate bar to break off a piece.

"What college do you go to?" I knew there was an insane amount of colleges in Boston, like fifty or sixty plus.

"MIT," he answered, standing up and walking toward the tree line.

I gaped. "I'm sorry. *The* MIT? You're kidding, right?" He seemed smart, but MIT smart was another level altogether.

"Nope," he answered with a crooked smile, retrieving a long thin branch to use as a makeshift marshmallow toaster. He didn't seem to mind my disbelief, but I needed more details. A part of me still thought he might have been kidding.

"What's your major?" I asked, trying to study his posture and facial tics as if I were a criminologist.

"Petroleum engineering." His voice didn't hold any of its usual conviction. His gaze was focused on his marshmallow. He turned it slowly in a circle, toasting every side until it was a nice golden brown. I had to admire his dedication. My usual method involved setting the marshmallow on fire and devouring the sugary carcinogens.

"Huh." I sat there dumbfounded and he finally looked up at me, saving me from my misery.

"Do you want proof?" he asked with a half-smile.

"Yes." I wanted to trust him, but it just seemed so odd.

He put his weight into his right leg and pulled out an old brown leather wallet from his back pocket. With a little flick, he opened it and pulled out a white card.

When he handed it over, I held it gently in my palm as if it was a piece of the Beck puzzle. It was his MIT student ID. He was pictured there in a tiny one inch by one inch square. He looked oddly serious. None of the features that made him breathtaking were present: his eye color wasn't visible due to the shitty picture quality, his dimples were tucked away, and his air of confidence was hidden. It was like looking at his evil twin or something.

Directly under the photo read: Beckham Dilan Prescott— Pet. Engineering Department Access.

Once I'd handed it back to him, we just sat there in silence. None of it added up. Why didn't he want to be an engineer if he was almost done with his degree?

"So what are you going to do for a liv—"

He cut me off. "Let's swim, Abby Mae. S'mores can wait."

Before I could reply, he went into the tent, zipped it up so I couldn't see the bottom half of him, and proceeded to change into a bathing suit.

My mouth hung open as my brain tried to catch up with the change of events. I was about to put a gooey marshmallow in my mouth and now I had to put a bathing suit on? I thought about saying that I hadn't brought a bathing suit, but it was the middle of summer in Texas.

He'd call my bluff.

"Is that water safe to swim in? What if it has a ton of bacteria or something?" I asked, standing up to clean our plates and clear the table.

I heard the tent unzip.

"Oh, it definitely does, but we'll be okay. You can trust me, I'm an engineer." He smiled a quirky grin.

I was about to utter a snarky remark, like "you're not one yet," when I finally registered his appearance. He was standing there shirtless with a pair of navy swim trunks resting low on his narrow hips. His smooth pectorals slid into well-defined abs, and suddenly I couldn't remember what I was meant to be doing.

Did they make petroleum engineers work out? It must have been part of the curriculum.

"I'll clean the rest, you go change," he said, heading toward me. I instinctively took a step back and then did an awkward pivot so that he wouldn't be standing right next to me. I understand that wasn't the smoothest thing to do, and I sort of looked like a flustered robot, but it was just A LOT to take in all at once.

CHAPTER SEVEN

I had to eventually give up trying to find a bright side to the bikini situation. Size-A boobs, giant scar across my chest, pale skin…there was no bright side other than the fact that I was pretty skinny and I had long legs. I adjusted the triangles over my boobs and then pushed them together one last time, forming a hint of cleavage. The moment I let go, the light pink material fell right back into place. I looked like a prepubescent boy.

"C'mon Abby. The sun's going down in twenty minutes!" Beck called.

"Okay, okay. I'm coming." I unzipped the tent flap and stepped out. Beck wasn't busy doing "campy" things; he was standing there, watching me climb out, just as I had feared.

I had to concentrate painfully hard on each of my

movements. *Take one step out of the tent.* Good. *Now another. Turn and zip the tent. Yes, he's looking at your ass.*

His greenish hazel eyes were brazenly taking in my bikini body, only pausing for a moment over my scar. I had to say something to break the awkward moment.

"God, if you stare any longer I'm not getting in that water with you."

He laughed, thought for a second, and then cracked up at that, throwing his head back and clutching his stomach. I shoved him playfully with my hand, but as I moved to walk past him, he caught my hand again and pulled me back so I couldn't keep walking.

I looked up into the green swirls around his irises and could tell he was on the cusp of revealing something. His dark eyebrows were pressed together. His lips were parted slightly and his gaze never wavered. But it didn't last. I could see him pushing the thought aside before he formed a new one in its place.

"You think you're going in before me?" he asked with a goofy smile. He dropped my hand and raced past me toward the water.

I stood there speechless, wondering what it was he had *really* wanted to say. He dove into the lake with no reservations, and then surfaced a moment later. Translucent drops of water clung to his chest and shoulders. Cedars rimmed the lake on all sides and the setting sun shone beyond that. I wished I could have taken a picture for Caroline. We weren't that far from the town, but it felt like we were in the middle of nowhere.

"Does it feel good?" I asked, creeping closer to the edge. There was no way I was going to jump in like he did. I wasn't certain, but it seemed like I shouldn't ingest any of the water. There was no telling what type of bacteria lurked in it and being immunocompromised meant snorting gross lake water was probably not the best plan.

"Perfect," he answered, treading lightly and waiting for me.

I waded in up to my waist, and then when I couldn't touch anymore, I swam toward him. He was right. It was so warm outside that the water was refreshing, just shy of freezing. Yes, my teeth were chattering, but it still felt good.

"It's not that cold," he laughed.

"I'm smaller than you. You probably have like ten layers of fat warming you up," I joked, knowing full well there was not even a single layer of fat on him.

"Want to go to the middle and back?"

I looked beyond his shoulder. The lake was huge and I hadn't swam in years, but I didn't want to admit defeat.

"Okay, but no going under. That's cheating," I stated.

"Seems reasonable. Ready?"

My teeth were still chattering and I could feel my lips turning blue (one more side effect of being so pale), but I nodded. But before he could countdown, I started swimming as fast as I could. I kicked my feet in time with my arms, leaving him in the wake of my splashes.

"Hey! Cheater!" he called, starting to swim after me. I don't condone cheating, but we both knew he was going to win. I just needed a little advantage. Not to mention, seeing him flustered was priceless.

I grabbed some disgusting lake slime and chunked it behind me to add obstacles to his path like those bananas in Mario Cart. When I peered back, the slime sat atop his brown hair and sludge was dripping down his face. I couldn't help but burst out laughing.

"Sorry!" I offered innocently, but he tossed it off with a determined look in his eyes. *Uh oh.*

I kept swimming, never looking behind me for fear that he'd be on my tail. The center of the lake was still quite far, so I hunkered down and tried to concentrate on breathing in and out. It's embarrassing how little I had worked out prior to that moment. I couldn't do anything before my transplant, and then after, I'd worked with a physical therapist, building a bit of my strength back. It obviously wasn't enough. My arms felt like lead weights and my stamina was quickly dwindling.

My lungs gulped in heavy breaths and I tried to push past the pain, but my body was deciding it had had enough. I paused and tried to catch my breath while I treaded water. That's when I looked up and saw Beck in the center of the lake, looking relaxed and happy. Damn, I hadn't even made it half way. I tried to swim closer to him, but quickly decided against it. Dying on the first day of an epic road trip would really put a damper on my plans for living.

"Are you okay, Abby?" Beck yelled when he realized I wasn't swimming any closer.

My breathing was still uneven, so I just gave him a feeble thumbs up. He didn't buy it. He dipped under the water and I assumed he was bee lining for me. I tried to recover quickly. He'd think I was a wimp if I was this tired before even making it to the halfway point. Maybe I could say that I was attacked by a group of lake monsters and had to fight them off. I'd faced Loch Ness and lived to tell the tale.

A second later, his brown hair popped out of the water a few feet away from me.

"Not a swimmer?" he asked, inching closer. If his plan had been to kill me on this camping trip, he should have done it then. I didn't feel like swimming back to shore and treading water was becoming harder by the second.

"Guess not," I mustered shallowly.

His brows furrowed and, without my permission, he swam up to me and wrapped an arm around my waist. I would have been angry, but the moment he lifted some of my weight off of my arms, I wanted to cling to him for eternity.

"To hell with feminism, please just carry me back to shore." I wrapped an arm around his broad shoulders, feeling his muscles move and flex under my touch.

A rumble of laughter moved through him in response to my request. "Could you wrap your arms around my neck as if I was giving you a piggy-back ride? That's probably the easiest way."

I shifted behind him and then instinctively wrapped my legs around his waist as well. It hit me like a meteor: I was barely clothed with my legs wrapped around a really, *really* hot guy. My boobs were pressed against his toned back. I looked up to the sky and mouthed 'thank you' to whoever might have been watching.

"—legs," he said.

Oh, God. "What?" I mumbled, realizing I'd missed whatever he had just said.

"Unwrap your legs," he repeated. My face turned ten shades past crimson. I had been clinging to him like a baby monkey. "You can kick with your legs or just lay there," he added, "but I can't really move my hips with you gripping them that tightly."

"Yeah, okay. It wasn't *that* tight," I grumbled, letting my legs fall back.

He laughed and started to swim us back to shore. "I

probably lost circulation *down there*."

I smiled at the thought. "Oh please, the water is cold. I'm sure there wasn't much circulating going on anyway..."

He grinned back at me and shook his head. The water reflected back at me from his hazel eyes. My heart pounded against my chest so hard that I'm sure he felt it as well. His pace picked up while I tried to ignore the shifting of his back muscles against my chest. Let me tell you, it was not an easy task.

The second we got back to shore, I grabbed my pajamas, my cell phone, and the black urn, and bolted from the campsite. I told Beck I was going to change and use the restroom before it got too late. In reality, I just needed a moment to collect myself. Clinging to him like that had felt amazing, and there was no denying how turned on I was. But I wasn't sure if I was supposed to feel like that considering he hadn't made a move on me or anything.

As I walked through the woods, I realized that I was just like my Aunt Dana's shih tzu that always humped my leg when I went to her house. Poor dog. I knew what it felt like to derive your pleasure from an unassuming patron.

When I found the restroom, I changed into my sleeping shorts and a tank top, but even that still seemed like too many layers. My fear that the temperature wouldn't drop at sundown was realized. It was somehow even hotter, and the air was stale and static. I pulled my hair into a messy bun and then threw my stuff back into my backpack.

There was one last thing I needed to do before I headed back to the campsite. I walked further into the woods, untaped the black urn, and then texted Caroline.

Abby: Short version: We're camping. Went swimming. I was a pathetic wuss and Beck had to carry me back to shore. Bonus: I felt his body and it was probably the best moment of my life.

Yes, you can relax. I checked like ten times to ensure that I had Caroline's name at the top of the text screen and not Beck's. I've seen enough sitcoms to know that I couldn't fall for that mistake.

After the text had sent, I put my phone down and twisted the lid off of the urn. I took a deep breath in preparation for the next moment, but nothing happened. The contents of the urn didn't budge. There was no wind, remember? Just static air. I looked down into the basin and waited for something profound, but instead I just stood in the forest, in my pajamas, holding an urn, and looking like a weirdo. I sighed and tipped the urn over a little bit, letting the top of the ashes spill out onto the ground. It was the definition of anti-climactic. The light gray ashes just fell to a pile on top of the dirt. There was a reason people called it *scattering* ashes and not *dumping* ashes. No one wants to *dump* ashes.

I tried really hard to have a spiritual or thoughtful moment, but I ended up just thinking that it was getting darker and that I didn't want to be eaten by a bear. My phone buzzed next to me on the ground. Caroline's face appeared and any hope of having a magical moment was lost.

I snatched the phone and clicked 'answer'.

"Hey. You just ruined what was supposed to be one of the most moving moments of my life," I proclaimed.

"Were you about to have sex with Beck?"

I snorted. "No. I was scattering the first bit of ashes."

"Ohhhh. Yeah, sorry about that. Do you want me to sing a song or something? Maybe say a prayer?"

I twisted the urn's lid back into place. "You don't know a prayer, Caro."

"I could *make* one up, Abs. Have a little *faith*."

"Oh my God. I see what you just did and it is so not funny." I still laughed because it actually was funny. "How's your bum liver?"

She sighed and I knew it was a bad prognosis. "They haven't let me go home yet."

"You're still in the hospital!?"

"Yeah, the doctors don't feel like I should go home anytime soon."

I chewed on my bottom lip and tried to think of something to cheer her up. Instead, I said, "It's not too late. I could come home. I really don't want to be away from you while you're stuck in there."

"You are the most stubborn person I know and I'm hanging up before you say anything else."

"Call me if you need me. Any time, okay?" I added quickly, knowing her threat about hanging up was real.

"Yes. Bye, Abs."

The moment I hung up and started heading back to the camp site, my phone rang again. Beck.

"You know, we'll be together for two weeks straight. We don't also have to be on the phone while I'm in the bathroom," I spoke, internally thrilled at the thought that he just couldn't get enough of me. Oh, who was I kidding.

"Where are *you*?"

His tone was anything but playful.

"What are you talking about?" I asked, thinking it was strange how dark the forest had become. When I'd left the restroom, twilight was still in effect, but now darkness was descending all too quickly. Suddenly, I started to panic. I hadn't brought a flashlight; the only light was coming from my phone's screen.

"You've been gone forever. I went to check the bathrooms and you weren't there."

Oh, crap.

"I'm sorry. I had to call my friend and then I guess I lost track of time."

I heard him take a deep, calming breath.

"Okay. No big deal, it's just that you probably shouldn't wander around by yourself at night."

I wanted to clarify that technically when I *began* wandering, night hadn't fallen yet, but he was right so I just kept my mouth shut.

"Do you know how to find your way back to the restroom?"

I thought I did so I said, "Yes."

"Okay. I'll meet you there. Don't hang up until you see me." I couldn't tell if he was overreacting or not. It probably *was* scary when he went to restrooms and I wasn't there.

I kept walking, angling the phone toward the ground so the soft glow would illuminate my path. If my wandering hadn't been too erratic, I was pretty sure the restrooms were just a few yards in front of me. Unfortunately, I had no way to be sure.

"I'm sorry, Beck," I murmured softly, feeling foolish all of a sudden.

"Hey, it's no problem."

Just then I saw a flashlight glow in the distance and a cell phone illuminating the cutest brown-haired boy in all of the woods. Unless, of course, Orlando Bloom was also camping there.

"I think I see a big dork next to the bathrooms," I joked, feeling an immense relief now that I knew I wouldn't be lost in the woods forever.

He chuckled and I saw his face pop up to look for me. It didn't take him long.

"What a coincidence, I see a lost gypsy girl walking toward me," he squinted through the darkness, "...in polka dot pajamas. And she has an urn in hand, so it's hard to tell if she's going for a good-girl or a gothic-type look?"

I burst out laughing as I stepped closer. *He was too much.*

"You're too much."

"Thanks," he smiled.

I was only a few feet away from him then.

"It wasn't a compliment."

He pressed end on the call as I stepped right in front of him.

"You promised me s'mores," I said with a smile.

He grinned and we started to walk back toward camp.

"Yeah. I thought I was going to have to eat them all while you got dragged away by mountain lions."

I hip-checked him, except our difference in height made it so that I ended up just hitting my butt on his upper thigh. So smooth.

"You were going to eat them even though I went missing?" I asked, feigning shock.

He shook his head and wrapped his arm around my shoulders, bringing me into his side. "Oh, Abby. Of course I would have. What was I meant to do? Just *leave* the s'mores at our campsite? That's ludicrous."

CHAPTER EIGHT

By the time we crammed ourselves into the tent, I was full of s'mores and thoroughly sweltering. Roasting by the fire hadn't been the best idea in ninety-degree weather, but it was definitely worth it for melted chocolate. The last thing I wanted to do was crawl inside my sleeping bag, so I just lazily fell on top of it— making a big THUMP sound. My limbs relaxed out around me, and in the next moment, Beck mimicked my pose on top of his sleeping bag as well.

"This is the life," I said, glimpsing the dark shadows of the night through the tent.

"Abby Mae, I think you might be right about that."

I rolled over onto my side and watched him laying there. "How old are you?"

He looked at me with such earnest concentration that I had to consider if I'd asked something else. Then he responded, "Between 30 or 40."

I laughed. "What?"

He shrugged. "I don't sleep much. The average person sleeps one third of their lifetime, so I figure I've lived about twice as long as everyone else my age."

"So you're twenty?"

"Twenty-one. You?"

"Hmm…I guess ten or eleven," I answered, playing his game.

His eyebrows shot up. "Jeez, you must be quite the snoozer."

I sighed. "I was in and out of the hospital my whole life until a few months ago, so I slept a lot," I admitted, instantly thinking of the scar beneath my tank top.

"Oh, wow," he answered, still facing the roof of the tent and letting my declaration take hold. I knew it would change things between us, but he would have found out eventually.

"I don't think it works the same for you," he declared, rolling over to face me. His t-shirt stretched over his chest and in the lantern light he looked like a dream.

"Why not?"

"I don't think having a life-threatening illness would take away years of your age. I think you might be wiser than the rest of us."

Maybe he was right. I knew what it was like to go to sleep at night worrying that everything would be the "last" thing in my life: the last time I ate dinner, the last time I hugged my parents, the last time I opened my eyes, the last time I heard someone say my name. But then I thought of all the things I had yet to experience. I didn't know what it felt like to be normal. What it felt like to go on a date or attend high school and go to prom. This was my first time traveling anywhere without my parents.

"Penny for your thoughts," he asked, pulling me out of my reverie. I'd been staring up at the full moon through the roof of the tent.

"Beck, could we kiss? I know that this is the first night of a road trip and I have no clue if you'd even want to, but I had congenital heart disease up until two months ago. I had a heart transplant and that's why I have this big ugly scar on my chest." I pointed to where the top of the scar peeked out of my tank top. "I promised my friend, Caroline, that I would be brave, but it's hard when you're clearly much more experienced than I am. Right? I mean you're really ho—"

I didn't get to finish my sentence. Beck leaned forward and closed the gap between us, sealing his lips to mine. It was the most romantic thing I'd ever experienced. He wrapped his hand gently around my neck so that his palm was pressed against my skin, bringing us even closer. Every bit of sense was focused on the feel of his lips on mine. I was in heaven. Until I did the unthinkable— I attempted to french kiss him. What sort of person tries to french kiss someone when they have no clue what they're doing? I ended up just awkwardly sticking my tongue down his throat and he pulled away laughing.

Yes. Beck ended our first kiss by cracking up.

"Did you just attempt to use tongue on your first kiss?" he asked, sporting his dimpled grin. I hated that he was laughing at me. Had that kiss not affected him at all? I leaned forward and covered his smile with my hand, but it only made him smile wider. I could feel his warm breath on my palm.

"I thought that's where it was heading," I groaned, wishing a bear would maul our tent in that exact moment.

"You can't make fun of me!"

His features suddenly turned serious and he reached up to peel my hand away from his face.

When his lips were finally free, he replied, "Abby, I don't see how I could possibly make fun of you for practically sucking my face off."

I narrowed my eyes and stuck out my tongue at him. His teasing was funny, but it still didn't change the fact that my ego was lying in a puddle on the ground.

His grin settled into a thoughtful smile. "I'm sorry that you were so sick until a few months ago, but I'm really glad you're healthier now and on this road trip with me," he declared so softly that it nearly broke my heart.

I couldn't do anything other than nod for fear that he would see the emotions written across my face. He said I needed to work on my poker face, and I wondered if he could see that I was royally flushed in that moment.

We laid there for a few minutes, just studying one another, when suddenly we heard a loud snap and then something heavy fell onto the tent, making it cave inward. I squealed and jumped toward Beck. I curled into him with my face buried in his neck. My heart was beating like a hummingbird and it took me a moment to realize that Beck was running his hand down my back…while laughing.

"Hey, Abby. I think it was just a branch of a tree breaking off and landing on our tent."

"Nope," I protested, not willing to pull my face out of the warmth of his neck just yet. "Please make sure it's not a bear or a serial killer."

"What should I do if it's a bear serial killer?" Beck asked, really pleased with how funny he was being at the moment. I could have killed him, if you know, the bear serial killer didn't get to him first.

I smiled against his skin. "Is that a bear that *is* a serial killer? Or a person that kills bears…serially?" I asked for clarification.

Beck laughed and then finally sat up, which sadly meant that I had to unwrap my body from around him. He didn't seem to mind me cuddling up to him, but then I thought back to the dreaded *first kiss* and any hope of future cuddles pretty much flew out the window.

He moved forward on his hands and knees and unzipped the tent. Then he poked his head out and peered in both directions before winking back at me.

"I'm thinking we're all clear. But we should probably set up night shifts to make sure. We'll each sleep for five minute intervals," he teased with a sexy smirk.

"Alright, alright. We'll probably be killed any minute now, but who knows," I paused and lowered my voice to a mere whisper, "*maybe* I overreacted."

Beck laughed and rezipped the tent. "I didn't mind the overreaction," he murmured, looking down at his sleeping bag.

I blushed and then tried to do a fake yawn to cover up my massive grin.

"I'm ready for bed," I said, suddenly feeling exhausted from our day.

"Me too. I'm not trying to be creepy or anything, but I usually sleep in my boxers. I won't do that to you tonight, but I definitely can't sleep with my shirt on in this heat. Is that okay?"

Like any man, woman, or child would have said no? "It's fine, I usually sleep with my eyes closed anyway, so I won't see." I smiled at my attempt at playing off my nerves, and then made a show of rolling onto my back to give him some semblance of privacy. But when he started to tug the shirt off, I couldn't keep my eyes focused on anything else. I watched the tanned muscles pull taut in his back as he threw his shirt into the corner on top of our backpacks. The second he was done, I flipped over to face away from him. The last thing I saw was his smirk that told me he knew I was watching the whole time.

"Night, Beck."

"Night, Abby."

• • •

Sleep was elusive that night. I tossed and turned so much that I'm not sure I slept more than one hour at a time. It was just so damn hot. I thought about stripping off my tank top and sleep shorts, but figured I should at least wait until the second night for that. Sometime after sunrise I finally turned over and realized that Beck wasn't in his sleeping bag. I pushed up into a sitting position and unzipped the tent to find him a few yards in front of me. He'd moved one of the camping chairs to the edge of the lake and was reading in the early morning light. It looked like a nice idea, so I grabbed my kindle, slipped on my sandals, and joined him.

The camping chair dragged in the sandy dirt behind me as I stepped closer. Beck glanced up from his book and I realized that maybe he wanted some private time. I didn't want to encroach on that, so I placed the chair a few feet away from his. Before I could sit, though, he gave me a silly look and reached out to pull my chair closer.

"I brushed my teeth already so you don't have to worry about my morning breath," he winked.

"Oh, well I just woke up so you won't be so lucky," I

grumbled, taking my seat next to him and folding my legs up into a pretzel in the chair.

"Ah, so no attempts at second kisses should take place this morning."

My head snapped up to meet his gaze. "Oh, so you think there will be more *attempts*?"

He smirked. "There will definitely be a second kiss in your life. It could even be with me if you play your cards right."

Confident, goofy, sonofa, jerk.

"Nah, I tried it that one time and it wasn't that great. I think I'll abstain for the rest of my life."

He laughed and shook his head. "What are you reading?" he asked.

I looked down at my kindle and wondered if I should make something up or if I should tell him the truth.

"An awesomely cheesy romance." I told him the truth.

His lip turned up in a half smile. "Nice."

"You?"

He held up his book for me to read the title: *The Curious Incident of the Dog in the Night-time*. The cover even had a die-cut of an upside down dog.

"What's the incident?" I asked, adjusting in my seat to get comfortable.

"I can't tell you," he replied.

"Hmph."

"Want to read for a bit?" he asked.

I nodded, but I just ended up staring off at the lake for a while, wondering where the rest of the trip would lead. Quite a lot had happened and we'd been gone for less than twenty-four hours. If the excitement of the trip was modeled on an exponential curve, we'd be having sex by tonight and I'd be pregnant and married by the end of the two weeks.

• • •

We'd packed our stuff and headed out toward greener pastures before noon, deciding that before setting out for Odessa and Marfa, we wanted to see the coast. Beaches in Texas aren't the most pristine, but as long as you steer clear of Galveston, the water isn't too murky. We were heading south and jamming to Ben Kweller when I asked Beck what he wanted to do with his life now that he wasn't sure about engineering.

"I don't know. Maybe release a studio album of guttural noises. It'll be white noise for hardcore rock fans."

"Like Yoko Ono?" I asked, pretending to take him seriously.

"Not even remotely similar. Mine will be much more guttural. Like, at least four times as guttural, maybe even twice as throaty."

He didn't give me any time to expand on that ridiculous topic.

"What do you plan on doing to make money?" he asked, peering over at me from behind his Wayfarer sunglasses.

"I have absolutely zero, negative zero idea of what I want to do." Just the thought of it brought back that immense pressure in my chest.

"On account of not really having a future before two months ago?" he asked.

"Exactly."

He nodded empathetically. "So now the world is your proverbial oyster and you're finding out that maybe shucking oysters isn't quite as easy as everyone makes it out to be. Oh, and there are far fewer pearls than you expected."

I nodded, thinking that I might have been in love with him in that moment.

"You could be the producer for my album," he suggested. That was the very first time he suggested a solution to my future-career woes.

"Thanks. I'll keep that in mind."

"Oh my GOD," he shouted out of the blue, and I jerked back against my seat in fear. Were we about to hit a car or swerve off the road?

"WHAT?" I yelled, pressing my hand to my heart.

"A sign back there said to exit in five miles for a Prehistoric Dinosaur Adventure Park."

Dear God.

There was no point in arguing, Beck had us turning into the nearly abandoned park less than ten minutes later.

"Abby, I realize you're containing your excitement because you're trying to remain mysterious and aloof, but please know that if you want to squeal or cry, I wouldn't think less of you."

I crossed my arms in front of my chest and kicked the gravel with my Keds. "I can't believe you're dragging me here."

"I can *feel* the excitement emanating from you. It's palpable, Abby. Wow. Minty."

I picked up the pace after that so that I could pay for both of us. Beck kept sneaking his card into every checkout line and I didn't want him thinking he had to pay for everything during the trip.

A pimply-faced kid was sitting inside of a crumbling kiosk. The remnants of the shack made it clear that at one point it had been painted vibrant colors, but the wood had started chipping ages ago and now it was just depressing.

"Two tickets please," I said politely.

The kid looked up from his Nintendo DS. "Two adults or two kids?"

I looked behind me. There was only one other car parked in the lot and there were no kids in sight.

"Oh. Two adults."

He took my cash without a second glance and started getting my change.

"Don't touch the exhibits. Don't sit on the dinosaurs. Don't take profane photographs using the dinosaurs as props," the kid droned on.

"People do that?" Beck implored excitedly as he stepped behind me.

The kid shrugged. "The rule is there for a reason."

Beck thought that was the funniest thing ever. As we walked away, he sidled up to my side and whispered in my ear, "That could be *your* job. You could be Ms. Prehistoric Dinosaur Adventure Park. YOU could tell people not to take sexual photos with the dinosaurs."

I veered away from him and started to take in the exhibits. The front kiosk had definitely foreshadowed the quality of the rest of the park. I had no clue what to expect, but it was about one-tenth the size of a normal zoo. There were cages set up with animated dinosaurs inside, but most of them had stopped working long ago. The ones that did work moved painfully slow and their growls came out sounding like distorted garbles.

It took us hardly any time at all to lap around the entire place, but we couldn't leave yet. It didn't feel like we had done everything the park had to offer. I was measuring my foot in one of the "Compare Your Footprint to a T-

REX" displays when Beck came up with his brilliant idea.

"I think you should sneak into one of the cages and climb onto a dinosaur," he whispered quietly, as if the kid up front could hear us all the way back there.

"Great idea," I beamed before dryly adding, "No."

"C'mon, Abby! The kid said it was against the rules, don't you want to do it?"

"Not in the least," I answered, acknowledging that my footprint was in fact MUCH smaller than that of a T-rex.

He stepped in front of me and blocked my path with his hands on my shoulders. "Abby. Someone has done it before, that's why there's a rule. Don't you want to be that person? Don't you want to have memories of this summer that don't include measuring your freaking footprint?"

I hated him for calling me out on the fact that I really was a goodie-two shoes, but living my life didn't mean I had to break rules. Though I wasn't sure how else I would feel alive. I'd never done anything like that before; maybe I didn't know what I was missing.

"Shit. Fine, I'll do it."

You wouldn't have said no to those greenish hazel eyes either. It really wasn't fair.

We picked the Triceratops in a cage near the back of the park because it was lowest to the ground. Beck laced his fingers together and I wedged my Keds inside his cupped hand so that he could help me over the fence. He couldn't come in with me because he was acting as my lookout and documentarian.

"Don't look at my ass."

"Wouldn't dream of it," he answered with a smug grin as I pushed off the ground and grabbed the top of the fence.

"Oh, please," I called as I hopped over and landed with bent knees in the mulch.

Holy crap. I was officially breaking the law. Right? Wasn't this trespassing or something?

"Move, Abby. You look like a deer caught in headlights."

I flipped him the bird, then crouched low and ran toward the dinosaur. I didn't want to be out in the open when I attempted to mount the damn thing, so I ran around to the other side. A couple of thumps on the dino told me that it was made of thick plaster; at least the thing would hold my weight while I was up there.

"Hurry!" Beck called.

I wiped my hands on my jeans shorts and tried to get a good hold on the back of its skull where there was that giant frilly curve. I stepped up onto the back of its bent knee. Then, with a giant grunt, I pushed off the knee and pulled myself up.

"Woohooo!" Beck called as I repositioned myself on top.

I knew I had less than a minute before the pimply kid looked up from his Nintendo DS, but I couldn't move. My heart was pounding a mile a minute. Adrenaline was shooting through every vein and I sat there reveling in the feeling of being wholeheartedly *alive*.

I looked over to Beck and saw him holding up his phone, ready to snap a picture. "Do something!"

I threw my arms in the air and squealed louder than I ever had in my life.

"Get down! Get down! Why did you just scream? The kid's coming over!"

I didn't want to get down. I threw my hands back into the air and pretended to ride the dinosaur like I was trying to rope cattle. Beck just stood there laughing hysterically and snapping photos. I leaned back and laid down, then bent my knee up like I was posing seductively. I looked right at Beck and bit my lip.

"Oh my God, Abby." He wasn't snapping photos anymore. He was looking at me like he wanted to devour me.

"HEY! GET DOWN!" The kid had finally arrived. I screamed and scrambled into action. My survival instincts kicked in and I jumped down and hopped the chain link fence with unusual dexterity. Once I was on the other side, Beck and I took off like we were sprinting for our lives. I'm not even sure if the kid chased after us, but we had a mission. We were the law-breakers, delinquents, and rebels without a cause trying to fight the man and get away with it. We kept sprinting through the exhibits, out of the park, and toward our car before Beck pulled my arm and stopped me.

I was at the passenger door, leaning against the glass. He was supposed to go to his side so we could finish our getaway, but he wasn't following protocol. He pushed me against the passenger door and pressed his lips to mine. It was a soul-stealing kiss, the kind that lifts you off your heels and makes your spine curl. I wrapped my arms around his neck and moaned into him. Our hearts were already beating rapidly from our run, but they blended together as Beck gave me the best second-first kiss anyone has ever had.

And that, future kids, is why in an old brown box tucked deep within my closet, you'll find a photo of me attempting to mount a Triceratops.

CHAPTER NINE

Abby: Hey C. We just arrived in Corpus Christi. We're staying in a hotel on the beach for the next two days. Kiss number 1: horribly awkward, I'll give details later. Kiss number 2: best experience of my life, details also to follow. PS. I sort of broke the law today!

Abby: Hey Mom! Sorry I haven't answered your calls. I wasn't at my apartment this morning because I was visiting Caroline. Don't worry. Love you and I'll call you later.

Caroline: What?! First & second kiss already AND breaking the law? I'm so proud. If I don't answer later, I'm probably napping- don't worry.

Mom: Oh, alright. Well that makes me feel better. I know we've been hounding you lately, but it's hard not to worry. I love you.

"Earth to Abby," Beck called as we parked the car in a spot outside of the beachfront hotel. We were splurging for the next two days; after camping last night, we felt like we deserved a shower and a real bed.

"Sorry, I was texting my friend Caroline," I replied, slipping my phone back into my purse.

"Is she a healthy friend or a sick friend?"

I wondered how he would even know to ask something like that. I guess being sick for so long meant that most of the people in my life would have also been sick.

"Very sick friend," I answered quietly. "She needs a liver transplant."

"I thought those were one of the easier organs to get?"

I looked out toward where I knew the ocean was. I could barely make out a thin layer of blue waves beyond the horizon. "Not if you still have cancer."

I couldn't see his reaction, but I could feel his gaze on me. He never said anything, because really what was there to say?

"Do you think we have time to go swimming?" I asked, narrowing my eyes and trying to fight the feelings of sadness looming just a few blinks away.

"Probably not tonight," he answered wistfully. "What if we went first thing in the morning?"

I glanced back toward him. "Sounds good. Can we order pizza and eat it on the bed while we watch a movie?"

He nodded, giving me a small smile. "After running from the law, we should probably lay low for the night," he joked, making me smile once again.

Our hotel room only had one bed. I pretended like I didn't care, as though I'd casually shared a bed with dozens of hot guys in my past, but inside my organs were flip-flopping around like crazy.

"Abby, please try and keep your hands to yourself tonight," Beck joked the moment we walked into the room.

Normal-Abby would have offered a witty comeback, but the alien inside my brain at that moment could only mumble awkwardly and evade eye contact at all cost.

We fought over both the pizza *and* the movie. We ended up just having to order two pizzas: one small vegetarian with pineapple and one medium supreme. Beck thought we should rent *The Conjuring* and I thought we should watch *Man of Steel*. I nixed the horror, he nixed the overdone superhero plot.

"I'm going to take a shower before our food gets here, but so help me if you purchase *The Conjuring* I will throw your pizza into the ocean."

"As if your miniature arms could fling it that far." He eyed me skeptically.

I gathered up my shampoo and floral scented body wash. "I will fling it as far as I can. If it lands on top of your grandfather's Camper, then so be it."

"I'm pretty sure *The Conjuring* is taking place in this room right now," he said with a hint of a smile.

"Are you saying that I'm possessed?" I asked, heading toward the restroom.

"If the devil-like-tendencies fit…"

I tried to come up with something as equally funny, but I couldn't stop the laughter from ruining my plan.

"I think I hate you as much as I like you," I admitted before shutting the bathroom door.

He mumbled something, but I couldn't hear it with the door closed. Instead, I imagined him saying that I was the funniest, prettiest girl he'd ever met. That was probably dead on.

After turning the water on to warm up, I pulled out my thermometer and my various pill bottles. My temperature was still normal, thank God, and the pills were swallowed quickly with the water muffling most of the noise as I stuffed the rattling bottles back into my bag.

Fifteen minutes later, feeling one hundred times better than I had with all that residual lake slime dried on my skin, I pulled on my pajamas and carried my stuff out of the bathroom. Our pizzas still hadn't arrived yet, so Beck was sitting on the bed with his back against the headboard, focusing on a text. I took the opportunity to look at the pieces of him I hadn't yet inspected: his long jean-clad legs, his broad shoulders, the sexy five o'clock shadow he would most likely shave soon.

I started brushing out my damp hair before asking, as casually as possible, "Who are you texting?"

He looked up, his hazel eyes locking onto mine, and grinned. "Mary Beth."

I huffed nonchalantly, "Sounds hot."

"Hmmm," he said, drawing his gaze down to my bare legs and then back to his phone.

"Are you guys dating?"

His grin widened, but he didn't look up at me. "It's not like that."

"Oh."

"You seem overly curious about me texting another girl." He quirked an eyebrow.

I shrugged and shifted slightly so that I could look at the hotel mirror propped above the desk. From my vantage point, I could see Beck watching me brush my hair. "Not in the least," I answered.

"Alright," he answered confidently, running a hand through his now disastrously-messy hair.

"How do you know her?"

He narrowed one eye, tilting his head back in thought. "Let's see… she made me a baby blanket when I was little, but I don't really remember our first meeting."

I loosened my hold on the brush, only then realizing I'd been tensing every muscle in my body. "Oh. Is she your grandmother?"

Cue the adorable half-smile that made my heart skip a beat. "The one and only. Grandmother aka Grammy."

I scrunched my nose. "Hah. So you aren't sexting?" I thought I'd win with that comment, but Beck never let me win.

"I didn't say that."

I laughed and shook my head. He wiggled his eyebrows playfully and tossed his phone down onto the bed. A second later, he started tugging his t-shirt off and I was left gaping like an idiot. The way his muscles stretched as he lifted his arms…the hard lines of his six-pack.

"I'm going to shower. If the pizzas get here will you pay with the cash I left out on the desk?" He walked away and I was left gaping like a sad guppy.

"Mhmm," I murmured dumbly. I wish I could say that seeing him strip didn't faze me, but it was so unexpected. We'd gone swimming together, yes, but being half naked in a hotel room felt much different.

I was still sitting there on the edge of our bed, with my hand wrapped loosely around my hairbrush, when a knock sounded at the door.

"Coming!" I yelled as I clambered off the bed and reached for my wallet. Like hell I was going to use Beck's cash with him not around; it was finally my turn to pay for something.

Ten minutes later, the shower cut off and I heard Beck drying off. My body was relaxed against the headboard with my pizza box propped on my lap. It felt scandalous to be eating on the bed, but just as my first bite was an inch away from my mouth, Beck walked out of the bathroom wearing nothing but a towel around his hips. It was sitting just under his stone-hard abs and angled dangerously low.

Ahhh.

"Seriously?! Seriously. Who just walks around like that?" I commented, dropping the slice back into the box and clapping my hands over my eyes.

He laughed and my fingers parted so that I could peek through them. I wasn't being subtle. There was just so much to look at it. His shoulders were impossibly broad and I could smell his body wash, clean and woodsy, from across the room.

"Some of us are trying to eat, you know…"

He laughed and shook his head. "What are you doing, Abby?" he asked, reaching into his bag for clothes and holding his towel together with the other hand. *Oh god, please let it fall open. Please let it fall open. Wait, no. I'm not watching. I'm enjoying my pizza.*

"Abby?" Beck prodded, peering over his shoulder at me.

Realizing I'd been caught peeking through my fingers, I scrunched them back together quickly. "I'm protecting my womanly sensibilities," I answered. "What are *you* doing?"

He shook his head, "Trying to break you out of your shell."

"Consider my shell cracked," I answered, dropping my hands and reaching for my pizza slice. Keeping my eyes focused on that savory pizza was training in will power.

Clothes successfully in hand, Beck made his way back to the bathroom. I thought I was in the clear, but at the last second, I glanced up and he dropped his towel. It fell with a thump right at the edge of my bed.

"BECK!" I yelled just as I was greeted by his tremendously-shaped backside. It was definitely the best butt I had ever seen, which is saying something because I saw Brad Pitt's in Troy.

When we were beyond full and the movie credits were rolling, I turned toward Beck.

"Did you work while you were in school?" I asked, wondering how he was able to splurge on our trip.

He scrunched his brows and turned toward me. "No, I took hard course loads and was an undergrad TA. Why?"

I shrugged and shifted my gaze to his worn-in t-shirt. "I was just wondering how you have money to splurge on a road trip if you're still in college."

"Ah," he nodded, and turned toward me. His brown hair fell over his forehead in a boyish mess and I thought for a moment to reach over and tuck it back into place. I gripped my shirt instead.

"I had a trust fund that became active when I turned twenty-one."

"So you're really rich?" I asked, probably breaking every social code.

"Stinking rich," he said with a silly grin.

"Like that movie where the kid gets a blank check?"

He laughed and then met my eyes with a fierce-intensity. "My grandfather started a publishing house. That business card I wrote my number on was his."

My mouth dropped and then I quickly shuffled off the bed and retrieved my purse. His grandfather's card was still tucked away in my wallet behind my buy one get one free frozen yogurt coupon.

"Do you want it back?" I asked. The card looked old and worn and I felt bad that I hadn't taken better care of it.

He scrunched his brows together and shook his head. "No. I like knowing you have it."

For a second I thought about arguing that he should keep it, but then I thought better of it. "Okay, it'll be in my wallet in case you want it back," I conceded.

"Thanks."

"So why don't you just go work for your grandfather's company?" I asked, crawling back onto the bed and pulling my long night shirt down.

"He sold it a few years before he passed away."

"Oh. Was it a family business?"

His features hardened at the mention of his family. In the few days I'd known Beck, I thought his entire personality was lighthearted and carefree, but in that brief break of character, I saw a deeper layer hidden beneath.

"It could have been, but my father's an engineer. He went to MIT as well." Another piece of the Beck puzzle fell into place.

"Let me guess…was he a *petroleum* engineer?" I was trying to lighten the mood, but I was doing a poor job of it. His gaze was focused on the never-ending abyss that filled the space between our two bodies.

"Ding, ding, ding," Beck mocked sarcastically, and I knew he was tired of discussing his father.

"Well my dad is a computer programmer and my mom quit her job when I was born," I answered, diverting the topic.

"Because of your illness?" he asked.

"I'll never be sure. She said she wanted to be a stay-at-home mom and never minded the fact that she had to focus most of her attention on me." I rolled onto my back and stared up at the popcorn ceiling. "I give her a lot of crap, but every day I lived past my life-expectancy mark was because of her. Because she never took no for an answer and demanded the best medical treatment and holistic care."

"Is that why you're a vegetarian?" he asked. I was surprised he'd picked up on that fact.

I nodded. "Tons of studies have proven that meat, especially red meat, is linked to heart disease and cancer, so obviously my mom nixed that from my diet when I was really young."

"Maybe I'll become a vegetarian with you," he declared with a half smile.

I glared over at him. "Good luck, Mr. Supreme Pizza."

"Oh man, that was *really* good. Maybe I'll just have meat until the end of this trip or something. I need a cut-off day so I can eat everything one last time."

"Sounds reasonable," I replied.

We laid there for a moment in silence.

"Let's go to sleep. I have a surprise for you in the morning," he said with a confident smile.

"Really?"

His gaze took in my wide grin.

"Yep, and it has to do with the ocean." He waggled his eyebrows.

I squealed and jumped up onto my feet. My hips bumped from side to side as I did a giddy dance on top of the hotel bed.

"Abby! What if you're getting your hopes up?" Beck called, jumping up to join me. I didn't care if I was or not.

"Not possible!" I yelled. "I've only been to the ocean one time and that was like ten years ago! I'll be happy with whatever it is."

We ended jumping around the bed and laughing as we tried out various mid-air poses. I attempted to do a herky jump, but I ended up just flailing around. He probably saw my bright pink underwear beneath my sleepshirt, but I didn't really care. We were friends. Beck reached out for my hands and I gave them to him willingly. His grip held mine easily, and then he started twisting in a circle so that I had no choice but to follow his lead. My feet dipped in and out of the mattress as we spun faster and faster until the hotel room was a blur behind him. Everything was a mess of color. His hazel eyes were the only thing in focus.

"Mercy!" I yelled, feeling the pizza in my stomach starting to protest our wild spins.

He let go of me instantly and we fell back onto the bed with exasperated sighs. Our quick inhales and exhales dotted the silence. A smile was permanently etched across my cheeks and I feared that I would end up going to sleep with it still there.

"A journalist," Beck said between breaths.

"What?" I asked, shifting my gaze to him. He had the same wild grin on his face that I did. His eyes were focused on a single point on the ceiling, but there was no mistaking the hope clouding them.

"I want to be a journalist. I applied for an internal transfer at MIT."

CHAPTER TEN

I woke up the next morning tangled in Beck. My legs were wrapped around him, his hand was under my shirt, wrapped around the side of my torso, and my arms were hugging his chest. I froze immediately for fear that he would wake up and assume that I was mauling him in his sleep.

My thoughts went something like this: *Mmm this feels good, he's so hot, OH MY GOD I'm practically feeling him up, GET OFF HIM.* I decided that the best idea was to move away from him like someone would rip off a band-aid. I counted down in my head. *Three, two, one.* Then I rolled away from him in one quick motion. Except I overcompensated because I was nervous and a little turned on from his zero percent body fat, so I ended up slipping off the bed and hitting my head on the wall as my body thumped onto the ground.

"Ouch!" I howled, pressing a hand to my forehead.

"Abby?" Beck asked with a hazy tone.

"Yes. No. Just go back to sleep." I stayed crouched on the ground, hoping he would go back to sleep and I could tend to my pride in peace. But a moment later, a head of messy brown hair peeked over the side of the bed. He had a silly grin and was blinking his eyes open one at a time. The expression on his face told me that he knew exactly what happened.

"You'd rather sleep on the floor than next to me?" he asked, but his words were muffled by the blanket.

I shrugged and pushed to my feet. "You're a blanket hog." *Yeah, good job, Abby. That sounded much cooler than you really are.*

"Is that why you needed to cuddle me for warmth?" he asked, stealing my smugness.

"I don't know what you mean by 'cuddling'," I lied, rifling through my clothes, trying to distract myself from his gaze. "But I'm going to go down and eat breakfast."

"Okay. I'm going to go for a quick run."

"Sounds good. I have some things to do as well. Want to just meet at the beach?"

Beck agreed and I went into the bathroom to change into my bathing suit and cover up. By the time I was done, he'd already left for his run.

I grabbed my beach gear and the black urn before heading down to grab a banana and some granola from the hotel's breakfast bar. I wasn't sure where I would attempt to spread the ashes considering we'd slept in so late that the beach was already crowded. Could you imagine if I opened the urn and the ashes spread out all over some kid's sandcastle or a family's beach picnic? I was tempted to try it just to see the madness that would ensue, but it seemed too cruel even for my dark humor. Instead, I hiked my beach tote higher on my shoulder and set out to find a more private location.

The moment I stepped outside, a wild breeze picked up strands of my hair and whipped them around. I walked down onto the sand and stuffed my sandals into my bag so I could feel the warmth beneath my feet. In a few hours the sand would be unbearably hot, but now it just comforted my soles as I walked along the shoreline.

I passed so much life on the edge of that ocean. Happy kids running toward the water and then stopping abruptly at the edge and squealing with excitement. Would I have screamed like that if I was healthy enough to go to the beach when I was that young?

Almost a mile away from our hotel I found a long fishing pier. There weren't any fishermen on it. Maybe the water was too choppy or maybe it wasn't fishing season. I had no clue. All that mattered was that I could traverse the wooden planks and have a perfect spot to spread some of the ashes. I dropped my bag and retrieved the urn. The tape was already starting to curl back from the edge, but I prayed that it would stay intact for the rest of the trip.

After a peek behind me to make sure I was truly alone, I peeled back the tape and popped the lid off. As soon as that urn opened, the wind picked up the particles of ash resting at the very top. I titled the urn a smidgen to the side and even more particles were carried off over the water. The ocean was a much better place to spread ashes than the center of the woods.

I watched the ashes twinkle in the sunlight. Most of them dropped to the surface of the water, but the wind swirled some around and around, taking them farther from the pier. No words or prayers came to mind, but a *feeling* settled in my stomach. Freedom. I smiled wide watching the symbols of my oppression being carried away by nature's invisible force.

By the time I found a spot under an umbrella near our hotel, Beck still hadn't arrived. Was he running a marathon or something? I pulled out my SPF 100 sunblock and peeled off my cover-up. I could already see a slight red glow dotting my thighs and shoulders. The perks of pale skin were endless.

Just as I was adjusting my navy bikini top, I heard Beck approaching. His signature laugh drifted toward me and I turned to see him talking to a girl I recognized from the hotel breakfast bar. How did he meet girls so quickly? I hadn't come across one guy in nineteen years that seemed interested in me, yet it seemed as if girls approached him daily. Maybe I was playing for the wrong team. Maybe being a lesbian would be easier.

"Yeah, hopefully we can make it." I heard him telling the girl. Wait, what?

"We?" she asked, and I quickly turned back around, hoping they hadn't noticed me watching. *Squeeze the lotion and put it on your arm like a normal person would do.* I ended up squeezing it too hard and the lotion darted a few feet to the left, landing on the protruding belly of an old man sleeping. Oops.

"Me and my friend, Abby."

"Oh," the girl answered with a dejected sigh. "Okay, sure. It'll start around eight."

Yeah, whore. That's me, his *friend*, Abby. Then the realization hit. Was I freaking friend-zoned?

"Alright, cya."

Oh god, I knew he was walking toward me then. I busied myself with reading the ingredients on the back of my organic sunscreen. Zinc Oxide, zinc oxide, zinc oxide. Beck plopped down next to me, jostling my shoulder slightly.

"Oh hi, Beck! I didn't see you there." My voice was an octave higher than usual and my smile exuded fake sweetness.

He gave me an odd look and then nodded back to where he was just standing.

"That girl is staying in our hotel. She invited us to a bonfire tonight on the beach."

"We or you?" I asked, and then instantly regretted my jealously. Why did I care? Beck could make out with her *in* the bonfire for all I cared, right? I uncapped the sunscreen and started lathering it down my arms.

"We're a packaged deal, Abby. Need some help?"

I almost refused, but Caroline's face popped into my head. She would have yelled at me for turning him down. "Oh, sure. I've only done my arms." I could feel my heart rate pick up and my hand shook a bit too obviously as I handed the bottle over. I'd watched enough movies to realize that a guy offering to put sunscreen on you meant that in about ten seconds he would *accidentally* untie my bikini top and then we'd have raunchy beach sex. Was I prepared for public sex? I hadn't yet mastered private sex. Or, you know, anything past making out.

My breath caught when his hand hit my back. His touch felt sensual and warm, but not in an inappropriate way. He wasn't trying to give me a massage or anything; it was just the way my body reacted to him. It felt like his palm was setting my skin on fire. I told myself it was the sunburn already sinking into my shoulders. Yep, that feeling was from the sun, not Beck.

"How far did you run?" I croaked, trying to fill the

silence.

"Just six miles," he answered, moving to the bottom of my bikini strings. His hands slipped under to make sure I didn't get burned if my top shifted. It made my entire body buzz with nervous energy. I heard myself moan under my breath. What the hell? Did he hear that? Distract him.

"Just?" I stumbled over the word like I was learning to speak for the first time. "I could maybe run one-tenth of a mile."

"We'll get you training soon enough."

I grunted with my disapproval.

"I ran track in high school and college. Obviously MIT isn't known for athletics, but it helped me stay in shape while I was hunkered down in the library for ten hours at a time."

I imagined him wearing glasses, holding a book, and running with no shirt on. "If you become a vegetarian after our trip, I'll go running with you tomorrow morning. Wait, no. I'll buy a skateboard and a dog. Then I'll hold the dog's leash and let him pull me along side you."

He laughed. "That's cruel."

"It would be a really big dog. Or maybe a wolf."

He rubbed the last bit of sunscreen into my shoulders and then handed the tube back to me. "Sounds good, let's swim. My surprise doesn't start for another hour."

I hated having to wait another hour, but at least we were at the beach. I'd been dying to jump into the water since first stepping out of the hotel, and now I was practically melting from the heat, even under the umbrella. I hopped up and was about to start walking toward the water when Beck grabbed my hand.

"You can't just mosey on in. You've got run in with me and dive into a wave."

He was already pulling me along, practically lifting me off the sand behind him. Little kids looked up just as we narrowly missed taking down their hastily-built sand castles.

"Beck! What if the salt gets in my eyes?" I asked just as my toes dipped into the cold water. It felt amazing. "My sunscreen hasn't soaked in!"

"Close them!" He didn't even pause to reassure me. He took me farther out until a wave hit my thighs. The wave after it hit my stomach. Each one rocked against my slight frame, threatening to break my connection with Beck, but he held on tighter.

"On the count of three, hold your nose and close your eyes!" Just as he finished his orders, I looked up to see the wave-of-all-waves rolling toward us. It looked like it would swallow me up whole.

"Beck!" I screamed, half-fearing for my life, half-giddy with anticipation.

"One, Two, Three!" he called. I plugged my nose and closed my eyes just as Beck pulled me under the surface so that the wave washed over us. The cold water met my face with an icy splash, and for a moment I forgot I was under water. I smiled wide and briny water slipped over my tongue. I didn't mind the taste and I didn't have long to consider it because in the next moment Beck was pulling me to the surface. He was laughing wildly and I joined in, feeling the laughter in every cell of my body.

I wanted more.

"Let's go out farther!" I shouted, starting to pull him away from shore. I knew the dangers of the ocean: rip tides, under currents, sharks eating me alive, etc. But I didn't care. I trusted Beck and I knew he wouldn't let the ocean harm me if he could help it.

"There's probably a sandbar soon. Let's try and reach it," he commanded.

I could still touch at that point, but the water was getting higher and higher as we went. My heart didn't kick into overdrive until the water hit my neck. I wasn't sure how long I'd be able to tread water in the ocean. Calm water in a lake was one thing, but something about the ocean seemed inherently scary.

"I think you'll be okay, but if you need to you can climb onto my back like you did in the lake. Okay?" I didn't want to *need* to rely on him, but I was glad the option was there nonetheless.

"Are you sure there's a sandbar out there?" I asked, trying to find reassurance in the unknown.

He stopped moving us forward and turned to look at me. "No. I honestly have no clue. We can either try to reach one and maybe end up getting eaten by sharks, or we can stay here and wonder for the rest of our lives if there was a sandbar just a few more yards in the distance."

I didn't respond right away. Our eyes locked together. Hazelly madness and sage green. I had to squint as the sun glistened against the water. Then, slowly, a grin unfolded.

"The shark would definitely want to eat you. You're much more meaty. So, really, I have nothing to worry about. Let's go."

I thought he'd start pulling me out to sea right away, but instead he leaned in and kissed the edge of my mouth. When he pulled back I had no clue what he was thinking. His features were indistinguishable and his gaze was focused on our goal.

Was that a kiss kiss, or did I have food on the side of my mouth from breakfast? Dear God, if I had granola stuck to my face, please let a shark eat me right now.

We started swimming, finally releasing our hands, but sticking close enough that our arms touched whenever our strokes aligned. I tried to control my breathing so that I wouldn't embarrass myself with my lack of endurance. I didn't have an excuse. I wasn't the sick girl anymore. My body was healthy, my heart was healthy. I could do it.

I took a deep breath and pushed against the waves trying to rock me back to shore. Beck slowed his pace so that we stayed together.

Then finally, he let out a cheer and I turned to watch him place his feet on the ocean floor and stand up. Not a second later I followed suit and felt my feet dip into sand. We'd reached the sand bar. My breaths were labored and heavy, but I felt like I'd accomplished something much more profound than simply swimming out into the ocean. I know it might be hard to understand, but two months before that I couldn't walk to the bathroom without feeling winded. The idea of exercising or using my body as anything other than a vessel for watching TV, reading, and sleeping, had seemed like a cruel joke.

So you see, when I swam to that sandbar, using my own muscles, my own blood, and veins, and heart, it felt like I could take on the world.

"Beck!" I squealed, and jumped so that water splashed around me.

"Abby!" Beck answered with excitement. He could've swam to that sandbar and back two dozen times, but he celebrated with me as if he knew how monumental it was.

"TAKE THAT SHARKS!" I screamed so loud that I'm sure any shark within a few miles fled for fear of my wrath.

Beck and I laughed and jumped around, splashing water. Then he completely side-swiped me.

"I LIKE YOU!" Three words screamed out into the ocean so confidently and carefree that I wanted to bottle them up to prove to myself that he had in fact said them.

I stopped splashing and I just stared at him with wide eyes and a gaping mouth. I know you might be thinking "he didn't say *love*, chill out", but before that moment, a boy had never told me he liked me. Waves crashed against my hips, and I just stood there silent, completely taken aback. Thankfully, he didn't wait for me to respond.

"C'mon! Our surprise starts in a little bit and we should take a quick break before then."

CHAPTER ELEVEN

Beck had arranged a surfing lesson for us through the hotel. After we'd returned to shore and I'd reapplied sunscreen (with Beck's help), a surfing instructor with longish blonde hair and an interesting Texas-meets-surfer accent found us under the umbrella.

"Are you guys Beck and Abby?" he asked, looking down at a sheet of paper in his hand. He wasn't wearing a shirt and I could tell he spent most of his time outside. His entire body had a deep tan and he was toned from surfing.

I wondered how he spotted us among all the other beach goers, but when I looked around, it seemed we were the only ones around without a cartload of kids. I guess it was pretty obvious.

"Yeah," we said in unison, and then stood to shake the sand off of us.

"Oh, great!" he said. "Let's get started. I'm Jason. I'll be your surfing instructor."

Of course his name was Jason.

I pulled a hair band out of my bag and tugged my long hair into loose ponytail so it would be out of my face during our training. Then we followed Jason over to the shoreline where he'd placed two longboards in the sand.

"Have you guys ever surfed before?" he asked, holding my gaze with a pair of dark brown eyes. He was not *at all* bad to look at and I decided I would enjoy my surfing lesson even more.

We both shook our heads and he placed his hands on his hips, assuming the teacher pose. "Surfing is an art and you guys won't master it during one lesson. But, we'll start with the basics on the sand, move to the board, then move into the water."

"We'll do it right here on the beach where everyone can watch us?" I asked, adjusting my bikini bottom. Oh who was I kidding? Nothing would fall out of my bikini while I practiced surfing on the beach.

"Yeah, it won't be so bad." He gestured to the few beachgoers that were focused on us. "They'll go back to doing their own thing in a few minutes."

We nodded and I looked over to watch Beck roll out his shoulders and stretch his arms. He looked so good in that bathing suit and I had a suspicious feeling that he'd pick up surfing much faster than I would.

"Alright, let's start in the sand on our bellies. We'll learn how to mount the board first."

"Hear that, Abby? You're going to learn how to mount." Beck thought that was quite clever. Jason had the decency to clear his throat and look away.

I rolled my eyes. "Beck, you were the one trying to mount me in my sleep last night. Don't think I forgot."

He grinned and narrowed his eyes. "That's not quite how I remember it. I woke up to you practically on top of me."

I choked out a laugh. Were my unconscious limbs not to be trusted around him?

"Alright, you two," Jason said, breaking us out of our little banter.

"I was AH-MAZING!" I cheered as we unlocked the door to our hotel room.

"Okay, okay."

I twirled around and then folded my fingers behind my head in a cocky stance. "Jason said I was one of the best students he's ever had."

"He was just trying to get in your pants." Beck gave me a pointed stare. He really *was* competitive.

I scoffed. "Yeah, right! I stayed on the board for like twenty seconds at the end!"

"Alright. You were…pretty good," he relented with a quiet whisper, barely loud enough for me to hear a few feet away.

"I'm sorry, I don't think I quite heard that." I smirked, taking a step closer to him and dropping my arms. I wondered how long he'd put up with sassiness.

He picked his head up and his hazel eyes met mine as he took a step toward me. He didn't stop until his body was touching mine. His bare chest was pressed against my cover-up and I could feel his diaphragm lifting when he took a steady breath. He ducked his head until it was level with mine, then he moved his mouth until it was right over my ear.

"I said, you were *good.*" A tingle ran down my spine; it was as if he was trying to seduce me. His breath hit my neck and I tilted my head so that even more of my skin was exposed for him. I wasn't in control of my body in that moment. Had he pushed me to the ground or to the back of the door or to the hotel desk, I would have given myself over to him willingly and he knew it.

He bent his head an inch lower and placed a kiss on the base of my neck.

I had no clue what we were doing. He liked me, and I obviously liked him. Maybe we could just have a road trip fling. That's all it would be, right? We had no clue what we were doing with our lives. I needed to apply to college and I'd probably move away. He was probably going back to Boston. I had to find out what I wanted to do with my life. What was the meaning of life, anyway?

"I can practically hear your thoughts churning right now, Abby," Beck said, taking a step back and smiling.

I nodded infinitesimally. "I think a lot."

"I know," he said, stepping away from me. I wanted to protest. "Do you want to nap for a little bit before the bonfire?"

"Sure, I feel like I could go to sleep now and not wake up until tomorrow morning," I said, stretching my sore muscles. The swimming and surfing had been more physical activity than I'd done…ever.

He shook his head. "Not an option. I've never been to a beach bonfire before."

I smiled. "Neither have I."

• • •

I'd stepped out onto our hotel's balcony to call my mom while Beck showered. My parents were becoming suspicious. I had never gone this long without seeing them, but I played it off by telling my mom that I needed some space. I don't think she suspected that I'd left town at that point. It was just so out of character for me, being so distant, and I hoped she'd just assume I was camped out with Caroline or something.

"Sweetie, I understand that you need some distance from your father and me. I just want you happy and healthy."

The ocean breeze whipped through the phone so that I could barely hear her. I know she could probably hear it through the speaker. Was it windy in Dallas?

"Mom, I promise everything is okay."

Silence.

"Alright, well are you feeling alright?" she asked. I'd taken my temperature that morning and it was normal. I took all of my medications, and other than feeling tired from surfing and swimming, I knew my body was doing okay.

"Yes, Mom. I feel great actually."

She sighed into the phone and I felt terrible for making her worry. "Caroline isn't doing so well," I admitted. Caroline hadn't picked up the phone the past two times I'd tried to call, but I told myself she was napping and couldn't hear the phone ringing.

"Yes. I spoke with her mom today." Her tone said it all, it encompassed the immense sadness and I couldn't bear to listen to another word. I knew it in my heart of hearts anyway.

"Mom, I have to go."

"Already?"

I couldn't take it. Talking to her was reminding me of everything I'd needed two weeks away from. Just then, Beck walked back into the hotel room wearing his low-slung towel and nothing else. Perfect time to end the call.

"Yeah, Mom. I need to shower and stuff," I said, trying to inconspicuously watch Beck through the tinted glass on our balcony. He was leaning down to grab clothes and I watched the muscles on his back pull and stretch. He'd developed a healthy tan from being in the ocean all day and looked even sexier than before. I, on the other hand, developed a red hue on my cheeks, but other than that I had stayed as pale as ever.

I stepped closer to the tinted window so that I could see him more clearly. I hadn't realized I'd pressed my face against the glass until Beck looked up with a bemused smile. My eyes bulged and I quickly jolted into action, pretending that I was cleaning something off the window. Yup. Just a smudge on the window. I shrugged and gave him what I hoped was a nonchalant expression.

"Okay, I love you," my mom said with a defeated tone. Oops, I'd forgotten I was still on the phone.

"Love you, too."

Maybe the two weeks apart was good for both of us. We would both get to stretch our wings a little bit.

I slid the glass door open and Beck swiveled around to look at me. His damp hair looked even darker than usual and I just stood there in the threshold of the hotel room watching him for a moment. Each second I lingered there, the smile on his face widened until we were both perfectly clear about my obvious attraction to him.

"Shower's free," he noted with amusement.

"Perfect," I replied, finally realizing that my limbs did in fact still work. I tossed my phone onto the bed and breezed past him, not taking my change of clothes with me. We'll see how much *he* likes it when I come out in nothing but a towel.

The entire time I was soaping up and shaving and rinsing my hair, my heart was going a mile a minute. I wanted him to feel as affected by me as I was around him, but what if he didn't even bat an eyelash? One eyelash, people, that's all that I asked for.

The moment I turned the shower off, I heard muffled chatter from the other side of the door. I wrung out my hair and then pulled it up into a towel before pressing my ear to the door to listen for other voices. If he wasn't alone, my plan of seduction would come crashing down around me. I wasn't going to prance around in a towel for multiple people. One hot guy was enough for me.

With my ear pressed against the door, I realized that I could only hear his muffled speech. He must have been on the phone. Good, maybe I'd distract him and he'd drool onto the screen or something.

I unwrapped the towel from my hair and then wrapped it around my body. It hit a few inches below my ass. A glance in the mirror reflected my long strawberry blonde locks still damp and flung sexily (or so I hoped) around my face and down my back. I still had a healthy glow from the sun. My scar was peeking out from the top of the towel, but I tried to ignore it. He could take it or leave it. That scar wasn't going anywhere.

As I creaked the bathroom door open, I heard him laugh into the phone, but as I rounded the corner, his laugh cut off suddenly.

Success. I was indeed a siren. An unstoppable, sexy minx. My baby toe hit the edge of his suitcase and I howled. Motherfucker. Stubbing your baby toe is the face of true pain.

I glanced over to him quickly, hoping my mishap hadn't ruined the moment completely. His smile froze and then his features slid into a shocked gape.

"Oh yeah," he nodded into the phone, never looking away from me. "That recipe is good, but my grandmother makes one with pineapple in it as well."

Silence filled the air as the person on the other end picked up the conversation. Why was he giving someone recipe advice? What guy even knew a recipe by heart? His eyes drifted down my body in a lazy manner, taking in my neck and chest, then drifting down the towel to the few inches of my creamy thighs exposed at the very bottom.

"No, not the whole can. I'll have her send you the recipe. She's right here actually; do you want to talk to her?"

Why would he ask that? Why would I want to talk to whoever was on the other end of the phone?

"Oh, okay. I'll tell her. Bye. Nice talking to you, too," he said before hanging up.

That's when I realized that the phone in his hand wasn't his. It was mine. God damn technology companies. Did we all need to have the same rectangular black phone? What happened to being unique individuals?

I stepped closer to him without even considering the fact that I was practically naked. "Who was that?" I demanded.

"Your mom," he answered casually before standing up. His height towered over mine and I clutched the towel tighter.

“What?! Why were you talking to my mom?” I reached around him and grabbed my phone.

He didn’t move away. There was barely an inch between our bodies and I could feel his warm breath on my bare shoulder.

“She called back twice while you were in the shower. I didn’t want her to worry, so I answered.” I know it didn’t seem like a big deal to him, but it was. My parents were already suspicious of me.

“Beck! I’ve never introduced them to a guy before OR even mentioned a guy to them for that matter!”

I hated that there was amusement flashing across his heavenly features. Why wasn’t he taking this as seriously as I was?

“You should give your mom more credit. I explained that I was your friend and that you were in the bathroom. She was confused at first, but then I introduced myself and we started chatting. I think she likes me.”

I didn’t have anything to say to that, so I wiped a hand down my face and stared up at him. If anyone could charm my mom, it was Beck.

“Were you giving her a *recipe* at the end?”

His lips unfolded into a confident grin. “It was for my Grammy’s banana bread. Your mom wants you to send it to her.”

I couldn’t help but smile then. He took me by surprise at every turn. There was no limit to Beck Prescott; he couldn’t be pushed into a mold. Of course he would talk to my mom about banana bread, because why the hell not?

CHAPTER TWELVE

"So how did you meet this girl?" I asked as we made out our way out of the hotel lobby toward the beach. The sun had set an hour ago so the bonfire was most likely in full swing. I'd thrown on a cotton striped dress that hugged my meager chest and waist before loosening out into a mini-skirt. On any other girl, it would've look sexy and short, but on me it just looked like a sweet dress a toddler could pull off.

"She bumped into me on the way out of the hotel earlier, after my run," he answered, scanning his eyes down my outfit. I instinctively reached up to run a hand through my hair. It was falling in loose waves down my back. There was no point in trying to do anything else with it while we were standing out in the salty night air.

"*Physically* bumped into you?" I asked, trying to

clarify the encounter.

He laughed and narrowed his eyes on me playfully. "Yes, she was walking next to me and tripped or something."

I stopped walking and gawked up at him. "Oh my god, you've got to be kidding me."

He paused and stared back at me. It wasn't the safest place for us to stop, considering we were walking across the street that separated the beach from the hotel, but there weren't any cars in sight.

"What?" he asked, scanning for traffic. "Do you have to stand in the road right now?"

"She did it on purpose! She was flirting with you." The thought annoyed me because he told me he liked me, he yelled it in fact, so the universe should have listened and turned all the other pretty girls away. I couldn't compete with them.

"So what if she was? Girls have flirted with me before," he answered with a strange tone.

I grunted and walked past him. If only I could have said, *guys have flirted with me before as well. ALL THE TIME IN FACT.* But since that would have been a big ol' lie, I walked past him and headed toward the giant fire now burning a few yards away on the beach. I couldn't hear his footsteps in the sand behind me, but I assumed he was following me. If not, he'd stayed out on the road and had probably been run over by now. I told myself I didn't care either way.

The bonfire was blazing and crackling through the dark night. It was the centerpiece of the party with groups mingling all around it. Off to the side there was a grill and a few coolers lined up. As I stepped closer, I tried to inspect the scene quickly and decide which area looked the least intimidating. There were more people there than I had expected, at least twenty or thirty. They all looked around my age or a little older.

"Beck! You made it!" the girl from earlier called. I never did catch her name, so I dubbed her She Who Shall Not Be Named in honor of the Dark Lord. I'm sure they had a lot in common. I knew Beck was a few feet behind me, so instead of waiting for her to make her way over and tackle him into the sand, I headed over to the drinks. I couldn't have alcohol because of my transplant, which sort of sucked in that moment. It would have been nice to take the nervous edge off a tiny bit, not to mention everyone would assume I was fifteen if I walked around all night with a coke can in my hand.

As I was reaching in the cooler for a bottled water, a shadow fell behind me and blocked the fire's light. I twisted around to find Jason, the surfing instructor from earlier, standing behind me. He looked surprised to see me, but definitely happy about the coincidence. *Huh.*

"Abby, right?" he asked, reaching past me to grab a bottled water and a beer. He handed me the water and then popped open the can of his beer so that it echoed through the night.

"Yup. Jason?"

He smiled wide and motioned for us to move so other people could grab their drinks. I followed him a few feet away, trying to take in more of his appearance. He was really cute in a slacker way: kind eyes, easy smile, messy hair. He had on board shorts and a surfing competition shirt. I tried to guess his age, but I had no clue. He was somewhere between 15 and 45.

"I didn't realize you'd be here," he offered, taking a sip of his beer and then tilting his head to the side.

“I wasn’t *really* invited. Beck was invited and he brought me along,” I admitted.

“Ah. Are you guys together or just friends?” he asked over the brim of his beer. His posture hinted that he might have hoped it was the latter.

What an interesting question. I glanced over to where Beck was standing with She Who Shall Not Be Named. He wasn’t smiling, but he nodded at whatever she was saying.

“We’re just friends on a road trip,” I answered truthfully, I think.

I didn’t miss the smile that took over his features. “That’s great.”

“How old are you, Jason?”

I think my direct question surprised him. “Twenty-three.” Not too old.

“How long have you been surfing?” I asked before he could ask me my age. I didn’t want to admit to being nineteen.

“My whole life. I grew up on the beach in California and then moved here to go to school for marine biology.”

So he wasn’t *really* a slacker, just looked like one.

“That’s so cool!” I answered, because I instantly pictured him befriending dolphins. Oh wait, I think that’s only people who work at Sea World. Alright, I had no clue what marine biologists actually did.

He nodded and took a microscopic step closer to me. *Smooth*. “Are you in school?”

I almost answered truthfully, but then I remembered how many details were involved, and I just decided he didn’t really need to know about my life. We were having fun at a party, so I lied.

“I start in the fall.” Damn, that sounded truthful. I was getting pretty good at this whole deceit thing.

He nodded and then we awkwardly stood there for a moment. We'd pretty much exhausted all of the small talk I could think of. What was Beck talking about with the Dark Lord? Did they have a lot in common? More than he and I had in common? Was she explaining how hard it was to have big boobs? Fuck girls.

I peered over to the spot where I saw them earlier, but they weren't there anymore. A sinking feeling developed in my gut like my insides were being ripped out. Did they go back to the hotel? Were they making out on our bed?

Jason took another step toward me and I could smell the ocean on his clothes. Or maybe I could just smell the ocean in the air. My head was spinning with images of Beck with another girl.

"Did you like surfing? You were really good at it." He was practically an inch away from me then and I could smell beer on his breath.

I forced myself to look up into his brown eyes. "Yeah, it was really fun. I'd like to do it again."

"I could take you again. Maybe in the morning?" His voice held so much promise of what else we could do in the morning.

I nodded and smiled up at him because I felt like crap and I wanted him to flirt with me. I liked the way it felt and I told myself it was okay because he was cute.

"Abby, there probably won't be time to surf before we hit the road tomorrow," Beck stated behind me with a sharp tone. My heart leapt into my throat and I turned to find him staring past me, toward Jason. She Who Shall Not Be Named was staring past Beck at me. Oh please, enough with the stare off.

"What? Last time I checked, our itinerary was fairly *loose*." I crossed my arms over my chest, wondering what his motive was. If he liked me then he should do something about it, not just stand there.

Beck answered me simply with, "Not tomorrow."

Interesting.

I pulled my gaze from him and looked toward the girl behind him. "I don't think we've met. I'm Abby," I mentioned, extending my hand out toward her. She looked down at it with a puzzled expression before reaching to shake it.

"I'm Lia," she answered with a genuine smile. I was offering her a truce, and in that moment, the tension in the air started to melt away. *Slightly.*

As soon as we released our handshake, a random drunk girl shouted from the other side of the bonfire, "Let's play Drink or Dare!"

I laughed because it seemed so cliché, but to my surprise everyone instantly agreed and started shifting chairs into a circle. I'd never been to a party, but it didn't take a rocket scientist to figure out the premise of Drink or Dare. Luckily, my drink of choice would be H2O. Everyone scrambled to position their collapsible chairs by their friends, and at the end of it all, I was stuck by Jason while Beck and Lia ended up on the other side of the bonfire. The hint of a smirk on her face told me she was pleased with the arrangement. Maybe she *was* a wizard. Witch. Whatever. Maybe she's a dude.

If this were a movie, that's the moment where I would have taken a big gulp of some kind of alcohol. Instead, I untwisted my water bottle cap and took a long sip. The same drunk girl that initiated the game a few minutes ago jumped up and clapped her hands.

"I'll go first! If you choose Dare, you can't chicken out and choose Drink after you hear the dare! Those are the rules!" she instructed with what she probably thought was a cunning stare, when in reality it looked like a she was a winking pirate. Argh. Maybe being the only sober one would have its advantages.

After she'd perused the entire circle, her gaze landed on the guy to my right that was swaying back and forth in his chair. I leaned away from him, which brought me closer to Jason. He smiled down at me and propped his arm on the back of my chair.

"Ian! Drink or Dare?" she called, stepping closer to him.

Ian grunted and stood up, obviously choosing dare. The entire ring of partygoers cheered and scooted to the edge of their seat in anticipation of his dare.

"Strip your clothes off and jump in the ocean!" she demanded. Wow, this girl was going for the full monty right off the bat. What would this game end with? A giant orgy on the beach?

Without a moment's hesitation, Ian turned to me and held out his beer, as if I was his assistant during his dare. I took it because I didn't really have a choice, and then he gave me a loose grin and started to strip. This guy was less than a foot away from me and he was literally giving me a strip tease like I was a bachelorette. Best bonfire ever. He unpeeled his shirt and then flung it around his head like a helicopter before tossing it to a girl across the circle. She caught it with a wild cheer while he started on his pants. He let them drop onto the sand, as if they weren't the second to last thing concealing his *member* from my gaze.

"I'm a GROWER!" he yelled as he dropped his boxers and took off in a wild run toward the ocean. Everyone was laughing, but I just sat there, holding his beer and looking down at his Star Wars underwear, thinking how he'd regret not having them once he resurfaced from his wild dare.

Jason leaned in and whispered in my ear, "That was quite an introduction to Drink or Dare." I heard him say it, but just as he began to speak, I shifted my gaze from Ian's boxers up to Beck. He was watching me with his trademark grin, except the bonfire shadowed its appearance so that his features were masked in a mysterious glow. Staring at each other over that bonfire, it became clear that there were one million ways to view the world, but that Beck and I saw everything in the same wavelength. Like life was one big private joke that we got to share.

Ian didn't return from his swim, and the girl that caught his shirt had wandered off after him, so the game had to continue without them. A girl sitting a few seats away from Lia volunteered to pick the next contestant. She stood and spun in a circle, but stopped on a dime when she reached Lia. Lia, of course, chose dare. The entire show seemed a little too rehearsed, and when her dare surfaced, I knew that it was.

"Lia! Kiss one of the people sitting on either side of you. Your choice!" My stomach contents felt like they were about to surface all over the bonfire. Her choice my ass. There was a stoned guy practically asleep on the left side of Lia and perfect, amazing Beck on the other side. Lia did a wonderful show of feigned innocence, cupping her hand over her mouth and giggling. *Best actress ever*.

Beck was trying to catch my eye over the bonfire, but I couldn't pull my gaze from Lia. She tucked a loose strand of hair behind her ear and shifted her body toward Beck. I wondered if she ever played the Virgin Mary in any church plays. She definitely had the act down pat.

"You okay there?" Jason asked, breaking me out of

my daze. I looked down to see my hands wringing out the plastic bottle in my hand. I'd completely destroyed it while I'd been staring daggers at Lia.

"Oh, yeah. I'm fine," I lied, dropping the bottle onto my lap in an attempt to look normal.

I didn't watch the kiss; I stared at the crackling flames and listened to everyone's cat calls. It was a strange experience to behold. Fiery jealously didn't sit well in my stomach and the longer I sat there while the game continued around me, the longer I thought I might explode. Jason got called on, but he opted to chug a beer rather than accept a dare. I was grateful for that. But then Beck was called upon.

The same girl that started the game off stood and pointed at Beck. "You have to give someone a lap dance. The hottest guy or girl here!"

I laughed, cracked up in fact, and the people around me shifted and gave me awkward stares. I admit that I looked crazy, but I just couldn't let the universe off on this one. It needed to know how God damn funny it could be at times. Lia blushed and her friends cheered and gave her encouraging words. Everyone assumed Beck would give a lap dance to the girl who had kissed him and who was clearly the prettiest girl at the party. *Predictable*. But then Beck stood up and started walking around the bonfire toward me and I started laughing even harder. A nervous laughter mixed with all the jealousy that had been building inside.

I hated Beck in that moment, but I almost felt like he was giving me the most thoughtful gift in the world. He was telling a group of strangers that he thought I was the one that deserved a lap dance. He stopped walking right in front of me and I stared at his stomach, hidden beneath a sexy black shirt.

"Ms. Abby Mae, may I have the honor of giving you your first lap dance?" he asked with a mockingly serious tone.

I finally tilted my head up to his face. "I don't think you can fit on my lap."

He quirked an eyebrow. "Is that a challenge?"

Despite myself, I cracked a smile. I could feel my whole body shaking with a nervous energy. I hated the fact that everyone was staring at us and I had no clue what Beck would actually do. He hung his arms in the air and started shaking his hips to the beat of the music playing from someone's iPod speakers. Everyone started clapping and egging him on. He turned around and shook his jean-clad butt in my face before I shoved him away playfully. He turned back around with a devilish grin, and in the next moment he shifted forward so that he was standing over me. I pressed back into my chair, feeling my adrenaline spike. I mashed my lips together as he stretched his legs on either side of my hips and leaned down so that his face was hovering over mine. It wasn't what I imagined he'd do. He was practically on top of me, pinning me to my chair.

He knew that I was squirming in my seat, so when he ground his hips down onto mine, making the entire female population of the party squeal loudly, I scowled up at him with an angry stare.

"Don't like it, Abby?" he challenged, knowing that I obviously did.

"You aren't even doing it right," I answered, trying to shift my head to the side so that our lips were farther apart.

"Show me how you do it then," he challenged with a threatening smirk.

Like fucking hell.

"Yeah!" everyone cheered in agreement. It wasn't their opinions that ultimately made me shift forward and push Beck back into the sand. It was the fact that Caroline would have been jumping up and down telling me to grow a pair and show Beck what I wanted. It was the fact that Lia was scowling over at us with a sour grimace. I was learning that jealousy was a pretty strong motivator.

Beck sat back in the sand with his hands propping him up. I shifted to stand in front of him and tried to think of every lap dance scene I'd seen on TV and in movies. Obviously, I'd never given one before, but I had good rhythm and a strong goal: make Beck lose his mind. I closed my eyes and let the world slip away, thinking of Beck and what I'd do to him if there were no consequences and no casualties (my ego). I strung my hands up into my hair and slowly shifted my hips to a slow rhythm. I felt sensual and powerful in that moment as my body twisted to the left and right.

I inched closer to him and he leaned forward to wrap his hands around my calves, slowly dragging them up and down, and warming my skin. With a gentle tug, he pulled me down onto his lap and I let my legs fall on either side of his hips. My knees dug into the sand and I dragged my hands down his chest, feeling his muscles beneath his shirt.

My dress rode up so that the backs of my thighs were rubbing against his jeans. His hands dropped to my legs, just to the edge of the hem, pressing it up an inch higher.

"You're so sexy, Abby," he whispered, and I rounded my hips in a slow circle like I'd watched women do a dozen times before. I was drunk on adrenaline and my own boldness. My body pressed down onto him as if we were suction-cupped together. It felt so easy to move on Beck like that, rolling my hips and letting my sexual prowess shine. His hands gripped my thighs, searing his skin to mine. His thumb was so close to a dangerous goal and I wanted him to reach it.

I could feel him responding to me, and I didn't care that we were at a party. The bonfire danced behind him, silhouetting his body and blocking out everyone else. I felt life coursing through me, exhilaration fueling my seduction. I strung my hands into his hair and pulled his head toward mine as I continued to grind in slow circles on his lap. We'd moved past public decency long ago, but I couldn't hear anything other than the sound of my heart thumping wildly. When his lips met mine, we kissed like we'd been starving for it. He swiped his tongue over mine and tangled his hand in my hair, gripping me against him. Our hips moved together and I was no longer in control of our lap dance.

We were having sex *with* clothes on, in front of twenty people.

"Alright, you two! Jeez, get a freaking room!" the ring leader's voice finally penetrated through my lust-filled haze. I pulled my mouth away from Beck's and pressed the back of my hand to my lips to conceal my overflowing emotions: elation, embarrassment, shock, and desire. He smiled up at me with hooded eyes. His brown hair was even more unruly thanks to my fingers.

I sat there frozen in lust.

"I'm not complaining, but if you don't get off my lap soon, this might not stay so innocent." He couldn't even hide the amusement in his voice. He squeezed my hips once more before I pushed off his lap and plucked myself in the seat Ian had previously been occupying. Beck took my old seat without a word. I brushed off the fine layer of sand coating my knees and calves. Then I straightened the hem of my dress out and tried like hell to keep from looking up toward the rest of the group. They were already focusing on a new contestant for Drink or Dare, but the flush on my cheeks wouldn't recede and I felt like I was on display at the zoo.

Jason leaned forward so he could see me past Beck. "What's a lap dance among *friends*, right?" His tone held a note of annoyance. Did he think I lied to him before? Beck and I *were* friends and we *weren't* dating, so it's not my fault that at a party I didn't feel like recounting our complicated-as-hell status to a random surfing instructor.

I couldn't look at Jason or Beck throughout the remainder of the game. Beck and I just sat there in silence until everyone started clearing out. I grabbed my phone out of my purse and motioned that I would walk ahead so I could make a call. I prayed Caroline answered.

CHAPTER THIRTEEN

"Oh my God, finally!" I felt the flutters of relief wash through my nervous belly when Caroline answered on the fourth ring. It was late for her, but when all you do is sleep, days don't seem to be divided quite the same as they used to be.

"Hey, Abs," she answered with a voice that sounded like it was being grated. None of her usual cheeriness was present either.

"Hey, did I catch you at a bad time? I could call back?" Maybe she was just tired.

She cleared her throat and I could hear the bed rustling like she was trying to sit up a bit further. "No. It's okay, just feeling extra crappy."

Usually she sugarcoated her illness. She would talk about being in the hospital like it was an extended stay in a hotel and nothing more.

"Is that why you haven't been answering my calls? I don't care if all we talk about is how shitty you feel. I miss you."

There was a long silence and I stared down at the sand. In the moonlight, it almost looked like snow. Warm, grainy snow.

"Abby, I want you to be happy and I've just needed some time to process everything."

My heart dropped.

"Process what?" I shouted into the phone with no regard for anyone around me. I didn't care what they thought.

"Abby…They gave me a new timeline."

A timeline. They gave her an expiration date. As if anyone could predict the fucking future. A timeline was statistics and nothing more. It didn't account for externalities. The fact that Caroline was the best goddamned human being I'd ever known and that she deserved longer than whatever timeline they decided to give her.

"How long?" I stopped walking and let my knees fall forward into sand. My butt fell back onto my heels. Snowy sand stuck to my legs, exfoliating my pale skin.

"Eight months."

Eight months of life is what Caroline had to plan for. What I had to plan for. I felt an overwhelming need to scream building within me, building in my stomach and winding up my trachea and throat, pressing into my lungs. Then, when it reached my mouth, I counted to ten. This wasn't my illness. This wasn't about me. Caroline needed me to be strong. She needed the best fucking eight months of her life.

"Can I come pick you up and take you on the rest of the road trip with us?" I asked, praying she would say yes.

"I don't know when I'll be out of the hospital, but what if when you get back we go on one. Just you and me." That sounded like heaven. I instantly thought of all the fun places we could stay together. We could go to Hollywood and walk the star mile and find every celebrity we'd ever pined over.

"Sounds perfect."

"Any updates for me?" she asked, and for the first time that night, I heard hope in her voice. She really was living vicariously through me.

I shifted around to see who was still around. The party had cleared out pretty quickly, but Beck was still on the beach a few yards away. He was sitting on his butt in the sand with his arms bent around his knees. His face was angled toward the ocean. The moonlight hit each of his sharp features. He was probably making sure I didn't get kidnapped, but I appreciated the privacy he gave me.

I told Caroline everything about the bonfire, the kissing, and the sandbar confessions from the other day. She eagerly listened to every detail. When I admitted that she was the devil sitting on my shoulder at each moment, she cheered into the phone.

"You're damn right I am. I've never been prouder," she admitted, and I could hear the smile in her voice.

"You would have loved the surfing instructor. He was straight off *Laguna Beach*."

"Meh. He doesn't sound as hot as Mr. Lap Dance."

I burst out laughing. "I should call him that from now on."

Once our laughter died down, the crashing waves settled in and I just sat there on the phone with her, wondering what she was looking at in her hospital room.

"Once we hang up, I'll take a picture of the ocean and text it to you."

"Thanks. I'll put it as my background," she answered wistfully.

"I love you, Caroline."

"I love you, too, Abs."

• • •

"That's a lot of pills," Beck mentioned as we drove out of Corpus. We'd left just after breakfast and I'd forgotten to take my medicine beforehand. My medicine bag sounded much more ominous when there was no music playing in the car, so I switched the stereo on low before I started rattling through each pill bottle.

"They're for my sex change operation," I quipped, not really wanting to get into the details of them.

"You're turning into a man?" he asked, eying me skeptically from his driver's seat. "I think you'd make a really good one. You weigh, what? A hundred pounds? Nothing says dude like chicken legs."

I dropped one of the bottles back into the bag and narrowed my eyes toward him. "They're not chicken legs!"

"I know," he smirked. "They're perfect." He'd slipped the compliment in so flawlessly that I almost missed it. "What are the pills actually for?"

He knew about my transplant, so there was no point in harping on it even more. "I'm one of those people that grows hair on every surface of my body. Have you seen those shows on discovery channel?"

He couldn't hide his playful grin. "You watch too

much TV, but sure, I'll let you stick with that answer."

I laughed and twisted my legs under me so I could sit like a pretzel on the seat while I finished taking each pill in quick secession.

A moment later, he hit his hand onto the steering wheel, like he'd just remembered something. "If you stop taking the pills, you could be the bearded lady at the circus." He paused and then looked over at me with such strong hope in his eyes that I thought for a moment he was being serious. "Except if you go through the sex change operation, you'd just be a normal dude with a beard."

He frowned and shrugged before turning his attention back to the road.

I didn't stop laughing until we crossed the Corpus Christi city line.

I thought Beck would, you know, *go* for it after my lap dance last night, but nothing happened after we returned to the hotel room. I was exhausted and the weight of Caroline's prognosis flitted through my mind every time I tried to close my eyes. I tossed and turned, unable to peel the images of her sickness from my mind. Her mangled lungs, her failing liver. I knew Beck was awake as well, but he gave me the peace that I craved.

"Alright, lightning round," I began, pausing to insert an awesome game-show sound effect. It, of course, wasn't lost on Beck. He appreciated every nuance of my humor. "Which of the following was not the name of a Spice Girl: Scary, Baby, Silly, or Posh?

"Silly," he answered quickly, sliding me a cocky half smile.

"What? C'mon, you can't guess it that fast."

"Why can't I guess that fast if I know the answer? It's called *lighting* round."

I crossed my arms and sat back in my seat. "Okay, let's play Desert Island instead."

He winked and I pretended to be staring off through his window when actually I was just studying his features while he drove. Sometimes I had to remind myself that he was real and sitting in the same car as I was.

"Let's do the TV show edition since we know you'll have an unlimited tap to draw from," he joked.

My grin spread wide, "Okay three TV shows each. You go first."

The music hummed from the radio while I waited for his answer. We were in the middle of God knows where, following any road that our hearts desired.

"The complete history of *SNL*, *LOST*," he paused to think for a second, "and probably *The Walking Dead* since I'm watching it now and I want to know how it ends."

"Wait. Wait!" I blurted, waving my hands up into the air. "You want to watch a show about being stuck on a desert island *while* being stuck on a desert island?"

He smirked. "The irony is too good to pass up, and Kate also happens to be my dream girl."

It was silly, but I instantly compared myself to Kate. We didn't have anything in common. Why couldn't I have adorable freckles??

"Okay. Your turn," he demanded eagerly.

I nodded, stalling for time so I could make sure I wasn't missing any of the good ones. "*The Office*, *Will and Grace*, and *Game of Thrones*," I declared, instantly regretting my choices. "No, wait! Maybe *House of Cards* instead of one of those. Or *Friends*."

His laugh filled the car. "You would choose to be lost

on a desert island with Michael Scott?"

"And Jim," I smiled proudly, imagining *my* dream guy.

We drove for another hour, heading north with no real destination in mind. I propped my feet up on the dashboard and stared at the landscape whipping by. At one point, I pulled my phone out and recorded a video through my passenger window to send to Caroline. It was just twenty seconds of dried grass and trees, but the sky was so blue and cloudy; I knew it would give her a taste of life.

Around lunchtime we were passing through a small town when I saw a huge sign that read "Texas' Largest Flea Market - 5 miles".

"Beck, have you ever been to a flea market?" I asked, shifting my gaze toward him. He'd slipped on his Wayfarers so I couldn't see his eyes, but there was a little bit of stubble dotting his chin. I thought if I were his girlfriend, I'd make him keep it like that. It morphed him into something even hotter, that slight shadow of facial hair.

"Not that I remember. I saw that sign back there too."

"Could we go?" I asked, wanting to see if their claim about it being the 'biggest in Texas' was true.

"Do you think we're ready for a flea market date? I heard that usually doesn't come until later on in the relationship. I mean we *hardly* shared a lap dance last night." How he could tease me and make me smile all in one sentence, I wasn't sure, but I sat there staring at him like I'd been searching all of my days to encounter that very moment. Was I supposed to comment on the fact that he was joking *or* that he had called it a date *or* that he mentioned "relationship"? I ended up not saying much of anything. I grunted awkwardly and turned toward the window, praying he couldn't see my blushing cheeks in the glass' reflection.

"That was the best lap dance I've ever received, by the way." *He wasn't going to drop it.*

I didn't shift back toward him. "How many have you had?" I asked, concentrating hard on the gravel road splashing rocks as we exited the highway.

"Just the one. But it was by far the best I've ever had," he spoke confidently.

I tried to hide my all-consuming smile. "Beck. Turn into the flea market."

"Alright, but there's no coming back from this experience," he declared, turning right into an expansive parking lot.

I know he was being silly, but his sarcasm wove around me, making it feel as though going to a flea market together actually *was* a big step. I shook my head clear of the thought, unbuckled my seat belt, and hopped out of the car. The sign a few miles back wasn't bluffing- it *had* to be the biggest flea market in Texas. The parking lot alone could have been a small metropolis. There were trolley cars looping around the perimeter, taking people to the entrance who didn't want to walk the half mile themselves. Beck bypassed them and started weaving through parked cars.

"Wait for me!" I shouted, picking up my pace so I could catch up with him. The wind whipped my hair and I turned toward the sky, noticing the dark rolling clouds blocking out the sun completely. At least the flea market was covered because the sky looked like it was going to open up any second. When I looked back down, Beck was studying me with a serious gaze— one that couldn't be mistaken for friendship. I stuck my tongue out at him and he pretended to lasso me toward him. I played along and he pulled me into him so he could kiss my cheek.

"Do you think they have real lassos here?" I asked with gleaming eyes.

"I'm pretty sure they just call it rope?" he answered with a hint of a private smile.

After hours of wandering around, we stood at the entrance of the flea market with our purchases in hand. We stayed together at first, picking out the most heinous items and containing our laughter until we were far, far away from the vendors. But then when I spotted a gift that I had to purchase for him, I decided we had to split up for a little while so I could surprise him.

"Alright, time to see who won," Beck said, sitting down on a bench just beside the front doors.

I followed him over and set my bag in my lap. "Who won?"

"Yeah, who found the better stuff?"

"Ah," I nodded, and unpeeled the top of my bag to look inside. "I got one thing for you, but it's not a gift or anything and it definitely doesn't mean I'm like pining over you. I just knew you had to have them when I saw them."

He smirked and opened his bag as well. "Well, that's okay because I found something for you, too. But mine definitely means I'm pining for you, so you should take it as such."

I rolled my eyes playfully and tugged out his gift. "Here," I said, handing him the tissue-wrapped items.

"You shouldn't have," he joked before he'd even unwrapped it. I hit my shoulder against his.

"Open it, you fool."

With a laugh, he tugged off the paper to reveal a pair

of ceramic salt and pepper shakers. In the shape of zombies. Really awesomely-realistic zombies. His mouth dropped open as he turned them in his hands.

"You win," he declared with a look of awe. Ceramic zombies will do that to you.

"Not fair," I poked him. "I should get to see what you got me before the winner is declared." Although I knew there was no way he was going to top my gift.

"Okay, here," he said, shifting the shakers into one hand and handing me a little cardboard jewelry box out of his bag.

I'd never been given a piece of jewelry before, so when I opened the lid and found an old tarnished locket, I was speechless. The heart locket was tiny, barely half an inch tall. It was made of gold, or fake gold, I couldn't tell and I didn't actually care. My eyebrows scrunched together as I felt tears burning the back of my eyelids. I couldn't cry over something so silly, but there was something deeply personal about the gift.

Beck was watching me with a steady focus, but I couldn't meet his gaze. Not yet. I fumbled with the clasp on the side until it gave and then peeled the locket open. Inside, there were two tiny black and white photos. On the left was a young girl with a bow and frilly dress. On the right was a soldier in uniform. They looked to be the same age and I knew they were a couple. This had been the girl's locket.

"Look on the back." Beck motioned for me turn the locket over.

I closed it and flipped it gently in my palm so that the back of the heart was facing up. Inscribed on the tarnished gold in perfect cursive were the words: *with this heart*.

"I thought we could replace the pictures," he offered

timidly. "Or you could be a creep and leave the old couple in if you want." It was so like Beck to do something extremely thoughtful and then follow it up with a joke to try and lighten the mood. I wasn't going to let him get away with it. So, I turned toward him on the bench and leaned forward to plant a gentle kiss on his lips. His mouth was slightly open so it was awkward, but the moment our lips touched, he pressed back into me with equal amounts of fervor. His empty hand wrapped around my neck and brought me closer to him. I opened up for him, letting him slip his tongue past my lips. He tasted sweet, like the funnel cake we'd shared earlier. I needed more of him and the way he gripped my hair told me he needed more of me as well.

There we were, sitting at the front of a flea market in the-middle-of-nowhere, Texas, with hundreds of people shuffling around us. He was holding onto zombies and I was holding onto someone's long-lost locket that now felt intimately mine.

Just as we were pulling away from each other with dopey grins, a grouchy old woman huffed past us. "I cannot believe the indecency displayed by youth these days," she declared, clutching her oversized purse closer toward her chest as if we were street thugs about to mug her.

Her equally-as-old friend emphatically agreed with her as the two waddled around us with snooty glares.

Beck gave me a scolding glance. "Abby, we're *indecent*," he muttered, unable to keep a smile from spreading wide. His eyes were alive with lust and there was a glow under his tan skin. I knew I looked the same.

"*So* indecent," I added.

"They acted like we were having sex or something," he added jokingly.

Without missing a beat, I declared, "I bought

condoms before we left for the trip. Magnum condoms." The announcement slipped out before I'd even thought about whether it was an appropriate response. The truth is, the condoms were burning a hole in my suitcase. I didn't want Beck to stumble upon them and get the wrong impression. Like I was planning on having sex with so many guys that I had to purchase different sizes.

"That's cool. I bought deodorant and travel toothpaste," he answered with a wicked grin. Just then, a window-shaking clap of thunder sounded from outside. The storm had finally reached us.

"They were so you and I could have sex."

Beck started cracking up. "They *were*?"

My face blushed twenty shades past red. I was pretty sure I looked like a cherry. A big loser cherry with too many condoms. I had no way to answer that without basically giving him the green light to have sex with me.

"Can we stop talking about sex in a flea market? I feel like those grannies are still listening or something." Another clap of thunder punctuated the end of my request.

He let out a chuckle and tugged me up off the bench. "We should get going anyway; we've been here way too long. I doubt we'll make it to the car before the rain comes."

CHAPTER FOURTEEN

Beck was right. The sky broke midway to the camper, which was still parked on the other side of the world. We started to run, shielding our purchases under our clothes, but by the time we reached the car, the rain had soaked into our every pore. He unlocked the doors as quickly as he could and then we crashed onto the leather seats, laughing hysterically and flinging drops of water off of our clothes.

Just as I started to close the passenger side door, the wind picked up and worked against me to keep the door open. Rain drops slapped against my face and I couldn't blink fast enough to keep the water from dripping down into my eyes. Beck leaned across to help me tug it close. With both of our strength combined, the door slammed shut and we fell back onto our seats with contented sighs. My clothes stuck to me like plastic wrap and no amount of force could pry them off.

"So you think it was the biggest in Texas?" Beck asked, buckling his seatbelt.

"That's what she said," I answered, because the outdated joke was too good to pass up. Forgive me.

"Nicely done. You can use that while you're stuck on a desert island with Michael Scott," he commended, sliding his gaze over to me. His dark eyelashes were stuck together from the rain and there was a slight dewiness to his skin, like he'd just slid out of the shower. I sat there giving his beautiful demeanor a moment of silence- it deserved it. His shirt was stuck to his skin, accentuating every masculine detail hidden beneath. He wasn't bulky, he was a runner, but his arms were strong. Strong enough to pin me against the passenger door so that I wouldn't be able to budge an inch. My eyes drifted across his skin like he was mine for the taking, as if I had the right to peruse his body.

But then he started the engine and cut off my indulgent daydreams. We weren't going to have sex in the parking lot of the flea market. The angry grannies were probably parked directly next to us. I'd be seconds away from my first orgasm and the granny would tap onto the window with her wrinkly finger, damning Beck and I to hell for all of eternity.

"What are you thinking about?" Beck asked as he pulled to the end of the long line trying to exit. There must have been a hundred cars in front of us and the rain wasn't helping expedite the process.

"Oh, nothing. Did I see a CD in that bag of yours?" I asked quickly, fumbling for a safe topic.

"John Denver. Want to put it in?" he asked, motioning to the bag sitting in the cup holder.

"I've never listened to him," I answered, grabbing the

bag and starting to peel off the plastic encasing.

"What?" Beck exclaimed. "He's *the* iconic road trip musician. I'm surprised we've made it this far without him guiding us."

"That sounds really serious."

"Everything about John Denver is serious."

"Oh, is it?" I said, spinning the CD around my finger and pretending to drop it.

Beck nodded with a smug grin. "That's fine, Abby. Disrespect the road trip gods; watch what ends up happening to us."

What ended up happening to us was the longest exit line that has ever existed. We sat there long enough for John Denver's CD to repeat twice. I didn't care about "country roads" or "jet planes", I needed to pee. Stat.

"Holy buhjesus," I complained, smashing my face to the window for the fiftieth time. I suppose I thought that if I pressed my face into the glass hard enough, I'd finally be able to see what was going on up ahead.

Beck laughed and shook his head. "I don't want to blame the traffic jam on you, but I think it's fair to assume that it's one hundred percent your fault," he declared with a hint of amusement.

"What?!" I snapped, peeling my gaze away from the rainy line of cars.

"John Denver is demanding penance for your sins," he explained with a silly grin.

I laughed indignantly, "Ah. I'm *sorry*. I didn't realize he was God."

Before Beck could respond to my sarcasm, a police officer dressed in a long, bright-yellow raincoat tapped on

Beck's window with the tip of his index finger. Rain fell in sheets around him so that his face was shadowed under his hood. Beck rolled down his window and the officer leaned in through the threshold.

"Sorry for the hold-up. There was a wreck up ahead because of the slick roads. We'll be redirecting traffic back through the town and I'd suggest not traveling much farther than that. The traffic is heavy and they've issued a flood warning for all of our surrounding counties." His instructions were direct and authoritative.

"Do you know how long the warning is supposed to last?" Beck asked respectfully.

The officer's mouth formed a thin line. "Through the night. Rain should lighten up in the morning."

It was a good thing we had no real destination in mind because Mother Nature was deciding our fate for us. We'd stay somewhere in this tiny-ass town for the night and start driving again tomorrow.

"Alright, thanks officer."

The officer tipped his head and then offered us a final "stay safe out there" warning.

"John Denver is not a merciful God," I declared once the window was rolled up.

Beck chuckled, "I guess you *really* pissed him off."

The line of cars finally started moving and soon we were pulling out onto a road that was barely visible beneath the sheets of rain.

"So," I started, "I'm drenched and it's almost nighttime. What if we just pulled in somewhere and called it a night?"

"In a motel?" Beck asked, turning his windshield wipers up to their highest setting, which still wasn't enough. The longer we drove, the more paranoid I became.

Country roads weren't safe and I couldn't see more than a few feet in front of our car.

"Or we could just sleep in the camper," I offered, dreading the idea of searching for a vacancy in that tiny town.

He nodded and kept driving. We passed through Main Street, where shops and businesses were all closing their doors for the night. People darted for their cars and one old man tried in vain to stay dry using an old newspaper. I wondered if the ink dripped from the articles onto his clothes.

I only spotted one motel on our path and it looked like it had seen better days. Half of the rooms had broken windows and doors falling off their hinges. There was no way it could still be open and operating.

"There's a rest stop a few miles up ahead, we can pull in there and stay the night," Beck declared.

"Is that safe?" Visions of rest stop serial killers danced in my head. We were in the middle of nowhere, but I'd seen Texas Chainsaw Massacre and I wasn't going to be the next victim.

"We'll be fine."

I grunted and stared out the window, wondering what the night had in store for us. The idea of sleeping together in the back of the car seemed oddly romantic, but I didn't think Beck thought of it that way.

We only had to drive a few more minutes before exiting the two lane highway and driving into a recently renovated rest stop. It was, dare I say… *nice*. It was made of stone bricks and topped with a metal roof. Tall street lamps dotted the path toward the front entrance.

"Want to go scout out the bathrooms?" I asked after he parked in the spot closest to the doors. There were a couple of other cars parked near us. I assumed they were waiting out the rain as well.

"I guess there's no point in changing in there since we'll just get drenched again?" Beck asked, turning toward me with a defeated frown.

"We can change in here when we get back," I answered simply.

"Pfft, so that you can sneak a peek?" He shot me a wink that stole my common sense, and then bolted from the car. I hopped out and ran after him, shielding the rain with my hands and fingers. By the time we reached the rest-stop entrance, my wet underwear was wedged so far up my ass that I didn't think it would ever come out. Beck held the door open for me and we darted inside to the soundtrack of my howling laughter.

"What's so funny?"

"Nothing," I said, trying to edge toward the ladies room without turning around. I was sure he'd be able to see my bunched up underwear beneath my soaked dress.

"Mmhm, I bet. Meet me back out here after you fix your underwear!" Beck grinned and I pinched my eyes closed in embarrassment as I pushed back against the swivel door.

After using the facilities, I checked my appearance in the mirror. I was prepared for the worst, so my wet rat appearance actually wasn't *that* bad. I ran my fingers through my soaked hair, trying to de-tangle the long strands, but it was hopeless. My jade green eyes looked eerie in the fluorescent lighting and my skin appeared like alabaster marble. I was freaking cold standing in the air conditioned bathroom, so after I washed my hands, I held them underneath the drier for a few minutes, letting the warm air coat my skin.

When I finally walked out, I was greeted by Beck standing in front of a group of vending machines, gathering the various "courses" of our dinner.

"Oh jeez, I don't even want to know what you're getting out of there."

"Unless you want s'mores for dinner, you'll appreciate my vending machine hunt."

"At least get a granola bar or something," I muttered, stepping closer to him.

"It's all taken care of," he answered, shoving the food wrappers under his shirt so they wouldn't get soaked in the rain. "C'mon!" He motioned for me to follow and then darted for the door.

Once we were back in the car, my body was shaking from head to toe from the cold rain. There was no way in hell I was getting out of the car again before the rain stopped. I was tired of being wet and cold.

"Do you have a towel or anything?" I asked, rifling through my bag for a change of clothes. I pulled out an oversized t-shirt and a fresh pair of underwear. My sleeping shorts were somewhere in my bag, but I'd look for them when my teeth weren't about to crack from chattering so hard.

"No, but you can use one of my shirts," he offered, and then climbed into the back with me. The space was small, but we could both fit easily. He tossed a t-shirt over and I caught it just before it hit my face. His scent overwhelmed me.

"Mind if I change, too?" he asked, already working the hem of his shirt up.

"Ahh," I muttered awkwardly, trying to think of the correct answer. I didn't want to seem like a prude, so I shrugged and turned away from him to give us both some privacy.

I heard him digging clothes out of his bag behind me, so I took a deep breath and tried to pretend he wasn't watching as I crouched onto my knees and peeled my dress over my head. I was in my underwear and bra, but they were both wet and I'm sure completely translucent. Fortunately, the important sections were facing away from Beck.

I kept expecting him to say something or to make a joke, but he stayed silent as I reached for his shirt and dried off my arms, stomach, and back. I sat down and stretched my legs out to dry them off. I could feel his eyes on me, amplifying the goose bumps covering my skin. My ears were focused for any movements in my direction. Sadly, the only thing I heard was the rustle of a new shirt being put on. No hanky panky in the camper for me. I tugged my oversized shirt over my head and then reached under to unsnap my wet bra.

"Abby," Beck huffed agitatedly, and I twisted around to look at him. He was bent down onto his knees as well.

"What's wrong?"

"Did you just take your bra off?" he asked.

My brows scrunched together and then I looked down at my lacy size 34-A bra still resting in my palm. It could have fit an American Girl Doll. Was I not supposed to take it off?

"It was soaked," I answered with a confused scowl.

He wet his lips and looked up at the roof of the camper for help. His hands rested on his hips and when I inched toward him, his jaw clicked a millimeter tighter.

I tilted my head and gave him a small smile. "Did you want me to leave my bra on, Beck?"

"No… No, just will you put some pants on?"

I was making the cool, funny Beck uncomfortable in that moment. The second I got a taste of that power, I wanted more.

"I was going to look for my shorts after I changed my shirt," I explained. "Were you watching me take off my clothes?"

"Of course I was," he answered with a grin and a shrug. He was already collecting himself and I couldn't let that happen.

I inched closer to him on my knees so that we were only a foot apart. The air in that Camper smelled like summer rain.

"Because you *like* me?" I asked, tossing my bra onto my bag.

"Ah, so you did hear me say that?" he asked with amusement in his hazel eyes.

I mashed my lips together before answering, "You kind of screamed it in the ocean."

He laughed and then narrowed his eyes on me. "I had to be sure you heard it." The tone in that Camper morphed in that moment. We were being silly, and then suddenly all of the spare oxygen was zapped from the tiny space and we were left floating on unspoken lust and desire.

"I think everyone in the northern hemisphere heard it," I murmured, looking up at him from beneath my wet lashes.

I wasn't sure where we were going to go from there. But, of course, Beck had plans.

"I'm going to kiss you now, Abby," he said, bending low and erasing the gap between us.

My pulse spiked, "Normally you don't warn m…"

His lips cut me off and I was no longer in the back of an old VW Camper; I was wrapped up in Beck's touch, his mouth, his taste. He must have chewed a mint since the flea market because his mouth tasted like cool peppermint. His lips were soft and cold from the rain. My tongue traced across the seam of his mouth, and in an instant, his mouth opened for me and we were devouring one another, taking the kiss closer and closer into dangerous territory. I felt his hands glide up the sides of my legs, past my long shirt, and I welcomed it. I felt like I was inching toward bliss with every millimeter his finger crawled over my skin.

He'd pulled me up onto his lap so that his warm skin was pressed against mine beneath my shirt.

Our kiss never broke as his fingers reached slowly up my thigh. I wanted him. Oh, I wanted him so badly, so I inched my knees farther apart and pressed our bodies closer together. I didn't know how far Beck would take it.

I loved kissing him; I loved when he wrapped his fingers into my tangled, damp hair. But I wanted more. I needed to feel him between my legs; I wanted to know what his fingers would feel like there.

Beck broke our kiss and pressed his forehead to mine. *Please don't end this, please don't say that we can't take it any further,* I pleaded in my head. Maybe he saw the desperation written across my eyes because he didn't cut me off. He pressed his palm to the center of my chest, above my beating heart, and pushed me gently down onto my back.

"Lay down," he instructed.

I had so many conflicting emotions in that moment. The good, prudish role I'd been shoved into my whole life was fighting to surface. But the part of me that had never experienced such a powerfully sexy experience told my conscience to shut up and enjoy the ride.

My eyes were locked with Beck's hazel irises as his

hand pushed me down further. My elbows caught my upper body and then I slowly lowered myself back so that my head fell on top of my bag. There were clothes and unrolled sleeping bags shoved beneath me, but if you had asked me in that moment, I would have said I was lying on a bed of clouds. Every bit of my senses concentrated on the sinfully sexy look written across Beck's features. He looked like he was about to eat me for dinner and that thought sent a shiver from the base of my neck down to the tip of my spine.

"Lay down and relax," Beck whispered again with a wicked gleam in his eyes.

A nervous laugh escaped my lips. How the hell did he expect me to relax? I needed to know what was coming next; I had to prepare my body for his touch.

Little did I know there was *no* preparing for Beck's touch. His palms encircled my ankles and I arched my back in response, trying in vain to find an outlet for the delicious tingles spreading up my inner thighs. The tips of his thumbs rested over the veins of my inner ankles. I could feel my erratic pulse pressing against his hand. He knew how much he was affecting me.

As Beck's hand inched higher up my legs, I couldn't meet his eyes anymore. My gaze flitted toward the camper's ceiling, and I tried to concentrate on the rain beating down onto the metal roof. But nothing could distract me from his searing touch.

My hips twisted in need, and the action tugged my shirt up higher so that my underwear was completely exposed. The same pair of wet underwear that I had yet to change, which meant they were practically see-through. I pinched my eyes together, telling myself to calm down. That he would have seen all of me eventually.

His hands drifted higher and he pressed his palms to my inner thighs, pushing them apart and exposing me to him even more. Adrenaline spiked my blood like a shot of tequila. What was he thinking? Did I look like the other girls he'd been with? Did he want to keep going or was he only doing it because I wanted to?

"Beck, this is really intense," I finally admitted with an exasperated breath. I needed him to know how many whacko thoughts were drifting through my brain. His hands immediately stopped their gentle massaging of my skin.

"Do you want me to stop?"

I hopped up onto my elbows and exclaimed, "No! No. Please keep going. I might want you to stop…later, but please don't stop now."

His hazel eyes held such earnest conviction that I wanted to tell him I loved him, just to see what he would say. I, of course, didn't *love* him. That's crazy and dumb. But his eyes were just so pretty and his hands felt like my only connection to earth.

"It's just that I feel like I can't relax because I don't know what you're going to do next. I don't know if you like what you're feeling or if you think my thighs look weird." Who thought thighs looked weird? I didn't know. I just wanted him to appreciate the whiteness of my skin and not think that I looked like a pale ghost.

Beck leaned forward and propped his chin on my bent knee. His teeth bit down on his lower lip and both of his dimples made an appearance. If I had a camera, I would have snapped a picture of him sitting in that pose. He looked so fucking silly and sexy; I wanted to pounce on him.

"What if I told you what I was doing or thinking before I did it?"

What? My eyes opened wide. "As in *say* the dirty things out loud?"

He laughed a dark, throaty laugh that made my panties feel wet for different reasons than before. But then he pushed himself forward and stole my nerves with a sinful kiss that lingered until we were crazy for each other. His body pressed into mine, our hips rocking together. I wrapped my legs around his waist and pulled him to me even more. His hands found my hair and he tugged gently as his tongue swept over mine. He groaned into my mouth and I shuddered at the sexy sound.

Just when I thought I'd completely lost myself in the kiss, he broke it off and pulled back with a sinister smile.

"I'm going to kiss down the inside of your thigh," he offered, right before his lips made contact with the skin just inside my knee.

"Ho…ly!" My spine arched and I had to clasp a hand over my mouth. "Wo…w."

Two more kisses toward my underwear. "You have the most beautiful skin; it's creamy and soft."

He could have told me that my skin resembled a crocodile's at that point and I would have run with it. His lips were seducing my every cell, drawing me further away from reality.

His hand pressed down on the base of my stomach, keeping me from moving my hips, and each time his finger gently dug into my flesh, it sent a new wave of delicious shivers through me.

"Your underwear is still damp from the rain." *And other things*, I thought, but didn't dare add.

"Mhm," I mumbled in a high-pitched tone, finally collapsing down onto my back once again. His finger skimmed over the cotton material covering me. It was feather-light, but it was enough to split my world in two. How had I gone so long without this feeling?

"I'm going to kiss you here, Abby," he murmured with a raspy voice.

There was no time to offer a rebuttal or approval. His mouth found the cotton material and my eyes squeezed shut so tightly that I saw dancing stars. His lips pressed against my underwear and then his tongue found the same spot and licked slowly up and down. The cotton material was doing a poor job of protecting my nerve endings; if anything, the sensation of his tongue through the cotton only served to make each lick even more dramatic.

I tried to find words to fill the silence pressing against the camper's dewy windows, but noises of pleasure were the only sounds I could muster. My hands found Beck's unruly hair and I braided my fingers through it, pressing him against me harder.

Holy. Mother. Of. GOD.

He responded to my goading. His finger found my underwear and he stroked up and down as his tongue worked tortuous magic. I knew I was seconds away from orgasming in the back of that old camper.

"Abby, I'm going to push your underwear aside," Beck declared, and my mouth fell open. I pushed my tongue to the roof of my mouth, trying to calm my nerves as he brushed the cotton against my inner thigh. His warm breath hit me and I was helpless to anything but my need for pure, carnal pleasure. My back arched and I dropped my hands to the floor so I could dig my fingers into the clothes beneath me. I raked my nails against the fabric as his breath fell closer to my sweet spot, to the bundle of nerves that needed attention or I would combust into a flame of unfilled desire.

"You're so beautiful, so perfect." Beck complimented me with his deep, gravelly voice as his finger found my me and rubbed in slow, sensual circles. How many times had he done this to a girl? He was good, too good, to be as inexperienced as I was. That thought should have made me feel self-conscious, but his words and touch emboldened me. I didn't care what girls he'd learned on, I just wanted him to use his skills on me.

"Beck, I've never…" I gasped out as a crash of pleasure snaked up my spinal cord. "It feels so…" The pad of his finger found the exact spot that curled my toes under. "Ahhh," I spoke with an uneven tone, not understanding what parts of my brain were forming my words in that moment.

The next few moments happened in quick frames. His fingers were rubbing me into oblivion, and then his mouth joined. He lapped me up like I was the best thing he'd ever tasted, like I was ice cream melting down the side of a cone, too good to spare even a drop. I was riding each new wave of pleasure. Just as his finger pushed inside me, his tongue stroked my clit and I moaned his name again and again as he brought me to a mind blowing orgasm.

"Jesus…oh my…God, BECK," I moaned, collecting small pieces of the world around me: my fingers digging into his hair, my hips pressing up to meet his mouth, the rain pelting the roof of the Camper.

"Did you just include me in the Holy Trinity?" he laughed, shifting to sit back on his heels so he could see my face. I took the opportunity to stretch out like a cat; the awkward confines of the Camper had finally sunk into my achy muscles.

"You freaking deserve it." I smiled up at him, still coming down from my orgasm-induced high.

"You should take your underwear off. They're still wet," he offered, already beginning to drag them down my hips. The cotton slipped down past my knee and I helped kick them off the rest of the way.

I should have felt weird about being partly naked in front of a deeply sexy guy, but he'd already done something so intimate to me that taking off my underwear seemed like nothing.

"I don't want to stop yet." I smiled up at him and shot up onto my knees. His bemused smile was all the answer I needed.

CHAPTER FIFTEEN

"There's no rush, Abby. We have the rest of the road trip, plus you don't even have the nerve to tell me your true feelings yet." He held a wicked gleam in his eyes. He was fishing for my feelings. A hot, way-out-of-my-league guy was all but begging for me to tell him what I thought of him. What a joke. Life could be so fucking funny sometimes.

So I started laughing and couldn't stop. I laughed at his beautiful hazel eyes and brown hair. I laughed at the dimples that dotted the edges of his mouth, tugging at my heart in ways I could never have imagined before. I was laying there with crazy, rat hair in an oversized shirt and zero makeup. I had a scar the size of Montana on my chest while his chest was perfectly unmarred, tanned, and chiseled.

"Beckham," I started in a serious tone, "you are the strangest, hottest, funniest person I've ever met." I paused to let my compliments sink in, and then I cupped my hands around my mouth.

"I LIKE YOU!" I shouted so he'd know how I felt when he'd screamed the same words to me in the ocean. My voice ricocheted through the Camper, finding its mark when Beck's smile spread twice as big.

"Have you ever said that to someone before?" Beck asked with a quizzical brow.

I huffed and glared at him. "Don't flatter yourself, bucko."

He nodded but couldn't wipe the grin off. "Who else?" He reached out and wrapped his hands around my hips, tugging me closer to him. Our breath mingled between our mouths.

I rolled my eyes. "Countless movie stars. Dozens of them. You are hardly special at all. I tell Orlando Bloom that I love him pretty much daily."

Beck's head dropped forward as he chuckled. "Fair enough."

His hands snuck under my shirt, dragging across my skin and squeezing my hips. The move emboldened me and I leaned forward to kiss him. It felt like I lit a match. He pressed me down onto his lap and I rolled my hips, fighting the urge to just let him take me completely.

"Are we going to have sex?" I asked once he lifted his head again.

"Not tonight," he answered, squeezing my hips.

"Then I should probably put some underwear on," I answered.

"Probably so," he relented, letting me go.

I shifted around him and started digging in my bag for

a fresh pair and some shorts. The rain was still tapping on the roof, but it had lightened up since we arrived at the rest stop. Once I had all of my clothes back on, I grabbed a hooded sweatshirt out of my bag and picked up the black urn.

"Want to spread some ashes with me?" I asked, cradling the urn in my arm.

Beck had pulled on a hooded jacket as well and was still wearing his dark jeans. We looked like a modern day Bonnie and Clyde, on the run from the world.

"What's in there?" he asked.

"My dog, remember?" I answered swiftly. I feared he would ask again eventually, but I wanted to keep it private. He would make fun of me if I told him the truth.

"I still don't believe you. It's not your old heart, is it?" His eyes were glued to the urn.

"Ew! What? No, I don't know what they did with my heart after the procedure. It's in a biohazard bag somewhere probably." The idea of spreading the ashes of my old heart *was* poetic, but mostly just plain disgusting.

Beck nodded with a hint of a frown. I think he secretly thought he'd been right about that this whole time.

"Where do you want to spread them?" he asked, climbing into the front seat so he could exit on his side.

"Just around the rest stop," I answered.

"That's so gross, Abby," Beck laughed.

"Not where people will walk or anything!" I exclaimed, feeling defensive. "Maybe they have a garden or something."

Surprisingly, the rest stop had no garden. I guess your tax dollars don't allow for those sorts of things. Instead,

Beck hummed the tune of that sad song they always play on dog adoption commercials as I dumped some ashes onto the grass behind the bathrooms. It stuck to the ground. The rain made it instantly soggy, like a gray soup. The whole time I tried to be somber, but in the end it didn't work. Beck made me laugh all the way back to camper. It was impossible to be sad with him around.

While he unrolled our sleeping bags and made a little pallet for us to sleep on, I found my phone to check if I'd missed any calls from Caroline or my mom. The screen was black when I tried to swipe it open. Dead. I'd forgotten to charge it the night before and now any missed calls would have to wait for the morning.

"Is your phone dead as well?" Beck asked from behind me.

"Yeah. Stupid rain storm," I huffed, tossing my phone back into my purse. "Can we eat our vending machine meal now?"

Beck winked. "Only the best for you."

• • •

The next morning, Beck and I woke up late and ended up wandering into a diner to charge our phones and get some much-needed food. Crackers and cookies could only tide me over for so long.

Angie's Southern Diner looked straight out of the 1950's. The booths were covered in red and white striped upholstery. The tables had a red gloss coating. Elvis blared from the crackly speaker system and waitresses with tired expressions walked around in pink poodle skirts

"This place is awesome," I said, sliding into the booth

seat. There was an outlet just beneath the table, so Beck and I both plugged in our phones so that they could charge while we ate.

"Agreed, let's open up a place like this back in Dallas."

"I'm in," I answered, taking the menu from the waitress and offering her a quick 'thanks'.

Beck ordered us two waters and then looked back toward me. "What would we call it?"

"A and B's Vending Machine Emporium," I offered.

"How about just: Abby Mae's."

I laughed. "We can't serve any meat though."

Beck's eyes lit up. "Let's replace all the meat with chocolate cake."

Just then, the waitress came back and we had to scramble to decide what we wanted to order. I ended up ordering a salad that was "maybe organic" and Beck ordered a burger, fries, and chocolate milkshake.

"That's disgusting." I scrunched my nose when the plate of heaping food was set in front of him.

I started picking at my salad with my fork. Suddenly, I was no longer satisfied with my heart healthy choice.

"It might be terrible for me, but it is definitely *not* disgusting," Beck clarified.

I rolled my eyes playfully.

"How's the salad?" he asked after swallowing a big bite of burger. I didn't answer right away. I was distracted by his burger. It looked amazing. It had a meat patty, bacon, cheese, lettuce, onion, tomato, all shoved inside a buttery bun. The sounds Beck made as he chewed made me pierce my lettuce with a tad too much angst.

"It's great. Really… *fresh*," I answered without meeting his eye.

"So you definitely don't want a bite of this burger? I mean, of course you wouldn't," he teased before taking another big bite. I watched him chew with a look of pure ecstasy written across his face.

"You'd hate it anyway. It's cheesy and juicy. Definitely not your style," he added, wiping his mouth while holding the burger with his other hand.

Before I thought better of it, I pushed off my seat and leaned across the booth to take a giant bite out of his burger. It hardly fit in my mouth, but I chewed with a big smile on my face anyway. Beck sat there stunned, his hazel eyes locked onto my mouth. My taste buds weren't prepared for the flavor at first, but after another moment my mouth adjusted and I closed my eyes, appreciating the fatty amazingness.

"When's the last time you had meat?" Beck asked, continuing to stare at me with amazement.

"Over twelve years ago," I said with a full mouth, not caring how unladylike I was being.

"Damn, that was hot." A slow grin unwound across his lips.

I didn't take any more bites of his burger. That first one hit my stomach with a thud and I knew that if I had any more, I'd be paying for it later. We paid and waited for our phones to charge up before heading back toward the Camper. The plan was to head to San Antonio next. They have a Riverwalk with tons of shops and restaurants you can stroll down. It would be the final stop before we headed toward Odessa.

We hopped in the Camper and were heading toward San Antonio when I turned my phone on. A cluster of 'Missed Calls' popped up onto the screen. Most of them were from my mom and dad, but then there were a few from Caroline's mom as well. A dark, twisted feeling pierced my gut.

I pressed play on the first voice mail.

"*Abby, please call home as soon as possible. I have no clue where you are, but if you don't respond soon we're going to contact the police. I need to talk to you about Caroline, sweetie. Please call me back immediately.*"

I didn't even hesitate; I dialed home and pressed the phone so hard against my ear that it was cutting off circulation.

"Abby!" My mom exclaimed. She picked up after the first ring.

"Mom, I'm fin-"

"Where have you been?" she yelled into the phone, cutting me off.

I pressed the tips of my fingers into my eyelids, trying to stay in control of my emotions.

"I've been on a road trip, kind of. What's wrong with Caroline?"

She breathed into the phone and I knew she was trying to pick her priorities. If Caroline was okay, she'd yell at me for leaving. If Caroline wasn't okay, she'd worry about my punishment later.

"Sweetie. You have to come home. Caroline was really sick. Last night they-"

I cut her off. "*Was* really sick?"

"Abby…" My mom tried to soothe me through the phone, but there was nothing she could say. My heart rate was picking up. My hands were shaking. I lost focus of my vision so that the world became a messy blur.

"Is Caroline better now?" I asked with a hollow voice. My world caved in on itself like a collapsible tent. The sun seemed to shine too brightly, the air streamed too loudly out of the vents. Beck's driving seemed slow, as if he didn't realize that my world was slipping through my fingers with each passing second of this phone call.

Her silence said everything I needed to hear.

But finally she began. "No…Honey…Caroline passed aw-" she whispered, and I felt bile rise through to my throat.

"I'm coming home. I'll be there tonight," I muttered, and then hung-up. My phone slipped out of my shaking hand and tumbled down to the floor of the camper.

Caroline.

Caroline died.

Caroline was no longer experiencing life.

She was no longer a person. She would never answer the phone if I called her. How can that be possible? They say you appreciate something more when it's gone. That's bullshit. I loved Caroline through every second of our friendship because we knew it was always terminal. We were never meant to be friends forever. When we first met, we both had timelines that weren't even supposed to reach a new calendar year. Five years later, she was dead and my timeline was eternal in comparison.

"Stop the car," I demanded. We were on an empty stretch of highway with no other cars in sight. The sun was hanging high in the sky, heating the landscape and boiling my emotions even more.

Caroline lied to me. She told me she had eight months to live and she didn't even have eight days. That selfless asshole. There was nothing but desert until the horizon met the sky. I had the black urn in my right hand. I left my shoes in the car and the sharp rocks were piercing the tender soles of my feet, but I didn't care. I hoped I stepped on a million rocks. I hope they dug into my skin and drew blood.

Releasing a soul-crushing scream, I threw the urn as far as I could, watching it soar through the sky and then shatter into a million pieces once it collided with the ground. Wind picked up the dark grey ashes and spread them through the desert air. They moved organically, like a tiny tornado, but it wasn't enough. I picked up rocks and threw them to where the urn had shattered. I reveled in the sound of rock hitting pottery. It dotted the landscape along with my angry sobs.

I felt guilt like a red hot iron branding my stomach. I'd left her in that hospital room so that I could go on a dumb road trip with a dumb guy who didn't fucking matter.

"You let me go!" I cried. "You TOLD ME TO GO!"

How dare she decide what was best for me. She didn't want to show me her sickness? She wanted me to live? I'd fucking show her. I picked up rock after rock, stepping closer to the urn and chunking them as hard as I could.

"YOU'RE A COWARD!" I screamed toward the desert sky. "I hate you! I HATE YOU!"

She told me to go on a road trip when I should have been with her. I should have been there to give her ice chips or for comedic relief. I would have done anything, truly anything, but she didn't let me. She was being selfless, anyone would have agreed. But in that moment I had to believe she was actually being selfish or the guilt of last night would be too much to bear. She was dying and I was having my first orgasm. She was choking on her last breath and Beck was helping me spread ashes that weren't even fucking ashes!

I heard rocks crunch beneath Beck's weight behind me and I turned toward him. "You know what was in that urn?"

He just stood there, trying to gage my emotions as best as he could. It pissed me off that he wasn't as angry as I was. His hands were shoved into his front pockets and his eyebrows were scrunched together in concern. There was pity etched across his features and I wished I could wipe it off and replace it with something else.

He never answered. "Well I'll tell you anyway. I burned up old medical pamphlets, instructions for medications, preparations for the transplant, guides on how to prolong life with a debilitating heart condition. I burned everything up and shoved it in that urn because I wanted to be poetic and dramatic. I wanted to shed my old skin and move on from my old life. But you know what? While I was gallivanting around the country dumping burnt-up paper, my best friend was dying!"

"Abby." He moved to step closer to me, but his touch would have seared my guilty flesh. I didn't want it.

"I'm alive and she's not. Caroline died because nothing in life is fair." I looked up into his hazel eyes. They were staring back at me with such conviction. "She was a better person than me. When we first met, I wanted to ignore everyone in our support group, but she came over and sat next to me. She kept asking me questions and forcing me to answer. I thought she was weird and overly friendly. I made fun of her in my head. The nurses and doctors all loved her. Everyone who knew her fell in love with her."

"She didn't deserve to die," Beck answered for me.

"I did," I muttered toward the ground.

"No one deserves to die over other people."

I scoffed, thinking of all the serial killers that clearly deserved to die instead of good people every day. "Let's go. I have to go home."

I shoved past him and headed for the Camper. I wanted to be home. I needed to be home. I should have never left.

CHAPTER SIXTEEN

I hardly remember our journey back to Dallas. We drove straight there, stopping once for gas and a bathroom break. I'd broken down in the dirty bathroom stall, crying tears that I was too stubborn to shed in front of Beck. I collapsed on that disgusting floor, trying to make sense of life. I stayed in there for so long that eventually an attendant had to come bang on the door and demand that I let other customers use the restroom. Her palm shook the cheap plastic door and I wondered if the stall could collapse on top of me. The only thing I decided in that bathroom was that I didn't want to live in a world without Caroline.

Beck didn't mention anything when I got back into the car with puffy eyes. He put on a podcast of 'This American Life' and gave me my peace. I didn't want to talk about it; I just wanted to wallow in my sadness and guilt.

Empty landscape morphed to urban sprawl and concrete. We drove straight to my apartment without a word. He helped me bring my luggage up, and then we stood in the threshold of my apartment in silence. My throat was tightening up and tears burned the back of my eyes. I clenched my teeth together as a last stitch effort at remaining composed.

"Do you want me to stay?" Beck asked. His dark brown eyebrows were tugged together and his hazel eyes had lost all of their joy. He looked like he had in his MIT ID photo. My jaw tightened even more and I swallowed past the lump in my throat.

"No," I answered, keeping my eyes locked on the door jam.

"Are you sure?" he asked. I wanted to yell at him, to take my anger out on something, but I just mumbled a yes.

He nodded slowly and then inched backward. "You did the right thing," he said before turning on his heel and fading down the stairs. I pressed the door closed and then slid down onto the linoleum, wondering what he meant by that. Did I do the right thing by leaving Caroline to die? By coming home when I found out she passed away? By telling him to leave? By taking a road trip with a stranger?

I had no clue how to get beyond the questions. They were suffocating me from within. My apartment felt like a furnace, so I got up, grabbed my keys, and left.

Once I was in my car driving toward downtown, I dialed my mom.

"Sweetie, are you home?"

"I just got back," I answered, putting my blinker on and changing lanes to enter the highway.

"We're coming over!" she said, and I could already hear her shuffling around to get her shoes on.

"I'm not there, I needed some air. I'll come over to the house later."

"Are you sure? I could take a walk with you?" She was so sweet. She wouldn't have been this forgiving if Caroline hadn't died. She would have been royally pissed about my road trip.

For a moment, I considered letting her come with me. It would have been nice to have her for comfort, but I wanted to be alone.

"No. I'll see you later," I answered, and then cut off the call. I tossed the phone onto the passenger seat and focused on driving toward an unknown destination. I exited when I felt like it, turned left and then right without conscious thought.

I ended up on a street with a row of bars and trendy restaurants. It was nearly nine at night, so most of the places were in full swing. I parked down the street and then walked along the sidewalk, looking for a venue where I could drown my sorrows. They all had interesting names like The Flying Squirrel, O'Doyle's Pub, and The Hippy Hollow.

One bar caught my attention out of all the rest because of the wild dancers in the window. They were scantily clad and swaying with easy confidence. Music was streaming through the doors. It was a Rihanna remix with heavy bass that seduced me enough to pull my wallet out of my back pocket. I had no clue if it was an eighteen-and-over bar or not, but the bouncer at the door was busy arguing with another guy, so I just walked right in like I belonged. A dark black staircase led me up to a second floor and the moment I hit the landing, the music and bass multiplied tenfold. Bodies shuffled in every direction and I pushed my way through, trying not to make eye contact with anyone for fear that they'd realize I was too young to be there.

I wasn't in control of my emotions. At any moment I could have crumbled into tears that wouldn't cease, but I kept walking deeper into the flashing lights.

There was a single spot open at the bar, smack dab in the center, so I slid onto the seat and let the club scene engulf me.

"What can I get you?" A voice asked. I looked up to see a well-dressed bartender smiling down at me. He was impeccably groomed: waxed eyebrows and gelled black hair. Damn, he was prettier than me.

"Could I just have a water for now?" I wasn't sure if he would ask for my ID and I didn't want to get kicked out. My fingers laced together and my foot tapped nervously at the foot of my bar stool.

"Sure thing," he winked, and then grabbed a glass and filled it with water. His movements were fluid and moved to the beat of the music the entire time. When he was finished, he grabbed a small bowl and tossed a few Maraschino cherries inside.

"On the house, sweetie." He placed the bowl in front of me and offered me a genuine smile before moving on to the next customer.

I popped the cherries into my mouth one at a time, letting the pulsing music push away any thoughts trying to break through my facade. It turned into a cycle: I'd hear a snippet of the conversations around me or get distracted by the bartender and for a brief second I felt like a normal person. But then Caroline's death would snake into my consciousness and I'd feel a sharp punch to my gut all over again.

I wished she was at the bar with me. I wished she was sitting in the seat next to me instead of the couple shouting over one another to be heard. I stayed in my own little world, but she would have already had conversations with a dozen people. She drew people in like a fly trap and I always stood in the background in awe of how personable she could be to complete strangers.

I guzzled my water, trying to scrape away the sadness. People shuffled around me. The seats at the bar would empty and then fill again by a never ending stream of club goers.

My gaze was focused on my empty cherry bowl when a large presence filled the seat to my left. I didn't look up, but I could feel the person's energy. The scent of hair spray and a flowery perfume made my nostrils sting.

"Why the sad face, gorgeous?" A deep voice asked.

My eyes flitted up to see a sight that I have never beheld in all of my nineteen years. A drag queen, the most beautiful, over-the-top, sparkly drag queen I'd ever seen, was peering at me from beneath thick false eyelashes. I just sat there gaping, trying to take in as much of his/her appearance as I could. A bright pink wig spiraled at least a foot into the air. Her (I decided to go with her for the time being since I didn't know proper protocol) make-up was flawless: bright pink and purple glitter eye shadow that tapered off into a cat eye.

"Better close that mouth sweetie, or I'll find something to put in it," she said, and shimmied her shoulders playfully. Glitter particles flew into the air in every direction. Her sexual innuendo only forced my mouth open an inch wider.

"Javi, could you get us two shots of tequila, please?" she asked, pointing one long finger at the bartender. That's when it hit me. I hadn't wandered into just *any* bar. Nope. I'd wandered into a gay bar. Who knew they even existed in Dallas?

"What's your name?" she asked me as the two shot glasses were set in front of us.

"Abby," I answered shyly, staring toward the liquor. I wasn't supposed to have alcohol because of my transplant. It's not like one night would kill me. It was just one of those things that got cut when I already had so many obstacles working against my health.

"Well, Abby, You're in luck. You wandered into *my* club. I'm Queen Bee."

I smiled for the first time since listening to the message on my phone earlier that day. "I love that name," I answered, still not quite finding my voice. I sounded hollow.

"Good! Bottoms up, Abby. I need your help judging a competition and the rules state that the judges can't be sober!"

Queen Bee picked up the shot glasses and handed one to me. "To Abby!" She yelled it out so loudly that most of the people at the bar turned toward her in awe. "Who for the rest of the night will be named," she paused eying me up and down once, "Ruby Red!" Everyone cheered in agreement as I sat there shocked at the situation I'd stumbled upon. No one would believe me. Except Caroline. I had no doubt that she would have taken the shot glass and poured it down my throat for me.

"To you, Caroline!" I yelled, so loudly that it made my ears ring, before downing the shot quickly. The liquor burned going down and I didn't even think to hide the look of pure disgust on my face.

"Looks like we have a virgin over here," Queen Bee sang, shoving another shot into my hand that had appeared out of nowhere. I swallowed it without hesitation and felt the effect as the two shots hit my stomach. Everyone swarmed Queen Bee as if she was literally the queen bee. She air kissed the club goers and offered little greetings that they lapped up like loyal fans. I couldn't help but wonder how popular she was. Was this really *her* club?

"Now, Ruby Red, it's time to doll you up. You can't go on stage dressed like that." I looked down at my shorts and tank top.

"This is all that I have," I admitted, confused about what she planned on doing with me. She batted her eyelashes down to me and that's when I realized they had tiny gemstones at the end of each lash. She looked like someone straight out of the Capitol in the Hunger Games… only *more* insanely dolled up.

"I have everything you need!" she cheered, tugging my hand. "Follow me!"

She led me away from the bar and through the crowd toward a backstage area. There was a bouncer standing guard and a huge sign that read: "VIP". A small part of me felt like I should bolt and cut my losses, but a bigger part of me was curious about what Queen Bee planned to do with me. What could she possibly want me to judge? A drag queen contest?

"We don't have long, but I'll do your hair and makeup really quick and then we'll pick out something for you to wear," she declared as she pushed open a bright red, glossy door. The inside of her dressing room looked like what you would expect to find at the end of Candy Land. It was like a rainbow had exploded on every item in the room. Bright striped, neon walls housed racks of sparkly clothing.

"Are you my Fairy God mother?" I asked, feeling the warmth of those two shots begin to swirl in my veins. I wasn't drunk, but the sadness eroding my stomach all day was finally taking a backseat to a newer sensation. All thanks to Queen Bee, I could breathe without feeling like a hand was clamping down on my lungs.

Queen Bee threw her head back and laughed, carefree and wildly. "Let's say just for tonight that I am." She pushed me down into the chair and put her hands on my shoulders. I caught her reflection in the mirror; her bright brown eyes met mine. Her expression held a look of deep understanding, and before I realized the words that were forming, I started telling her about Caroline.

"My friend died last night. She was sick for a long time and she never got to live her life. I'm trying to live for the both of us." I blurted it out, never taking my eyes off her. Her grip on my shoulders tightened and her mouth flattened into a thin line. It was a brief moment of profound sorrow, but then she nodded and tucked those feelings away behind her beautiful mask.

"Then baby, living is what you're going to do!" She whirled me around and immediately started working on my hair. She teased it, pulled it up high, and twisted it impossibly tight. All the while I squeezed my eyes closed, trying to handle the pain. She gave me another shot when she realized how tense I was. "Beauty is pain!" she laughed before stepping back to secure my hair with more hair spray than I even realized could fit inside of a bottle. I coughed and hacked, trying desperately to breathe through the thick, chemically air.

"Ten minutes until show-time, Sugar Britches!" she sang. I laughed uncontrollably, not even realizing what was so funny. *Maybe I shouldn't have had three shots*, I thought as she layered on purple eye shadow. I knew I was going to look like a clown. Who wears purple eye shadow without looking like a clown? She swiped on mascara and smeared my lips in bright red lipstick. My face felt tight from all the tugging and pulling.

"Are you ready, Ruby Red?" she asked once she leaned back to eye her work. Her smile was genuine and proud, like I was her baby girl all grown up. Maybe she really was my Fairy God Mother. When she turned that black chair around, my mouth hung open. I didn't look like a clown. I mean I looked crazy, like a Texas Pageant Queen, but somehow I still looked beautiful. The eye shadow made my sage green eyes pop and the mascara made me look older and sultry.

"This should fit, although it'll be a little loose," she said as she disappeared behind racks of clothing and then came back with a tight red dress. It was a cotton-blend material, and when I slipped it over my head, it clung to my skin like a wetsuit. It fell mid-way down my thighs and the spaghetti-straps criss-crossed between my shoulder blades.

"Now! In true Fairy God Mother Fashion, I have a single pair of gem-stone encrusted pumps. They're size eight and they used to belong to Professor Luscious, but she moved to San Francisco and left them here." I smiled at the drag name as she handed me the shoes. They were gorgeous and definitely a modern take on the glass slipper. Glittery gem-stones, which looked like fake diamonds, coated the entire surface.

There was only one problem. "I'm a size seven, they'll slip off," I lamented.

Queen Bee arched her impeccable brow at me and shook her head. "Fake it till you make it, that's how we work in this business."

I thought she was referring to slipping some stuffing into my shoes so they would fit, but the next thing I knew she was slipping falsies down the front of my dress so that my size-A boobs now looked like a size-C at least.

"You look like a mini-me! Now let's go!" She tugged my hand and the room spun in a hazy mix of glitter and color. I had to hold her hand with both of mine so that I wouldn't stumble in the stiletto heels.

The second we walked out of the VIP dressing room, cat calls sounded throughout the bar. Every single person stopped their conversations and held their drinks up in a wild salute to Queen Bee and me.

She kept tugging me behind her until we were on stage. A short guy dressed as an angel, complete with giant white feathered wings, handed a microphone to Queen Bee and then bowed in humble servitude. Any cheers that had followed us onto the stage completely died out as Queen Bee started to speak.

"Good evening!" she whispered seductively into the mic. "As you all know, every Tuesday at the Trancing Pranny we hold a little contest…" The crowd erupted in response. Whatever contest I was about to judge was clearly loved by everyone. "We have very *well-endowed* contestants tonight, but before we begin, I'd like to introduce you all to my guest judge for the evening." The spotlight swooped over to me in response. It was so bright that I had to hold my hand up to shield my eyes.

"Her name is Ruby Red and she's my little Cinderella, so let's all give her a big welcome!" The crowd whooped and hollered. For one moment I wavered on a precipice. I could sober up and remember the tragedy of the day. I could leave immediately and go home to my empty apartment and cry for Caroline in peace. Or I could let the tequila, the bright lights, the make-up, and the crowd, take its effect and pull me away from the demons crouching in wait just outside of the club. Luckily for me, the decision wasn't mine to make.

A second later, a wild club beat started bouncing from the speakers and right on cue, a stream of deliciously sexy men danced out from behind backstage.

CHAPTER SEVENTEEN

Each of the guys was better looking than the next. They were all different types. Tall, short, tan, and muscled. None of the men were dressed in drag; they had on normal, albeit very stylish, club attire. So what exactly was I going to be judging?

"Ladies, Queens, Sisters…" Queen Bee began, "We have ten of the SEXIEST gay men Dallas has to offer here on stage for you." She paused for a rowdy round of applause. "They'll each have three minutes to dance their asses off and show us their best moves!" She stepped closer to me and wrapped her hand around my shoulders. "Our little Ruby Red will be picking the winner, so they'll have to do everything in their power to impress her!" She waggled her eyebrows suggestively, and I peered back to see a few of the men shoot me silly winks or blow kisses in my direction. I blushed a dark shade of crimson that I prayed the spotlight didn't amplify.

The same Angel that had given Queen Bee the microphone earlier scurried onto the stage to place a pink barstool behind me. I didn't miss the shy smile he shot one of the men standing in line behind me. I turned to see a sexy blonde guy blow him a kiss.

Suddenly, Queen Bee pushed me back toward the barstool and I did my best to climb onto it without revealing my underwear to the entire crowd.

"DJ! Hit it. It's time for contestant number one to strut his stuff!" Queen Bee clapped her hands and moved toward the edge of the stage. The blonde guy who'd grinned at the Angel started clapping his hands above his head. He strolled forward with a confident prance, throwing his arms up to get the crowd going even more…and then the real fun started.

He reached for the hem of his shirt and started tugging it up. Screams erupted from the crowd and I cupped a hand over my mouth as he pulled the shirt completely off. The next thing to go was the button on his jeans. He demurely popped it open and then shimmied his hips around in a circle before locking his eyes onto me. *Oh crap.* His finger pointed directly at me and his tongue licked his lips slowly.

I pressed back against the barstool and reached down to grip the seat with both hands. Was he going to touch me? Were they allowed to touch me? He strolled toward me until he was a few inches away from my chair and then dipped all the way to the ground and back up again, worshiping me like I was some goddess. I couldn't contain my giggles or my blushing cheeks. Tequila will do that to you.

Sober-me would have been crawling out of my skin.

The music hit a new crescendo and he dropped his hips and swayed them back and forth seductively, then turned away from me and backed his ass up until it was almost touching my knees. I let out a nervous laugh as the crowd went wild. I had no clue what they expected me to do. His legs were spread eagle and his ass was popping up and down faster than I'd ever seen someone move.

So, I did what any logical girl would do. I reached out and spanked him, just once. I had no clue what came over me. It felt like an out-of-body experience.

"There's our little Ruby Red!" Queen Bee sang into the microphone, and I clasped a hand over my mouth in response.

Contestant number one finished his act and then stepped back in line, not even bothering to retrieve his scraps of discarded clothing. The next contestants passed in a blur of body parts and sexy dance moves. I saw flashes of male body parts I'd never seen before.

My favorite contestant, however, was the last one to go up. He was younger than the rest of them and had brown hair that reminded me of Beck's. The crowd didn't cheer for him in the beginning, and I instantly wanted to help him out.

I whistled and clapped my hands, and he shot me an appreciative smile. The contestant started clapping along with the beat, getting the entire crowd to join in with him. When he was satisfied that everyone was paying attention to him, he bolted off the stage and made his way through the crowd, crashing through people along his way. When he reached the bar, he hopped up on top and started working his magic. He was the best dancer out of all of them; he must have been classically trained because the kicks and spins he pulled out on that thin wood surface were too good to be accidents. I had to prop myself up onto my barstool to see over the crowd and I smiled when I saw him pick up someone's drink and toss it back.

I lost sight of him for a few seconds and then his brown hair popped back out through the crowd. He was bee lining right for me with something held in his outstretched hand.

When he stopped in front of me, I looked down to see him holding the stem of a glistening cherry.

"A cherry for you, Ruby Red," he winked seductively, and then held it up so that I only had one option: to bite it off the stem while he held it out to me. I chanced a glance past him toward Queen Bee. Her grin was wide and approving. I leaned forward, meeting the contestant's light brown eyes, and bit off the end of the cherry. The sweet juices coated my tongue and for a brief moment I pretended that the brunette contestant standing in front of me was Beck. The tequila made their similarities pop, so I leaned forward and kissed him, smack dab on the lips. His mouth tasted like strawberry Chap Stick and I pulled away giggling.

"I've never kissed a gay man," I admitted, loud enough for Queen Bee's microphone to pick up the faint echo. My voice projected throughout the club's speakers and everyone paused for a moment before going wild.

I looked over toward the final contestant and threw a hand over my mouth. He looked *nothing* like Beck. I was a tipsy fool and I didn't care one way or the other.

I dubbed contestant number ten the winner. There were balloons, confetti, and a crazy light show. My head was spinning by the time I slid off the stage with Queen Bee.

"Thanks for letting me go up there with you," I said,

walking out from behind the partition after I'd changed back into my normal clothes. My hair was still twirled in pretty waves and my make-up seemed thick enough to last a few years.

Queen Bee looked up at me from her director's chair. "It was an honor. You're welcome back any time. The crowd loved you." She smiled at me, and we stood, taking each other in for a moment.

On stage, her drag queen get-up fit in so well, but now that we were back in the dressing room, I could see the glitter starting to sweat down her cheeks and one of her false eyelashes was starting to peel off at the edge.

"Could I know your real name?" I asked boldly. I had no clue how the politics of this world worked. Was I supposed to understand that when we were in this club and when he was dressed up as a she, *she* was known as Queen Bee?

She looked at me for another second, tapping her manicured finger on her crossed knee. "Danny."

I nodded in appreciation. It felt like he was letting me in on a little secret by revealing that to me. "My friend's name was Caroline. I missed her death because I was in the middle of a road trip."

I could already feel the tears fighting to fall.

Danny nodded twice slowly, letting my confession sink in. "Do you think she was upset about that?"

I thought about his question and then smiled at the memory of Caroline threatening to call in a bomb threat about me. "No. To be honest, I don't think she was upset. I just wish I could've seen her one last time."

The closure of a final goodbye seemed like it'd been ripped from my hands by fate.

"Are you going to finish your road trip?" Danny

asked, starting to unpin his pink wig.

Finish the road trip? I hadn't even had time to consider it. Yes, we'd had fun, and the main reason for taking the journey hadn't been even been accomplished. But I pushed the thoughts away. I couldn't think of anything beyond dealing with Caroline's death.

"I'm not sure," I answered truthfully.

After I'd collected all of my stuff, I hugged Danny, took his business card, and then bid my farewell to the best place on earth. No, not Disneyland. The Transing Pranny.

But the moment I passed through the doors, the hand clamped around my lungs once again and I struggled for breath.

Caroline was gone.

CHAPTER EIGHTEEN

Even though I was mostly sober by the time I exited the club, I still opted to take a cab to my parent's house. I texted my mom to tell her that I was on my way. It was late, and she hadn't seen me in almost a week, but she didn't seem upset when the cab pulled up. She and my dad opened the front door and enveloped me in a tight bear hug, squeezing me until my organs protested.

"What were you thinking, going on a trip without letting us know about it? And why is your hair and makeup done like that?" my mom muttered. I knew her questions were rhetorical because she threw me into another body-squeezing hug before I even had time to formulate a response. I let her tug me closer. I was coming down from my drag queen-induced high and the security of my parents' embrace threatened to break the seal on my tears.

My mom was still hugging me when she whispered into my ear, "Honey, I'm so sorry." My hands, which a moment before were gently resting on her back, grasped her shirt for dear life. My fingernails dug into the thin cotton fabric. I squeezed my eyes shut, but tears still found their way down my cheeks. Hearing her say it out loud was more than I'd prepared myself for on the cab ride over. Caroline's emaciated face melted into my thoughts. Her sunken cheeks, her sad, dark eyes. Our last conversation on the phone was too short. Had I even told her I loved her? Did she know that I would have never survived treatment without her?

She was gone.

I melted into my mom's arms and let her hold my weight as I surrendered to the sadness. I felt all of it. I didn't shirk away from the absolute, all-encompassing pain that threatened to bring me to my knees. I'd experienced death and dying. Some could argue that because I knew Caroline was going to pass away, that my grieving process would have been different, but it was a different kind of grief that I felt.

I was enraged for Caroline's sake. Yes, I was sad that my best friend would no longer be my best friend and that I had a gaping hole in my life, in my heart. But I was just so livid at the world for ripping Caroline's life out of her hands. She was slow to anger, sweet and kind in every instance. If anyone deserved to *not* have cancer, it was Caroline. So I was left with this pit in my stomach that shattering a thousand urns would never fix. I was too young to be so cynical, but there was no way to avoid it when you learned that being good all year didn't mean Santa Claus left you toys; it meant that no matter how hard you fought, the cells in your body were going to do anything they wanted. We were helpless to the mechanisms that made us humans. They controlled destiny, not us.

"When did she pass away?" I asked once I thought I could speak without a sob breaking through.

"Late last night," my mom answered.

I breathed in silent sobs, inhaling whiffs of my mother's perfume.

"Her funeral is on Thursday," my mom offered.

Two days. Two days to think of how I would commemorate Caroline's life in a eulogy.

• • •

I fell asleep sobbing in my old room while my mom tried to console me. I'd wanted her to stay with me last night, and when I woke up, she was still by my side, sleeping peacefully on her back. I reached over to kiss her cheek before gathering all of my stuff and sneaking out of the room. The stairs creaked as I made my way down, but my dad must have still been sleeping as well because no one greeted me at the bottom. I slipped my shoes on and sent my parents a text about heading back to my apartment so they'd know where I was when they woke up.

My car was still sitting in the lot outside of the club from last night, so I took a deep breath and started my trek to get it back. I decided to take a cab most of the way, but when we were close to the street I had the driver drop my off so that I could walk the last mile. It was a pretty morning in Dallas. The summer sun had just barely risen, so it wasn't scorching hot yet. I desperately needed a change of clothes and a shower. The awkward glances from fellow pedestrians told me how crazy I probably looked with my slept on curls and make-up.

In an effort to avoid any more judging stares, I pulled my phone out of my purse and checked the missed text I'd spied earlier. It was from Beck, sent right after midnight.

Beck: I'm really sorry about Caroline, but don't give up on humanity just yet.

I didn't have much longer before I reached my car, but I still hit 'call'. The phone rang and rang. I walked a city block and he still hadn't answered. Before I could think of hanging up, the call dropped to voicemail and Beck's gravelly voice filled my ears.

"Hey, this is Beck. Leave a message."

Short and sweet, but it felt good to hear his voice. I didn't leave a message. Calling him had given me an idea, and when I reached my car and was in the security of my own space, I dialed Caroline's number.

It rang, filling the silence of my car, and I wondered if maybe her parents would pick up. Did they have her phone? What happened to a person's phone when they died? Someone had to be charging it.

Then the voicemail clicked on and my heart dropped when I heard her voice.

"Hi! This is Caroline. I'm sorry I missed your call. Feel free to leave a message." I sat paralyzed for a second, but then the electronic beep went off and I started to talk to her as if she would pick up any moment.

"Caroline, it's Abby," I broke down, letting my head fall forward onto the steering wheel. "I miss you so much. I can't believe you're gone…I broke my urn in the desert when I found out you lied to me. Why'd you lie to me

Caroline? Or were you hoping for the best?" I paused as a sobbing hiccup hijacked my vocal cords. "You just left me. I went on a road trip and you didn't stop me…You should have stopped me! I would have been there in a second. You're my best friend, what am I supposed to do without you?" I paused and ran my finger along the worn leather. "I have so much to fill you in on…"

So I sat in my car, leaving her voicemail after voicemail until the tears overpowered my vocal cords.

I had to sit in that car for an hour before my eyes cleared enough so that I could see the road on my drive home.

CHAPTER NINETEEN

I was the last person to speak at Caroline's funeral. I'd tried my best to stay composed as her parents and family recalled stories and anecdotes about her life, but it was a losing battle. I bent down to light the Donut Shop candle that was meant to smell like coffee and then stepped behind the podium. My heels sank into the soft grass as I shuffled back and forth, eying the note cards in my hands and willing my voice into submission. When I finally looked up, the sun was shining through one of the trees overhead so that I had to squint to keep my eyes from watering.

"My name is Abby Mae McAllister," I began, and the microphone rang out a high pitched noise causing everyone to groan and cover their ears. I cleared my throat awkwardly and shifted a few inches away before trying again. "Um… I never knew Caroline when she was healthy. We met when we were both sick and staying in the hospital for treatment. She was wearing this pink bow headband the first time I met her…" I held my hand over my head to show them how high the bow had been. "We met in a group for sick teens that I had planned on skipping. My mother eventually talked me into going, but I wasn't in a socializing mood. I remember sitting on a metal chair moping when Caroline plopped down in the seat next to me. This was a support group for kids in the hospital, mind you, so it wasn't surprising that most of the people there had a gloom and doom attitude. But, not Caroline. She wouldn't stop talking. She yammered on forever and eventually I had to cave and answer her for fear that she would never stop."

"She was an in-your-face type of person. She weaseled her way into my life and took root until one day I woke up and couldn't go a single day without talking to her. We bonded over everything: boys, books, annoying nurses." I half-smiled toward the nurses who'd come from the hospital. "We talked about our funerals as most sick kids do. It takes the edge off. As if by talking about death, suddenly it no longer holds power over you." I cleared my throat and shuffled behind the podium, pleading with my tears to stay in the corner of my eyes.

"She had a few demands for today." I looked down at the note cards shaking in my hands so much that I couldn't actually read the scribbled words anymore. I recalled the night in the hospital when we were supposed to be sleeping in our separate rooms, but the nurses looked the other way. We stayed up late laying out what our funerals would be like as if it was one big joke.

"She wanted all of her old friends from school to be here." I looked up to where a group of teenagers sat wiping tears away with tissues. I hadn't seen any of them visit Caroline in recent months. "She wanted the service to be outside. A place she rarely got to visit in the last few weeks." And then I smiled at the last request. "She also demanded that I bring Orlando Bloom as my date. I tried to contact his people, but I never heard back, so instead I brought this." I motioned toward the lifeless prop next to me. I'd searched everywhere around town and could only find a cut-out of him dressed as an elf from Lord of The Rings. The top of the cardboard was bending forward so that his bow looked rather limp.

I cleared my throat and pressed on. "I told her that I would play "Sweet Caroline" as a joke. She forbid me under penalty of death," I paused at the finality of that word before taking a deep breath and continuing, "but Caroline was my best friend. We were there to push each other's buttons, so in one last attempt to annoy her…"

I bent down and hit play on the iPod lying next to the podium. Neil Diamond's voice began to croon through the speakers as I took a step back. I had to stay up front while the song played so that I could take the iPod and candle off at the end. My eyes scanned the rows of people, taking in the crowd. They all held sad smiles and wet tissues. I didn't recognize most of them. They must have been her relatives. So many of them shared her dark brown hair. My parents were up front with Caroline's mom and dad.

My eyes kept scanning until I passed by her old high school friends. Then I looked toward the last row of seats that was occupied by a single person: Beck.

He sat with his hands folded between his legs. He was wearing a fitted black suit with a black tie that sat crooked around his neck. He looked like he was a boy on the cusp of manhood. His unruly brown hair wasn't styled or anything, but it was still longish on top, curling at the ends. He filled out his suit perfectly, as if he'd owned it for years but only recently grown into it.

I couldn't believe he was there. And yet I'd hoped he would be.

He was watching me with sad hazel eyes, and for the first minute of that song, our eyes never left each other. My gaze held immense grief, his held immense empathy. But then as the song kept playing and the crescendo hit, Beck sat up straight and lip-synced the words. His eyes closed and a smirk spread across his lips. He put his heart and soul into each syllable and then when the "bum, bum, bum" of the trumpet hit, he punched his hand into the air three times with the beat.

No one else could see him, but that didn't stop me from starting to laugh. Leave it to Beck to put life back into perspective. Caroline wanted me to be happy; she wanted people to sing at her funeral, not cry. So I reached down and spiked the volume of the speakers until the sounds of sniffling were drowned out. The song's happy tempo blasted on and Beck and I brought it home, singing loudly and pointing to each other when the lyrics called for it. We were separated by an audience of grief, but our singing pushed through it.

When Neil's voice trailed off and the song ended, I stood there for a moment, gathering my resolve and tucking my grief away for now.

One moment it was silent and then in the next life carried on. Caroline's mom welcomed everyone to her house for food and drinks, and people began standing up and chattering amongst themselves.

I picked up the cardboard cutout and my stuff, and then kept walking until I reached the last row of seats. Beck stood to greet me and I took in his handsome features. He ran his hand under his cleanly-shaven chin, taking me in from my kitten heels to my sad smile.

When our eyes locked, I exhaled a deep breath, letting it carry away everything: a pound of immense sadness, my worry that things with Beck had changed, and the nerves from speaking about Caroline while attempting to hold it together. It was the feeling you get when you fall face first into bed after a long day. That's what being near Beck felt like.

He stepped toward me, stuffing his hands in the pant pockets of his form-fitting suit, and offered me a sad smile. People shuffled around us, making their way to their cars. But we stood there, communicating without words and letting the moment sink in. I ran my fingers through my long hair and tilted my head to the side.

"I missed you," he offered quietly.

I smiled despite the circumstances. "I kissed a gay guy and I judged a strip-off at a gay club."

His features morphed from thoughtful repose to complete shock, mixed with humor in a matter of milliseconds.

"Wow." He cocked his eyebrows.

"Are you mad?" I asked. My hand was still wrapped around cardboard Orlando Bloom.

He shook his head and stepped closer. "I'm *impressed*. That must have taken some skill. Was he a better kisser than me?"

I thought back. "His lips tasted like strawberries and I was just tipsy enough to convince myself that he looked a little bit like you."

Beck rocked back on his heels and laughed. "So… he had brown hair?"

I mashed my lips together and nodded. "That was the only similarity it turns out."

Beck squeezed his eyes closed and laughed harder.

"But, no. He wasn't better than you," I clarified, looking away to find my parents, or so I told myself. They were making their way over with confused expressions. Oh right, I was communicating with someone from the opposite sex.

"That was such a good speech, Abs. Caroline would have loved it," my dad offered when they reached me. He wrapped his arms around my shoulders and tugged me closer, then looked up at Beck. There was an awkward silence for a moment before I realized I was meant to introduce everyone.

"Um, Mom and Dad, this is Beck."

"Oh!" my mom clapped her hands together in recognition of his name. I guess it wasn't hard to remember the one guy that had ever answered my phone.

"Hi Mrs. McAllister, Mr. McAllister." Beck offered his hand respectfully. I chanced a glance up to my mom to see her beaming from ear to ear.

"So you're the boy that whisked my daughter away on a secret road trip?" My dad joked, but his tone held an edge of sternness.

"Paul!" My mother swatted my dad's arm playfully.

"Actually your daughter whisked me away on a road trip." Beck shot me a private smile.

I just gripped Orlando Bloom and prayed that he would come to life and save us from this awkward moment.

"Will you be joining us at the Pruett's house?" my mom asked with a hopeful glint in her eye. Shouldn't she hate him? Sure, maybe it wasn't his idea to go on a road trip, but he was still a young guy who was most likely a bad influence on me.

His gaze flitted from mine toward my mother. "Actually, no, I have a family dinner, but I wanted to come and show my support for Abby." His words were so sincere. I wanted to kiss him in front of my parents, at my friend's funeral, with Orlando limply watching on.

"Oh," my mother answered, flitting her gaze between us, most likely trying to pin down what exactly was going on. "Okay, well it was wonderful meeting you. Abby, we'll be in the car." I loved my mother extra hard for dragging my father behind her and giving Beck and I one last moment of privacy.

"You're wearing the locket," Beck noted. I hadn't taken it off since the flea market. It rested around my neck, just above my scar.

"I haven't changed the photos yet," I shrugged, playing down the fact that it was now one of my most favorite possessions.

"I like it," he murmured. I looked up at him from beneath my lashes.

"Do you really have a family dinner?" I asked.

"Just with my dad," he answered with narrowed eyes.

I nodded. "You don't seem so excited about it."

"He doesn't know about my MIT transfer yet. I imagine it won't be a very pleasant meal."

I frowned, wishing I could help him bear the burden.

"Do you want to take Orlando Bloom for support?" I offered him a half smile.

Beck dropped his head and laughed. "Nah, I'll let you keep him. I don't think my dad would get the joke."

The conversation seemed over. I thought he'd turn

and head toward his truck, but instead he asked, "Are we going to finish the trip?"

My mouth hung open as I waited for my brain to catch up. I didn't know the answer to that. My grief over Caroline was a living thing. It grew and slept, dormant at times, and then wild and all-consuming when I least expected. Would she have wanted me to finish the road trip? Probably, but I didn't agree with her logic anymore.

"I'm not sure." I stared at my Mary Jane heels.

"It was just getting started, Abby. Think about it," he answered before dipping down and kissing my cheek. I inhaled his scent and warmth before he turned and walked away.

• • •

I *did* think about it. I thought about it as I grocery shopped with my mom. I thought about it as I went to my weekly check-up. My doctor was reprimanding me about missing my appointment and then she mentioned something about increasing my medication dosage. My mom took notes while I thought about Beck's question and stared at Dr. Pierce's mahogany desk. When I'd come in for the appointment, I tried to find Alyssa, but I guess she wasn't working that day. I still had the note she gave me tucked safely inside my wallet. It was taunting me. The fact that I had the address on me at all times. Maybe I'd never use it.

My mom dragged me back to the career counselor for another hour-long session. At least this time my counselor had the results from my career aptitude test. Apparently, I was most suited to be one of the following:

1. Park Ranger
2. Biomedical Engineer
3. Accountant
4. Writer

How in the hell she had arrived at any of those four jobs was beyond my understanding.

"I'm not sure I want to do any of those," I admitted, looking up toward Dr. Lucas.

She smiled knowingly toward me. One of those slow, condescending smiles that basically said *'oh, sweet naive little girl'*.

"Those are just starting points, Abby. From here, we'll narrow down other career paths and then decide where you should apply for college."

I zoned out and decided to spend the remainder of our meeting thinking of Caroline and Beck. They would have been good friends. They were both optimistic and friendly. I would have been the cynical glue that held the group together.

I texted Beck later that day.

Abby: I'm apparently suited for one of the following jobs: Park ranger, writer, accountant, and some weird type of engineering…

Beck: Who told you those were your career options?

Abby: My life coach.

Beck: Seems like the sort of thing you find out by living and trying different things out…

Abby: Do you want to be my new counselor?

Beck: Conflict of interest...
Abby: Oh...

I smiled at the idea that he still liked me, but I wasn't going to question it. Maybe the stars aligned perfectly when he walked into the funeral home and he was helpless to my alluring charm.

Abby: How was dinner with your dad?

Beck: He wasn't too thrilled, but he isn't paying for my school, so there isn't much he could do about it. I know I'm making the right choice though.

Abby: I'm glad you told him.

Beck: Me too.

Abby: Could you send me your address?

Beck: Why?

Abby: Reasons...

CHAPTER TWENTY

This time it would be different, I called my mom and told her what my plan was. She wasn't comfortable with the idea of me road tripping around the state with a relative stranger, but she knew there was nothing she could really do about it. After all, we'd already done it once and survived.

I packed everything I needed, sans urn, and shoved it all into my car before heading toward the address Beck had sent over last night. The roads were empty since it was early on a Saturday morning. I'd planned ahead, thinking it would take me longer to get to his apartment, but when I pulled up next to his grandfather's Camper it was barely seven am. Whoops. He was going to kill me.

I tried to pass some time, rearranging my CDs and making sure the iPod speakers would work sitting on top of my car. After the sun had fully risen and there was nothing left to do, I hit call and waited for him to answer. He didn't pick up until the fifth ring.

"Sorry that I woke you up!" I exclaimed into the phone before he had a chance to groan at how early it was. "I didn't have a choice. I couldn't sleep and so I left my house earlier than I had planned, and there was no traffic."

"What are you talking about?" Beck laughed, but his voice still held tones of sleepiness.

"Come outside after you put some clothes on."

"How did you know I wasn't wearing clothes?"

My cheeks reddened at the thought. "You told me you slept in your boxers usually and I was guessing, but wow…now that I know that you're naked..."

"Did you call me at seven to have phone sex?"

I laughed an embarrassing laugh to cover up how much his question flustered me.

"I'll be out in a second," he answered, and then hung up.

I scrambled out of the car and set up the speakers so that they would face his apartment building, then got ready so I could press play on the iPod as soon as I saw him. My heart raced. I was so nervous; I was putting my feelings on the line and if Beck laughed or thought I was a cheesy dork, I wasn't sure how well I'd take it.

There was a thumping of feet on the stairs and I peered up to see him making his way toward the first-floor landing. I panicked and hit play as quickly as I could. John Denver's guitar started streaming through the speakers followed swiftly by his soft melody. I reached over and turned the speakers up high right as Beck rounded the staircase and came into view.

His dark hair was disheveled and curling at the ends

even more than usual. He'd thrown on a white t-shirt and workout shorts that hugged his solid frame. Once his eyes locked onto me, he dropped his gaze to my jean cut-offs and took his time taking me in. He grinned and his smile momentarily stunned me. There was something about him that seemed different as he stepped closer to me. He was more confident, more in control of his next step. The song kicked up another notch and Beck's eyes flitted to the speakers resting on my hood. John Denver was in the middle of singing about saying goodbye.

"Are you about to leave without me?" he asked, turning back to me with a sexy half-smile.

I wouldn't make it two miles without him in the Camper with me. "No. I just think we started our last road trip off on the wrong foot," I shrugged, and crossed my arms to wait for his next move.

"So now you respect the power of John Denver?" he asked, stepping another inch toward me. I caught a whiff of his shampoo. He must have showered right before going to bed. I stared hard at his white t-shirt, willing him to close the remaining gap between us.

"Maybe I do…"

I caught a glimpse of his smirk before he enveloped me in his arms and picked me up. We were standing in the parking lot of his apartment complex with his hands wrapped tightly around my waist. My hands clasped around his neck and my feet hung a foot above the ground.

"Hi," I said, looking into his eyes and trying hard not to smile like a buffoon.

"When do we leave?" he asked. He was fighting a smile as well and I thought it was so silly that we were attempting to play our attraction off as anything less than clothes-tearing, soul-stealing, gut-wrenching madness.

"Right now."

"Now?" he asked, quirking his eyebrows.

"Well, after you pack and go pee," I smirked.

"Ohh, are you not going to make any stops for me?"

"Depends on how good you are at begging…" My cheeks flushed after those words slipped out. I was *not* a flirt, and the fact that my brain seemed to momentarily forget that had my cheeks burning bright red. "Um, you're still holding me, you know," I muttered quickly, trying to change the subject.

"You're such a romantic, Abby," Beck began, completely ignoring my embarrassment, or maybe he was trying to rub it in. "You drove to my house and played me a song. That is straight out of an 80's movie. You *love* me, don't you? Oh my god, Abby Mae McAllister, you can hardly keep your hands off me!" He swayed his hips so that my body swung back and forth like a pendulum in his arms.

I squirmed, trying to make him let me go. "Beck! You're being ridiculous. Don't read into it! It was more about John Denver than you anyway." God, my face was about to explode I was blushing so much. I didn't love him, or *maybe* I did, but I just couldn't stand him looking at me like that. His hazel eyes were masked with amusement, but beneath that was a deeply sweet guy staring straight into my soul.

"Are you going to let me down now?" I asked, finally relenting and going limp in his arms.

He narrowed his eyes on me for a moment and then leaned forward to give me a sweet kiss. It felt funny not having to arch my neck to reach his mouth for once. With him holding me, our heights were perfectly matched. Our lips were aligned and my arms grasped his neck, right under his hair line, pulling his face toward me even more. I think in the beginning that kiss was meant to be sweet and playful, but our mouths had ulterior motives.

Beck pressed my body against his as hard as he could without hurting me. My breasts were pressed against his chest, and before I knew what I was doing, I wrapped my legs around his waist. His hand found the hem of my jean shorts. We were in public, in broad day-light, yet Beck's fingers still slid past my hem, skating across areas that made me moan into his mouth.

I was lost in the moment, not realizing what a few days apart from him would do to my body. Every part of me craved to be closer to him. Straddling him in the parking lot wasn't cutting it.

"Beck," I mumbled, breaking our kiss.

"Abby," he answered with a heavy breath. His athletic shorts were thin and I could feel him against my jean shorts.

"Let's go up to your apartment…" I suggested, embracing the moment for what it was. There was no argument from him. In a quick flourish of movement, he set me back onto the ground, took my iPod, and grabbed my hand to tug me upstairs. I ran after him, clicking the button to lock my car at the last moment before we started running up his stairs.

We crashed into his apartment. I tugged everything out of his hands and tossed it onto his couch for safe keeping. He tugged his white t-shirt over his head and then grabbed me with every ounce of conviction in his body.

"Beck!" I squealed as he gripped my hips and pressed me back against his living-room wall. I guess we weren't making it to his bedroom this time. I was gripping his hair so hard I expected him to yelp. He unbuttoned my jean shorts and let them slide down my legs toward the ground. I owned a singular pair of sexy underwear and I knew I'd made the right decision putting them on that morning. They were pink and lacy where they hit the top of my thighs.

"You need to stop me now if you want this another way, Abby. We can go into my bedroom and take it slow. I don't want you to regret—"

I grasped his face and shoved my tongue into his mouth to break off his statement. I didn't want it slow and sweet. My body needed Beck more than I've ever needed anything else. The last few days had been a living hell and being there with Beck felt like I was putting a healing salve on my heart. At the heart of everything, I just needed him to take me against the wall of his living room and make me feel more than I'd ever dared imagine.

My hands found his shorts and I pressed them down so that he was left in his boxers. He groaned, deep and husky, into my mouth as my fingers brushed against him through the material. I wanted him so badly that I thought I might tear his boxers off with my hands. But I wasn't a cave woman and I'd probably end up trying and failing, thus looking like an idiot. He tugged off my shirt and bra, leaving us pressed against his wall in our underwear.

My heart skidded to a stop and then it picked up beating twice as fast as I realized how close we were to the final act. I pressed my hands against his chest and pushed him away from me gently. I didn't want him to stop; I just needed one moment to savor the flavor. It was the feeling you get when you cut a big piece of chocolate cake and you know your taste buds are about to be overloaded with decadent sweetness. I just needed to look at him and let the moment sink in so that I could enjoy every single bite.

His hazel eyes were dark and sexy. His hair was tousled from my hands. His chest was just as I remembered from watching him swim: tan and toned with just the right amount of six pack hardening his entire appearance. There was a story behind his smile as his eyes met mine. He was thinking thoughts I wished desperately to know.

"You're so beautiful," he told me.

"You haven't even seen the best part," I joked.

His hazel eyes turned a shade darker as he stared toward me. "I've already *tasted* it, Abby." Visions of us in the back of the Camper swept through my mind, turning my desire up another notch. I stood there in a daze as he bolted from the room, only to return a second later with a condom in his hand.

"Aren't you getting a little ahead of yourself?" I teased as he stepped closer to me.

"Am I?" he dared, kissing my neck.

"No," I murmured.

Our eyes locked as he trailed his hand down my stomach while the other rested against the wall beside my head. He had me trapped in the best possible way and I felt my insides quiver as his fingers trailed over my belly button down to the bottom of my stomach. That skin was so sensitive; it wasn't accustomed to being touched by seductive fingers.

"Beck, have you had sex before?" I asked, not even realizing the question was brewing in my mind until I heard the words pass between us.

His lip curled up on the edge. "Yes, Abby."

Now that the knowledge was out there, my mind was brimming with questions.

"Were they with pretty girls or just girls you met at a party?" I asked, needing to know everything. "Were you dating them?"

His finger trailed along the top of my underwear,

pulling the fabric a centimeter away from my skin so that his finger could replace it. I felt my stomach quiver with desire even as I waited for him to answer.

"I hooked up with a few girls that didn't mean anything, and I've had sex with girlfriends before. I always used protection, and no, I never loved any of them." That answer shocked me. He didn't love them? How is that possible? With that many girls, I would've thought at least one would have wormed her way into his heart like I was trying desperately to do.

"None of them?" I asked while arching my back so that he could have easier access to the edge of my underwear. He grinned in acknowledgment of what I was doing.

"No," he shrugged, obviously wanting the conversation to move onto more *pertinent* things.

"I don't love you," I blurted, because I felt like I did and I needed to feel like I had control of the situation again. He was pushing me toward a precipice and it felt like he knew what I felt before I'd even acknowledged it. It wasn't fair and I needed him to know that he didn't hold all the cards.

"Are you sure?" he asked before stealing a kiss. My eyes fluttered closed. Had his mouth not been stealing every ounce of will power from my body, I would have grinned at his cheesy confidence. It was like he *wanted* me to love him. He was daring me to let myself fall, and for a brief moment, I decided that I would accept his challenge. *Bring it on, Beck.*

My hands pushed his boxers down and a moment later my underwear was following their descent. We were beautifully naked and I tried hard not to feel self-conscious. I let his skin consume mine and I let him press me back against the living room wall once again. Except this time he didn't trap me with his hands. He trailed kisses down my neck, down my stomach, taking each breast into his mouth and swirling his tongue around my nipples. I arched into his mouth. He kissed down my stomach, licking a trail over my flushed skin. He continued his descent until he was on his knees, looking up at me with a cheeky grin.

"I think this is my favorite angle of you." He smirked and I tried to imagine what he saw. His face was right at the base of my stomach. His gaze sloped up my stomach and my breasts. My wild strawberry-blonde hair was fanned out around my face as I stared down at him.

Then I watched as he dipped his head and licked me there once, slowly, ending right before he reached the spot where I needed him the most. My mouth fell open as I watched him trace along my sensitive flesh. Holy. Then he held my eye contact as he dipped his tongue lower. Meeting his eyes felt like another dare. He looked sinful and confident and I didn't blink once.

I stared down at him, pushing my tongue to the bridge of my mouth whenever he circled closer to a sensitive part. Tingles spread from where his tongue met my skin. My hands fell back against the wall, trying in vain to grasp the flat surface. He finally flicked his tongue across my clit, slowly and teasingly, making sure I was more than ready for him to enter me. I needed something to balance it out, but I couldn't find anything. My knees started to buckle and Beck paused to look up at me with a cocky grin.

"Beck!" I moaned, pressing the heels of my hands into my eyes, unsure of what I needed. I didn't want his mouth to budge, but I wanted to dig my heels into his back as he pushed me against the wall. I wanted to experience the life that Caroline never did. I couldn't waste the moment life had presented for me on a silver platter.

I heard a crinkle of paper and dropped my hands to see Beck rolling the condom onto himself. His abs flexed as he bent forward to slide it on and I gawked like a fool. It was the sexiest and most terrifying thing I'd ever seen. I had no clue what I'd actually agreed to, and now that it was about to happen, fear spiked my blood and turned my heart rate up another notch.

"Beck, this is going to hurt, I know it is," I rambled with shaky hands. "Crap." Then I started laughing because I said crap right before I was about to lose my virginity. I thought it was supposed to be more romantic than that and I was ruining it. I tried to shake out my nerves, but it didn't help. I couldn't get out of my own brain.

Before I knew what was happening, Beck had his hands around my body and was carrying me away from our pile of clothes. Our naked bodies pressed together as he dragged me through a doorway and playfully tossed me back onto his bed. My head fell onto a sea of pillows and my smile was too wide to contain. A fresh clean laundry scent swirled around me.

"We're going to do this the slow and easy way, Abby. I'm not going to take you against the wall when you're shaking." I couldn't argue with that. My playful, goofy Beck had left the building entirely. This Beck looked like he was about to attack me and I gulped, staring up into his dark hazel eyes.

He was still hard, wearing the condom proudly as he dipped lower to crawl over me. Each touch of his skin meeting mine completed the current of electricity running between us and I could feel our skin crackle. His chest hit my legs, his mouth found my hip bone and my lower belly. His lips teased every nerve ending they touched. My hands clawed his sheets. I didn't even register the color of his bedding or the details of his room. All of that existed on the fringe, in the periphery of my consciousness.

His hand trailed up my thigh, and his finger sunk into me, testing how ready I was. It was such a sexy move, but it also scared the crap out of me.

"Uh, Beck," I murmured, and he looked up to meet my eyes. "I'm excited…I really am, but I also feel like I might cry or puke or something." My lips twisted into a playful frown.

It wasn't about being ready. I was more than ready, and I was confident in my decision to lose my virginity, but my brain wouldn't shut up. I couldn't just live in the moment.

His features relaxed instantly and his once dark hazel eyes lightened to their usual luster. "I think we're being too serious about it."

"Maybe so…I mean I know your penis is meant to fit inside of me, but it just looks really…*big*."

He barked out a laugh and let his forehead fall onto mine. "It will fit, Abby."

"Are you calling me loose?" I laughed.

He pecked my lips. "You're so ridiculous."

When he rested his forehead against mine his body had shifted over me. We were perfectly aligned. His hips were pressing mine down into the bed so seductively. His mouth captured mine so that his tongue and hips moved in the same rhythm. He was driving me insane.

"Okay, okay, I want you to do it. Please." My breathing picked up and I could feel my heart thumping against his chest.

He grinned down at me. His eyes held mine in a sweet exchange as he reached between our two bodies and worked the head of his penis inside of me. It felt foreign and much, much too big, but then I realized I was clenching every muscle in my body, including my jaw.

Beck held up his weight, but let his mouth fall against my ear. "Relax, Abby. Relax." His words were soft and sweet and I found myself heeding his instructions. I took a deep breath and he pressed into me another centimeter. One more deep breath.

It hurt like hell. Television and movies have it completely fucking wrong. It felt like my skin was tearing and I couldn't breathe. I could only concentrate on the excruciating pain.

"Beck, I don't know. I don't know," I kept repeating because I didn't know what was supposed to happen. It didn't feel good and I knew it was a vicious cycle. The pain made me tense up more and then the less relaxed I became, the more it hurt.

"Abby," Beck whispered into my ear, shushing me and calming my erratic heart. "Stay with me, Abby. Relax and breathe. Your body is ready. There's lube on the condom, but you have to relax."

I was about to argue and tell him how badly it was hurting, but then I took a deep breath, and in that moment the pain seemed to lessen. He was more than halfway inside of me and the worst of it was over. Each passing breath took with it the remnants of the pain. Beck kissed my neck and coaxed my hips wider apart and circled his fingers over me a few millimeters above where he was penetrating me. It was like a whole new world of pleasure unfurled before me. He was reminding me of why we were doing this in the first place. The feel of his fingers rubbing me as he slid into me hit me like a bolt of lightning and I moaned his name. Loud and unrestrained.

"That's it, Abby. Let me touch you." His words were magic. His fingers were magic.

"You're like Houdini," I moaned, and he let out a low husky laugh. Now that the pain was over, I felt silly for making it such a big deal.

"It hurt so bad." I could feel tears drying on my cheeks. I hadn't even realized I'd cried.

His movements paused and he looked up and met my gaze. "Does it still hurt?"

I wrapped my arms around his back and dragged my nails across his skin. Not hard enough to draw blood, but hard enough for him to realize that I was no longer in pain.

With one sweet groan, he pushed all the way inside of me. My head fell back against the pillow as I tried to get accustomed to the feel of him. All of him pressing against every single part of me.

After another moment he started rocking his hips, making sure to keep the pace gentle enough so that he wouldn't hurt me. His fingers, slick with remnants of us, rubbed my clit with gentle circles, edging to the exact spot that made my insides tumble upside-down. I ground up to meet him, pressing us together harder until his finger swiped once more and I exploded into tiny little pieces. It wasn't like last time, coming with him inside of me felt carnal. I came harder and longer, as if my body had something to hold onto to make the pleasure last as long as possible.

"Beck," I heard myself moaning as he kept thrusting into me harder. It still felt tight, but his movements didn't hurt. My body accepted him more than willingly and I watched with wonder as his face contorted from absolute control to absolute bliss. He came with a hard thrust into me. His stomach muscles clenched in tandem and his groan was sexy enough to almost bring me to another climax.

"Holy hell, Abby," he groaned, stretching each syllable into a love letter. He let some of his weight fall on top of me, and I stared up at the ceiling feeling all things at once, but mostly I felt wholeheartedly in love with this boy.

CHAPTER TWENTY-ONE

So our start time was slightly later than I had planned, but we still made it to our destination before dinner time. Odessa, Texas. Home of football. Football. And more football. Traveling to Odessa was the whole reason the road trip came about in the first place. Everything else had been fluff. Really nice Beck-filled fluff. It felt less momentous traveling without my urn, but I didn't regret smashing it. It was a symbol of my oppression, and now that it was gone, I felt one step closer to being free.

"So where do we head from here?" Beck asked, pulling into a convenience store parking lot so that we could plot out our journey. I pulled my wallet out of my purse and retrieved the slip of paper that Alyssa had given me at my doctor's office. The piece of paper that could get my doctor, Alyssa, and the hospital, all in major trouble. I had to use it wisely.

Once the address was staring up at me with its black ink, I turned to look at Beck. He was wearing the baseball cap he'd worn that first time I'd met him. His face was easy and open; a small smile dotted the side of his mouth. His default setting was happy. That's what I loved about Beck. He looked at life like it was a journey, like we were meant to enjoy every step of the way. Idling in a convenience store parking lot was a treat. Caroline didn't get to idle anymore, so I was glad that Beck didn't take it for granted.

"This piece of paper has the address of a house that we're here to visit." I introduced the subject to him lightly, unsure of how he would take it.

He nodded his head, his hazel eyes falling in and out of the shadow of his hat's brim. "Ooh..kay," he answered, obviously hoping for more information.

"We're *borderline* breaking the law, but you know, it shouldn't be a big deal. So just head to Main Street and then we'll—"

"Slow your roll. 'Breaking the law'? How? Do you have a restraining order with these people or something?" he asked, slightly kidding.

"What do you take me for?" I gawked at him as he put the Camper in drive.

"A sexy, slightly-dysfunctional girl," he answered with a smirk as he turned left out of the parking lot.

I smiled at the first part of his comment and chose to ignore the rest. "We're going to see the kid's parents, who y'know, donated my heart," I answered under my breath, hoping the music would drown out my confession.

"What?! We're going to visit the family? Do they know we're coming?"

I slashed my hand in the air to silence his worries. "Those are all minor details. I'm not going to spill the beans to them. I just want to talk to them. I feel like I have some right to know about the kid whose heart is now pumping oxygenated blood around my body."

I plugged in the address from the paper into my phone and told Beck to turn left in half a mile.

"So we're going to do what exactly?"

"Maybe scout it out a little bit first," I answered, absolutely clueless as to how the plan would pull through in the end.

"Aren't there ways to go about contacting the family?" Beck asked gently.

"Yes, Mr. Moral Compass. There are ways, but it takes forever and it's not a guarantee that the family will establish communication."

"You make it sound like adoption," Beck smiled, slowing to stop at a light.

I snorted and looked down at the tiny map on my phone. We were only minutes away from the house. Would they even be home?

We stayed silent the rest of the way until we pulled down a nice suburban street that looked straight out of a movie. There was a tire swing in some of the lawns and most of them had white picket fences.

"Looks like it'll be a nice family," Beck offered as I inspected the numbers painted on each curb. 1039, 1041, 1043…1045.

"Stop! It's that one!" I pointed to a blue house with cream shutters and a bright red door. It was a bungalow style with ivy wrapped beautifully along the fence. There were two cars parked in the driveway: a Prius and some kind of SUV.

"They care about the environment."

Beck smirked and swung his head to look at me. "Because they have a Prius?"

I half-smiled, unable to peel my gaze away from the house. "I bet they recycle. I bet their son was the president of the Recycling Committee at his school."

Beck's smile fell. "He was in high school?"

Don't do it Beck, I wanted to say. We can't let emotions ruin the plan. "Yeah. A senior."

Beck mashed his lips together until they formed a thin line and then turned back to the house. A second later, the back gate opened and a middle-aged man with a cool goatee trotted around to hop into the Prius.

"Duck!" I said as soon as he came into sight. I lifted the latch on the outside of my seat and flew the seat backwards until I was lying as horizontally as possible. Beck groaned but followed my instructions until we were both mostly out of view.

"This is ridiculous. He totally saw us."

I squeezed my eyes shut, unwilling to give up. "No, he's leaving. Let's go talk to the wife while he's gone."

Before he could offer a rebuttal, I moved to hop out of the passenger side door. Except my shoe got caught on the door because I wasn't used to rolling out of a vehicle. I face planted into the grass with the second half of my body still lying on the floor of the Camper.

To his credit, Beck asked if I was okay before completely losing it to hysterical laughter. "You'd make a terrible spy."

"Oh please! We would have been caught if I didn't tell you to duck," I fought back while I picked grass out of my mouth. We hurried across the street. I feared we didn't have much time. Maybe the husband was running to the corner store for ice or something.

I tried to inspect my surroundings while we waited for someone to answer the doorbell. The lawn was recently mowed and there were children's toys strewn around the front yard. I was inspecting a bright red wagon when the front door started to open.

"Can I help you?" A sweet voice asked. I turned to see a woman with light brown hair piled into a messy bun on top of her head. She was wearing a simple pair of khakis and a button down cotton shirt.

"Oh, hi," Beck began, and I cut him off.

"Hi. Um, I know this is awkward, but our Camper broke down and neither of our cell phones are dead. I mean charged. Neither of them are *charged* from our camping trip last night. Is there anyway we could use your phone?" It was possibly the worst lie I could think of, but I was hoping that she wouldn't read too much into it. Did we look like criminals? I should have made Beck take his hat off. Did he look like a drug dealer? Usually not, but now that I was looking at him out of the corner of my eye, he *did* have the build to be in a gang.

The woman's face morphed from confusion to pity. "Oh, wow. Yes, come in. I'll grab a phone."

Overwhelming guilt smacked me all at once. I wanted to yell at her for being so trusting. Beck said I was slightly-dysfunctional; this poor woman shouldn't have let us in. She kept leading us back toward a living room and then turned to face us. "Are you two from around here?" she asked politely, apparently wanting to make small-talk before finding the phone.

I didn't trust Beck's manipulation skills. I was the one with a mission. "We are, but we moved here recently," I paused trying to hold my tongue back, but it was no use. It was now or never. "We knew Colby though."

The woman's hand flew to her mouth. "Oh no, I'm so sorry. Please have a seat, let me get you a drink and the phone." She flew out of the room and Beck grabbed my arm. "Abby, what are you *doing*? That wasn't subtle at all," he hissed quietly.

I shook out my hands, feeling like I'd just held up a bank and now I was stuck with hostages that I didn't know what to do with. "Okay. Okay. I'm sorry. I didn't know what to do," I whispered, trying to calm my breathing.

"Here you go, you two," she said as she reentered the room with two glasses of lemonade and the phone. Lemonade. God damnit woman, don't serve us sugary drinks when we're manipulating you!

Beck bolted over to help her with the drinks and then he took the phone. "I'll go… call a tow truck," he fumbled, and the woman gave him an awkward glance.

The second he was out of earshot, she sat down and patted the couch cushion next to her. "Were you a friend of Colby's from school?" she asked gently. I tried to morph her features to see what she would look like as a teenage boy, but I failed miserably. I couldn't picture what Colby could have looked like at all.

"Um, yes," I lied, and then took a giant gulp of lemonade. "I mean, I knew of him, but we weren't really friends," I added once I had swallowed. I didn't want to lie to his mom anymore than I had to.

"Do you have any pictures of him?" I asked.

The expression that passed across her features was impossible to discern. "Oh, um, no, we don't."

Strange.

I nodded and tried to think of another question that wouldn't reveal the fact that I actually didn't know her son in any way.

"Could you tell me about him? If it's not too painful?" I had no clue where my question landed on the spectrum of red flags, but she furrowed her brows and set her lemonade down on the counter.

"I thought you said you went to school with him," she answered, not meeting my gaze.

"Right. Yeah. I'm sorry." She wasn't going to make this easy and I couldn't blame her.

"He was on the basketball team, did you know that?" she smiled as if recalling a memory. "He was the star of the team and all of the girls loved him, as I'm sure you know." She winked.

I smiled and nodded reassuringly as if all of that was old news. So he was an athlete.

"He was a giver. Everyone said he had the biggest heart."

I choked on my lemonade, spewing clear liquid across her coffee table.

"Oh dear, are you okay?" She leaned over and patted my back before I jumped to my feet.

I wiped the remaining lemonade from my mouth with the back of my hand.

"I'm so sorry. Let me grab some napkins." I darted into the kitchen only then realizing how awkward it was to be running around her house without her approval. I had no clue where she kept the napkins and my head was still spinning from her 'heart' comment. What are the odds that she would use that phrase? It was destiny. I was supposed to meet her.

"Ma'am," I began, twisting on my feet and starting to run back into the living room. I grabbed a towel from the counter as an afterthought. "Colby was my donor. He gave me his heart. Your son saved my life."

The woman was leaning over the table, moving papers out of the way of my lemonade spill. When I said my spiel, her gaze lifted to mine and she looked as if she'd seen a ghost. "Oh, sweetie. I'm not Colby's mom. His family moved out of Odessa shortly after his death."

What?

My shoulders slumped in defeat and I dropped her towel onto the coffee table. What did she mean they moved? Why hadn't they updated their address with the hospital yet?

"What? Do you know where they are?" My hand flew to my mouth. Crap. This was just a random stranger. I was lying, spilling lemonade, and now crying in front of a total stranger.

"I don't have any idea. They didn't tell anyone. I was just a neighbor of theirs. We moved into this place so we could have more space for our family." Her family that did *not* include Colby. What the hell.

The front door opened. "Alright, Abby, the tow truck driver is on his way, but I think I figured out our problem. It looks like the alternator was short circuiting with the cable that leads to the ignition. I just swapped it out with…a spare we had in the back," Beck rambled awkwardly. He really was a terrible actor. I don't think any of those sentences actually made sense.

"Colby's family doesn't live here. This isn't his mom," I muttered, feeling the tears starting to build behind my eyes. I could hardly look up toward him. Beck grimaced, eyeing the woman apologetically before walking over to me. He wrapped me in his arms and I stuffed my face in the crook of his arm.

"I'm so sorry, Abby," he whispered into my ear.

"It doesn't matter," I tried to cover up my sadness, but it felt like the treasure at the end of my hunt had been stolen by thieves without me even realizing. I'd needed this light at the end of the tunnel. I'd dragged Beck across the state for absolutely no reason. What a colossal waste of time.

Then I thought of something. "So you didn't really know Colby?" I asked the woman, pulling away from Beck. I needed to know if her story about him having a big heart was true or if it was just hearsay.

The woman frowned and shook her head, unable to meet my eyes.

I nodded and then reached down to wipe the lemonade off the table with the towel. It was the least I could do after barging into her house and feeding her lies.

"Oh, you know what! We have a neighborhood newsletter that comes out every few months. I keep them all in a little folder so I can stay up to date with community stuff," she shook her head clear of her tangent, "Colby was in a few of them. Let me grab them for you."

She hustled into the kitchen and I could hear her shuffling through papers. I studied the towel that had soaked up all of the excess lemonade before looking back toward Beck. He was watching me with worried eyes and I gave him a crooked smile to let him know I wasn't going to breakdown on the spot. I'd wait until we were alone.

"Did you really call a tow truck?" I asked.

He wiped a hand down his face. "No, and I felt terrible lying about it."

"Here you go!" the woman sang as she reentered the room with a folder held safely in both hands. "These are the ones I think you should have," she said, offering them to me. I didn't even hesitate; I took them from her and lunged forward to give her a massive hug. I felt guilty for lying to her, but now she'd given me another chance at completing my goal. I needed to know about Colby. About the boy who gave me his big heart.

CHAPTER TWENTY-TWO

"She said he had 'the biggest heart'?" Beck asked with a raised brows.

"Technically she said 'everyone said he had the biggest heart', so it almost doesn't count," I clarified, wiping my hands with the napkin. We were tucked away in a booth at a random dive bar in Odessa.

The folder's contents were lying out before us, beckoning me to start investigating. I hadn't wanted to read them until the food was cleared from the table for fear that we'd spill something on the last connection I had with Colby.

There were three newsletters in total. The first two had front pages that were centered on community festivals or school sports, but the last one had a large black and white photo of a boy on the front cover: Colby. It was clearly his school picture. It had that cloudy staged backdrop and he didn't have a real smile, just a cheesy fake one. Underneath, in large title casing it read: "A Neighborhood Loses One of Its Greatest." I tried not to dwell on the headline.

"I competed in UIL competitions for headline writing," Beck offered after finishing a drink of his beer. I guess he'd seen the newsletter as well.

I furrowed my brows in confusion, glancing up at him in the dim lighting. He'd dropped his hand on the table and was running his fingers through his sexy mussed-up hair.

"Headlines as in newspaper headlines?" I asked with a bemused smile.

"Yeah."

A half-smile still peeked through my teasing. "Who *does* that?"

He cocked an eyebrow. "Cynical Girl Misjudges Brawny Hero."

I threw my head back and cracked up. "Wait, where is the alliteration?"

Beck nodded and quickly made amends. "Cynical Girl Cuts-down Cute…"

"Cunt," I interjected.

"That." He pointed the rim of his beer toward me and narrowed his eyes. "Look at that. Very creative, Ms. Mae. Would have loved to have you on my UIL team."

"So did you win?" I asked with a hidden smile.

"What a Boar! Slumbering Swine Snoozes, Loses State Championship," he recited animatedly, swiping his hand across the air as if reading off a marquee. You would have thought the competition had taken place earlier that morning rather than four years prior.

I couldn't stop laughing. It was just too much. "You

won with that?"

"Women threw their underwear on stage when I recited that headline." He grinned, sipping his beer.

"Spare me."

"What did you do in high school?" he asked as I reached for the first newsletter.

"Nothing," I answered.

"Nothing?" he rubbed his chin.

"No. My parents pulled me out when I was a junior. When it looked like I wouldn't get the transplant," I clarified, remembering how somber my timeline had looked then. "Before that I wasn't really involved in anything." I shrugged and started flipping through the newsletter. Beck took a different one and we started working in silence, scouring the pages for any mention of Colby's name.

I kept flipping through, seeing one cliché small town thing after another: Bake Sale, Founder's Day carnivals, Town Hall meetings. Then finally I saw a tiny section of sports that covered everything from Odessa elementary to Odessa High School. There was a tiny, grainy photo at the bottom of the page that looked like an action shot from a basketball game. I skimmed the article underneath until I found his name. "*Colby Brubaker leads varsity basketball team to winning season.*" To my dismay, it was impossible to discern which of the tiny pixilated bodies was his in the photo.

"This one mentions his basketball achievements. I guess he was pretty good." I pointed to the article so that Beck could read it as well. I couldn't help but wonder how he died. He seemed like a really healthy kid.

Beck nodded, pressing his finger down to mark a spot on the newsletter. "I found something about his work with the National Honor Society. Apparently he set up a blood drive for the high school three years in a row."

I nodded appreciatively and grabbed the newsletter in the center. This is what I wanted. I wanted Colby to be a quasi-super hero, right? But to be honest, in that moment, when I found out that Colby was, in fact, a much better contributor to society than I could ever hope to be, I felt like shit. It was the same feeling that washed over me when I found out Caroline had died. If given a vote, would people have chosen Colby's life over mine?

My hands fell to my lap and I stared down at where they rested on top of my blue sundress. I picked the chipping red polish off my thumb nail, contemplating the peacefulness that comes with defeat. I could let a ghost haunt my life forever, or I could make the decision to carry him with me, not as a burden, but as a talisman.

I didn't bother reading about how Colby died. Two minutes prior, I would've done anything to know the details of his life, but now? Now there was no point in dwelling on the fact that this poor guy had passed away. I needed to use his heart the way he would've wanted it to be used.

Without consulting Beck, I slid out of the booth and hunted down a bartender.

"Do you guys do karaoke here?" I asked with a shaky voice. My hand was fidgeting with the hem of my dress as I attempted to meet his dark beady eyes.

The old, burly man eyed me skeptically. "Does it look like we do karaoke here, lady?"

I couldn't argue with that. The bar was filled with tired, sunburned patrons, trying to take a load off after a long day. They'd be more likely to have an old-timey western shoot-off than host a karaoke night. I turned back to the bartender and read his name tag: Dave.

"Dave, what about just this once?" I gave him a pleading smile. "I'm attempting to get out of my comfort zone and I'm afraid that if I leave here without doing this then I might never work up the courage again."

He shook his head slowly, not even bothering to look up at me. I gripped the side of the bar while I watched him retrieve a cold beer for a patron. Was I going to walk away? No. I couldn't leave Odessa like this. If he wasn't going to cooperate than I had no choice. I turned back to see Beck eyeing me skeptically from the booth, and then with one last breath, I hopped onto the bar.

Dave yelled for me to get down, but I didn't listen. I turned to face the crowd. All ten small town Texans and one adorable Beck smiled up at me in awe.

"Um, hello everyone." Only a few people had stopped their conversations, but by the end of my greeting, the bar was maddeningly silent. What kind of bar had no background music playing at least? "I'm going to sing a little song for you."

"Get the hell down!" Dave yelled, throwing his towel on the bar next to my feet. Beck hopped out of the booth, ready to grab me if the situation escalated. He looked menacing with his baseball cap pulled low and his arms crossed over his chest. He kept walking until he was right under me and I smiled nervously down at him.

I flitted my gaze over to Dave and gave him my best puppy dog eyes. "Please, it'll be quick…" I pleaded. He huffed and then rolled his eyes. That was as much of an approval as I was going to get.

I pinched my eyes closed and took a deep breath, preparing the sorry excuse for vocal cords I was about to subject everyone to.

"This is for Colby," I murmured, staring up at the

dirty fluorescent lights.

With no musical accompaniment, I was left high and dry as I started to hum the opening strands of "Your Song" by Elton John. I wasn't certain that I'd be able to hit all of the notes, but I closed my eyes and pretended I was standing alone in my shower. I began to sing the first words so softly that I doubt anyone could even hear. It was painful and I knew my entire body was shaking with nerves.

But then I opened my eyes and looked down at Beck. One of his arms was wrapped around his torso and the other was propped up and holding his chin. I tried to focus solely on him as I kept singing.

Mind you, I've never had a single singing lesson in my entire life. But I let Sir Elton John lead me forward as I broke into the chorus without reservation. I was belting the lyrics, telling everyone in the bar that I was so happy that they were "in the world". A few of the patrons whistled and clapped their hands. I guess even in Odessa, Elton had some fans.

When I tried to hit a really high note and my voice cracked, I laughed, rolling with it. The adrenaline made the embarrassment roll off me like I was wearing a waxy shield.

When I had to repeat the part about hoping "you don't mind", the entire bar joined in with mismatching vocals. It sounded pretty terrible, but when I carried the song home, the entire bar was silent. They're eyes blinked up at me with such profound understanding. I knew they'd probably all known Colby. Or at least known of him. Maybe that song meant something to them as well.

The second I finished, I hunched forward and started laughing. It was quite possibly the worst rendition ever created, but Beck was grinning up at me with quiet admiration. He reached up to grab me. His arms gripped my waist securely, and as I slid down to the floor, he held me steady against his body so that our faces were level. I'm sure everyone in the bar was watching, but they were strangers and I didn't care. My hands gripped his shoulders, and when our faces aligned, we both had impossibly wide grins.

"You were amazing," Beck complimented me, pressing his forehead to mine.

I squeezed my eyes shut for a moment, trying to soak in the moment. "Don't think I didn't hear you chiming in at the end."

He chuckled and then pressed his mouth to my ear. "Am I allowed to love you?" he asked, making my heart sputter to a stop. I looked up into his hazel eyes and I knew I was a goner. I couldn't form words because I would have cried. My eyes filled with unshed tears and I bit my lip in hopes of quelling the surge of happiness. My gaze shifted to his chin and I nodded gently again and again.

He was watching my reaction with such sincerity that I had to say something. Something to douse the flames before he pressed me back against the bar and took me in front of all the nice patrons.

"You probably only love me because I'm a rock star now," I quipped, sort of mumbling over the "love me" part for fear that I was being presumptuous.

A dimple appeared next to his mouth and I focused on that as he started tugging me out of the bar. We left the newsletters in the booth— in the city where they belonged. The city that missed their golden boy enough that it wasn't my burden to hold onto him any longer. As Beck pushed through the bar's doors, I pressed my hand to the jagged scar above my heart and closed my eyes. I would carry

Colby with me forever, right where it mattered the most.

• • •

"Have you ever had sex in a seedy motel before?" I asked as Beck and I laid down staring at the popcorn ceiling above our heads. Beck chuckled next to me and reached to grab my hand. I smiled and then rolled over to straddle him. His eyebrows shot up and I internally applauded myself for taking him by surprise. His brown hair hung sweet and disorderly against his pillow.

His hands pressed against my back, just under my bra, and I rocked my hips over his, getting a slow feel for him beneath me. My hands tugged his shirt up so I could skim my fingers along his abs, memorizing each ridge that belonged to me. I kept tugging higher until most of his upper body was revealed to me. My hands roamed everywhere.

"That tickles." Beck wiggled beneath me as I roamed too close to his underarms.

"Oops, sorry," I smiled, and dragged my hands back down to his lower stomach. I traced the V that pointed to my end goal. Beck's hands ran under the top of my dress, skimming over my skin until he found the clasp of my bra. With a quick flick, he undid it, and I mashed my lips together. That feeling of him dragging his hand around my torso to cup my breasts beneath my dress sent a delicious shiver down my spine.

"Beck," I moaned, not realizing I'd been rolling my hips onto him the entire time. That was all the encouragement he needed. He hands cupped around each breast. My nails dug gently into his torso, letting the sensations take over. A moment later, he pressed up so that I could push his shirt over his head. He tugged my dress off and then threw it across the room. His pants followed.

His hands wrapped around my back so that when he laid back down, he took me with him. Our chests were pressed tightly together. Warm skin on skin as our mouths found one another. It felt empowering to straddle him like that as his hands gripped my hair, keeping us melded together. We ground our hips together in a sweet rhythm.

I pressed my hand to his warm chest. "Could I be on top?" I asked with a crooked smile. I had no clue if I'd enjoy it that way, but I wanted to try. Beck licked his lips and nodded, grasping me on top of him. I pressed my hands to his chest to support my weight as his fingers dipped down my body, rubbing me gently for a few moments.

I reached down and clasped over his hand, aligning us perfectly. Then I bit my lip and started to sink down, unsure of how painful it would be. My weight wasn't enough to push me all the way down onto him. I hovered in limbo, adjusting to his size. My fingers gripped his chest and my head fell forward with the weight of the pleasure. But then Beck's hands gripped my waist and in one fluid move, he simultaneously bucked his hips up and pressed me down so that I was filled completely by him.

"Beck!" I cried out as a flood of sensations came over me. His hands gripped my hips as his thumbs dipped lower. The feel of him inside of me as his fingers moved over my inner thighs, touching flesh that was overly-sensitized, felt like too much for my brain to comprehend.

I couldn't remember to breathe or to move my hands from their death-grip on his chest.

We hung there, unable to move for a few more seconds. Then Beck moved his hands up to my face. He brushed my hair away and titled my chin with his thumb so that our eyes locked in a sweet gaze.

Our eyes told each other everything. They said 'I love you' even before we could verbalize the phrase. He started rocking his hips below me, slow and sensual at first. I leaned back, resting my hands on his knees so that I could roll my hips and feel every inch of him inside of me.

His groans told me how turned on he was. I fed off them, letting my eyes flutter closed as we found a sweet, fast rhythm. His thumb found the spot that had me imploding only after a few quick rubs. But then we were shifting, Beck was rolling me onto my back and spreading my legs out wide so that he could pull out of me and then thrust back in with unadulterated passion. Our love-making was on his terms; he took what he needed and gave me everything in return. My second orgasm came quickly, too quick for me to even grasp on for dear life. I was gripping his hair. He was biting into my shoulder, and we were coming together, breathing each other's names and praying for the moment to never end.

CHAPTER TWENTY-THREE

I was in the hotel's bathroom the next day, showering and taking my medications. Everything seemed normal and I felt fine, but when I took my temperature, it was slightly higher than usual. 100.9. I made a mental note of it so I could let my mom know, but then Beck knocked on the bathroom room and distracted me by stripping down to his skivvies so that he could hop in the shower.

"Hey! I'm trying to get dressed here," I joked, watching him push his boxers to the floor and turn on the shower. Oh how I loved that rock-hard tush. I'd never considered myself a butt girl, but if you were there you would have checked it out, too. It was just so sexy.

He turned to give me cheeky grin and then stepped inside the curtain.

"So are we going to Marfa?" I asked, stuffing all of my toiletries back into my bag.

"You remembered?" Beck asked, poking his head so that his damp hair left drops of water on the floor.

I shrugged, moving to leave and so he could have privacy. "It was your one request this entire trip, and Odessa wasn't quite what I expected it to be."

"To Marfa it is!" he called out playfully.

• • •

Marfa is in the middle of nowhere, but only about three hours from Odessa. We'd driven through stretches of desert with no end in sight when finally we spotted a tiny oasis of sorts. It was the holy grail of pit stops. The mecca of road trip pilgrimages. There was a fast food restaurant, a gas station, a souvenir shop, and then a smattering of things that you would never in your life need in the middle of the desert: rubber snakes, astronaut costumes, and quilt patterns.

"So why did you want to go to Marfa?" I asked, handing him the bag of candy we'd purchased at the rest stop. He picked out three green Sour Patch Kids and then handed it back over. He knew to leave the orange ones for me.

Beck drummed his fingers on the steering wheel and thought for a moment. "I've heard it's a cool town, but I mainly wanted to check out The Lights."

I stared out the window, trying to discern the meaning of his sentence, but I eventually gave up. "The Lights? Of the town?"

Beck's mouth hung open like I'd just fessed up to the fact that I didn't know the name of our current President. Hello, Mr. Obama, if you're reading this.

"What?" I asked with a smile.

"Abby. The Marfa Lights! They're famous! No one knows what they really are. Some people think they're aliens and skeptics argue that they're just car headlights really far off in the distance, reflecting off the hills."

I nodded, trying to imagine what he was talking about, but all I could picture were little UFOs flying around. "So we're going to check them out?"

"Absolutely," he answered with confidence.

I couldn't stop thinking about them. I'd never heard of such a thing. "Are they small? What if we go and we can't see them?"

Beck shot me a skeptical glance. "We'll see them, Abby. I bet they'll be there."

But what if they weren't?

The remainder of our drive went by quick, and by early evening we were pulling into a camp ground that had come highly recommended by the owner of one of the gas stations in town. He said we had to rent one of the teepees. So we followed his directions and pulled into El Cosmico Campground. It was like a hipster's wet dream. There were genuine teepees set up next to propped up tents. Abstract sculptures dotted the landscape and punctuated the fact that we were *not* in a run-of-the-mill campground. There was a communal kitchen and an outdoor shower that had a rock wall for privacy. We lucked out. They had one teepee still vacant and we snatched it up before someone else could.

After we'd parked our car outside the campground, we trekked with our backpacks toward the center of the desert oasis. The sun was setting behind the shrubbery and cacti, illuminating the teepee in a golden glow. We untied the flap and hesitantly stepped inside. The decor was minimalist and awesome. There was a simple bed with a multi-colored quilt sitting on top of an animal hide rug. A vintage American flag hung over the bed. Some hippie architects had definitely designed the place.

"This is the best place we've stayed so far," I grinned, spinning in a circle in the center of the teepee. There were massive poles that merged at the center, almost twenty feet above my head. The sun was shining through gently, creating patterns across the pale canvas covering the entire space.

"I agree," Beck answered, tossing the stuff down on top of a vintage trunk at the foot of the bed. "I think I saw a bar and grill on the drive over. Should we check it out and see if they serve dinner?"

"Yeah, but do you mind if I freshen up a little bit?" I felt light headed and I wanted to change into something more appropriate for a bar. I hadn't put make-up on once since meeting Beck, but I'd packed a few random things in case the occasion called for it. Tonight seemed like as good a night as ever, especially considering the fact that a headache had developed in the past half hour and I felt less than sexy. But maybe if I freshened up and put some makeup on, my body would get the hint.

Beck went to scope out the campground while I got ready. I pulled out a wrinkled, but still pretty, aqua dress that had thin spaghetti straps. The cut was low in the front and normally I skipped over it so that my scar wouldn't be on display, but I didn't seem to mind that when I was around Beck.

I pulled out my bag of makeup that was stocked full with no help from me. My mother had done her best to provide me with things she thought I should use, but most of it looked like foreign torture devices. I skipped over the eye shadows and opted for some mascara, a touch of bronzer, and some cherry-red lip stain that brought out the bright red tones in my strawberry-blond hair. Mostly I felt like a little kid playing dress up, but I tried to talk myself up as I slipped on my strappy sandals.

When I pushed the flap of the teepee open, I didn't see Beck right away. The sun had dropped lower toward the horizon, finally allowing the temperature to hit a *tolerable* ninety degrees. My sandals clapped against the rocks and dirt as I wandered toward the center of camp and spun around looking for him. The abstract sculptures and teepees blurred by and then I saw him walking toward me. I stopped my spin and waited for him to get closer. He must have snuck into the teepee after me and changed because he was wearing a vintage Dallas Cowboys shirt that hugged his chest, over a pair of worn, sexy jeans. His hands were stuffed in his pockets and his eyes were locked right on me. That crooked grin was ever present.

When he stepped closer, he whistled, low and sweet. "Wow."

I looked down at my dress. There was a hint of cleavage and the bottom cut off well above my knees.

"How'd you sneak in without me seeing you?" I asked with a bemused smile.

Beck winked and shrugged before placing his hand above my heart, right over my scar. He leaned in and gave me a quick kiss, and I could feel my heart fluttering beneath his hand. "You look beautiful."

I couldn't argue with that.

We walked hand in hand to the Camper and then Beck drove us to the bar. I couldn't tell if it was the heat clinging from earlier or just me, but I grabbed a glass of cold ice water as soon as we walked into the bar, trying to lessen the headache forming behind my eyes.

The bar was a casual place; mismatched tables and chairs dotted the floor. A stage was set up on one side of the room. A guy was singing softly while playing an acoustic guitar.

Beck and I propped ourselves against the bar and ordered some appetizers. It was too loud to try and have an actual conversation, so we munched on our food and Beck sipped his Fat Tire beer. I didn't mind the crowd. In a small town like Marfa, it seemed like most of them knew each other. I people-watched until the bathroom called.

"I'll be back," I murmured to Beck before sliding through chairs to the bathroom. There was a long line of girls chattering, but as I stood against the wooden paneled wall, I closed my eyes and just rested. I realized then that I never told my mom about my fever. I wet some paper towels and dabbed my forehead and neck, telling myself I was overreacting, that it was just the desert heat. After using the bathroom, I fluffed my golden waves into submission and then pushed through the crowd to find Beck. Except the sight I was greeted by made my stomach drop.

The spot I'd been sitting in for the past hour was now occupied by a much prettier girl with her head dipped low to Beck. He was smiling and nodding. Her long blond hair fell pin straight down her back, and when she threw her head back and laughed, I thought the appetizers I'd just consumed would make their second appearance on the bar's floor.

I stood there for a moment, watching them talk animatedly to one another. It was a strange feeling. I'd never had a boyfriend, or even a boy I cared about. Before meeting Beck, I'd never experienced that tight twist in my stomach. The death grip of jealousy.

I took a deep breath and decided I had two options. I could be an adult and walk over to them and join the conversation, or I could save myself the trouble and just wander around the bar. There were back rooms that people kept meandering out of, so I figured I'd check them out.

With one final glance toward the bar, I backed up before Beck could see me and went in the opposite direction. The first archway opened up to a room where people were playing ping-pong. The next room held a pool table and a dart board.

The darts room was less crowded than the other one, so I walked in and sat down on an empty bench near the door. My head felt a little better when I rested it back against the wall.

There were two guys playing a game and then a couple of people waiting for their turn. I had no clue what the protocol was, so I relaxed on the bench and started to watch the current game, trying to forget about my fever and Beck.

It felt good to be anonymous and I didn't mind if people thought I was weird for sitting by myself in a bar. There were enough people watching the game around me that I didn't look like too much of a loner.

"Are you going to play?" a voice asked to my left. I tilted my head to look up into an unfamiliar pair of bright blue eyes. They belonged to a guy standing to the side of the bench, just a few feet away. He obviously didn't want to encroach on my space without asking.

"Oh, you can sit if you want, and I'm not sure, maybe if no one else wants to," I answered distractedly. The guy sat down next to me and I peered over at him from the corner of my eye. He had blond hair that fell a little longer on the top than it did on the sides. His face was handsome with stubble dotting his jaw line. When he sensed me staring at him, he turned to look at me and I smiled awkwardly before muttering, "Are you going to play?"

"I don't have a partner yet," he answered with a small smile. Smooth.

So he wanted me to be his partner. I didn't think it was a problem, so I told him I'd play him.

"What's your name?" he asked, peering at me gently.

"Abby."

He nodded and then offered his hand, "I'm Ethan."

Ethan looked to be in his early twenties, but it was hard to tell in the bar lighting. A small part of me felt guilty for walking away from Beck, but he seemed occupied, so I'd play one game with Ethan.

The two people before us finished up their game and set the darts back into the bucket underneath the boards.

"You ready?" Ethan asked, standing up and offering me his hand. I took it because I didn't want to be rude, but it felt strange. Mine fit in Beck's like a lock and key. But my hand felt awkward in Ethan's. I tried to look back through the doorway, but Beck's spot at the bar wasn't in my view. I chewed on my bottom lip and then turned to follow Ethan over to the dart board.

"I haven't played in a while," I muttered as I picked up three darts out of the bucket.

Ethan gave me an encouraging smile. “Well, what if we practice for a bit?” he offered.

“Yeah, okay, that sounds good.” I tried to shake out my shoulders and relax, but it was hopeless. My head was dizzy and I felt guilty about leaving Beck.

My first three throws were beyond pitiful. Like a blind monkey pitiful. Two of the darts hit the paneled wall beyond the dart board and the one dart that did hit the board landed on the far edge.

“Yikes!” I laughed, stepping up to retrieve my darts.

I looked back to see Ethan stifling a laugh. “I think landing them on the actual board is the goal, but you definitely get points for originality.” I smiled and scrunched my nose.

“Yeah, yeah. Let’s see how good you are,” I quipped, stepping back to stand next to him. With easy grace, Ethan landed all three disgustingly close to the bullseye.

“Pfft!” I gaped. “Be honest, have you been practicing all night?”

He walked backwards to grab his darts. “I’m good under pressure. Especially around pretty girls.” He winked and my heart dropped. But he didn’t give me time to say something awkward. He walked back to my side and started sputtering advice.

“Okay, try to aim your elbow at the board when you bend your arm backward.” I listened to his instructions and slowly bent the dart backwards. “Now it’s all in the wrist…try to let it flick out of your hand,” he continued. A second later, I tossed the dart and it sailed painfully slow across the room and into the ground about two feet in front of the board.

“Oh my god! This is pitiful!” I huffed, and turned toward Ethan. “Maybe I shouldn’t take your advice.”

He held his hands up in surrender. "True, even your first turn was better than that one."

I rolled my eyes playfully and turned back to shoot the next dart. I was assuming what I thought was an okay dart-flinging position, when suddenly I felt Ethan's hands circle my waist so that he could stand behind me and direct the shot. Yes, everyone, I was actually having one of those classic romance moments when the guy attempts to correct the girl's sports swing. Except it was with the wrong guy and his hands sent a terror down my spine.

"Abby?" I heard Beck's voice behind me and my entire body froze. I didn't want Ethan's hands on me, but I didn't have time to protest. Beck had chosen the worst possible second to find me. I twisted around, trying to get out of Ethan's grasp, but my dart scratched his arm in the process.

"Oh, crap! Sorry!" I murmured, my face flushing dark red from the embarrassment of the situation. Should I feel bad about Ethan touching me? Yes. But that girl was touching Beck at the bar.

"I've been looking everywhere for you." Beck stepped forward, his features were hard and accusing.

His tone pissed me off. We were both in the wrong and I didn't deserve to be talked down to. With a huff, I turned and flung my remaining two darts as hard as possible at the board. They landed ridiculously close to the bullseye. Maybe I had to be angry to play darts well.

"I came back from the bathroom and my spot was taken, so I decided to check out the rest of the bar," I explained calmly, turning back to Beck. His arms were crossed and I realized he stood a good half foot over Ethan. I was angry with him in that moment, but you should know that he also looked dangerously sexy and I wasn't immune to that.

Ethan stood there awkwardly glancing between Beck and I. "I'm guessing you don't want to finish the dart game?" he asked, rubbing his arm. Poor guy.

I crossed my arms in front of my chest and shook my head. "No, sorry, I'm sure you can find another partner though." I gave him a genuine smile before brushing past him and Beck, wandering out into the hallway.

"Abby," Beck called, but there was no need. I wasn't running away from him. I just didn't want to have this discussion in front of Ethan. The dark hallway in the back of the bar was a *much* better venue for our first fight as a couple.

"We're together, Abby," Beck stated, coming to stand directly in front of me so that I was stuck between him and the wall. I still had my arms crossed in front of my chest, attempting to block him from pressing up against me.

"I know we are," I bit out, a little too harshly. I didn't want to admit to being jealous.

"So what was that? You were letting him touch you and you should have seen the way he was leering down at you. Like you were his latest conquest." Beck wasn't hiding his anger, but he wasn't yelling. That wasn't Beck's style, yet his tone gave me chills and for a moment I feared that I'd pushed him too far. We didn't know each other's limits. We still hardly knew each other.

"I didn't want him to touch me. I came back from the bathroom and that girl was sitting there and it annoyed me. I just…I don't know what I felt. I just didn't want to come over and have to stare at her pretty face and compare myself to her. So I went to play darts."

"I wasn't flirting with that girl. She's here with her boyfriend and they wanted to go check out the Lights with us."

My face flushed ten times brighter. Fuck my teenage logic. "Well, this," I motioned between the two of us, "is new to me, and I'm apparently still a nineteen year old, whether I'd like to admit it or not."

"You're my girlfriend. You can't let another guy teach you how to play darts. *I* want to teach you how to play darts." He unwrapped my arms from around my chest and then boxed my head in with his hands against the wall. His face dipped low to mine and I bit my lip in anticipation.

He just called me his girlfriend.

"He was a shitty teacher," I joked, staring up into the hazel eyes that were home to me.

Beck closed his eyes and smirked before leaning in and giving me a soul-stealing kiss. His lips met mine and I sighed into him, pressing my hands against his chest and giving myself over to the moment.

When he pulled away, I felt him take a little part of me with him. "I'm sorry," he offered quietly.

"Me too," I smiled wistfully. "But that was a pretty lame first fight. I think we should break plates and stuff next time. Maybe one of us slams the door and leaves for the night to 'get a pack of cigs'."

Beck shook his head so that his nose ran across mine. "How about we skip all of that and just have really great makeup sex," he offered, bending low to kiss my neck. My eyes fluttered closed and I desperately wished we weren't in the hallway of a bar.

"Oh…" I sighed. "Okay."

Please take me in the bathroom. Please take me in the bathroom.

"We have to go. Izzie and Tom are waiting to go see the Marfa Lights with us," Beck said, stepping back and reaching for my hand.

"Now?" I asked, surprised at how fast the plan had formed without me.

"Yep. There's a guy that offered to be our tour guide," Beck answered.

CHAPTER TWENTY-FOUR

There was a viewing platform in Marfa built so that tourists could have a good vantage point to view The Lights. It was made up of a small stone building with a large wrap-around porch. Our group made our way up the stairs that lead to the porch after we'd reconvened in the parking lot.

I'd briefly met everyone at the bar before we left. Tom and Izzie were from England and they were backpacking across the United States before heading off "to university". Izzie wore a black dress with her pin-straight blonde hair. Tom was dressed really well in a pair of ankle jeans, boots, and an army fatigue jacket. Drew, our tour guide, seemed incredibly odd, but I was happy to have a guide so I didn't complain.

"So do you guys know much about these lights?" Tom asked with a thick British accent as he started to roll his third cigarette of the night. He was chain-smoking. He'd pull out a bag of tobacco, roll it into a thin piece of paper, and lick it closed, repeating the process as soon as the previous cigarette was finished. I wondered when he had time to eat or drink.

"Beck told me a little bit about them. That they're supposed to be aliens?" I answered with a shrug. I tried to force my head to stop spinning by taking deep breaths, but nothing seemed to help.

Izzie smiled, "Yeah. That's all we've heard as well."

Drew, who'd been inspecting the perimeter of the rock wall for God knows what, stray javelinas maybe, turned when he heard us talking about the lights.

"They ARE aliens," he clarified with a sharp tone. Izzie and I shot each other a silly glance and I tried my hardest to stifle a laugh. *Okay* then.

"The Lights were first sighted in 1957 and there have been many studies that claim to explain what the lights are, but I believe they're examples of paranormal phenomena." Drew's facts were interesting, but his tone was going in one ear and out the other.

I turned my chin toward the sky and inspected the billions of stars floating over head. Beck and I had seen stars when we went camping our first night, but the stars in Marfa were on steroids. They were brilliant flickers of white against stark blackness. As I stared up trying to connect them all into made-up constellations, I felt closer to Caroline than I had since the last time I'd spoken to her on the phone.

"The lights are going to look like small flickers of white light way out in the distance."

I cast my gaze to where he was pointing, but still wasn't convinced.

"I only see that blinking radio tower," I muttered, confused how that played a role in alien activity.

Drew shot me an annoyed glance, as if to say 'dumb tourist'. "Everything to the *left* of the radio tower is Marfa lights. Everything to the right is just headlights."

I tried to comprehend what he was talking about. I could see the radio tower, but I didn't see lights on either side of it. Why were the lights on one side aliens, but not on the other side?

I didn't want to ruin the moment for Beck, so I shrugged and kept my mouth closed.

"I feel like you're pulling our leg," Tom laughed toward Drew, rolling another cigarette. Meanwhile, Izzie pulled out a bottle of cheap champagne from her backpack, apparently uninterested in finding the lights at all. Drew stared daggers at them.

"Will we know when we see them?" Beck asked.

"Yes," Drew groaned.

"Alriiighty then," Beck answered. He kept his arm wrapped around me and propelled us toward the ledge and away from the group.

We turned to look back out onto the desert landscape. To be honest, I didn't really think we'd see anything. It seemed impossible to find something when I had no clue what I was looking for. The stars were distracting and I had to concentrate hard to block out their appeal. Beck and I didn't budge. We stared off into the distance, trying to stay as still as possible. My eyes scoped every inch of the blackness, and then finally a glow of bright white light came into view.

"Beck!" I hissed, pointing toward the light, fearing it was about to flicker out.

"I see it, too," he spoke into my ear, and we stood

there completely mesmerized. It looked like a soft glow of a lantern in the distance, except it was a sphere shape. It bounced and moved around the horizon line until it faded away after a few moments. My eyes were huge when I turned to Beck. "Holy crap! That's so cool!"

"We missed it!" Izzie cried. She and Tom were taking turns sipping from the champagne bottle and Drew was standing a few yards back with his arms crossed. His constipated expression said it all.

"They'll be back, you just have to wait. That one didn't last as long as they usually do," he huffed, as if he thought we weren't deserving of the Light's presence. I tried to give him a small smile, but he wouldn't look in my direction.

We waited. All five of us stood at the edge of the porch in a line. No one said a word for fear that we would lose focus. I leaned into Beck, frustrated with my burning eyes. They were probably just dry from the desert air, but I tried to blink away the pain and focus on the night spread out before me.

If you've ever tried to see a shooting star, it felt a lot like that. You know, statistically speaking, that you're bound to see one eventually. You just have to be patient and wait it out.

"There!" Izzie called suddenly, pointing out to the left. My gaze flickered over and I spotted them right away. This time there were three dancing lights, flickering brighter than the first one we'd seen. We all shouted gleefully and watched them with sharp focus. They lingered longer than the first group had, growing in size and then dwindling to nothing.

The truth is, I didn't care what they were: headlights, UFOs, a mirage caused from the temperature gradients in the desert. They moved on a backdrop of black sky, pulling my attention and stimulating a part of my mind that rarely got used in adulthood: wonderment. True amazement in the fact that I had no clue why they were there.

• • •

The campsite was quiet when we returned. Beck had to use the flashlight on his phone to lead us through the tents. The desert air had finally chilled and I was happy to be in the warmth of the teepee when we stepped inside and tied the flap.

"Are you okay, Abby?" Beck asked with a concerned frown.

I was wondering how long I had until he asked me that question. I'd been quiet on the way home, fearing the worst but trying to stay calm about how sick I felt. Maybe it was just the flu. I didn't want Beck to worry though.

"I feel fine, just thinking about things," I lied, bending down toward my bag. I couldn't ignore my heavy heart, but I didn't want Beck to catch on. I shoved my clothes aside and retrieved one of the condom wrappers from the box.

Beck's eyebrow arched when he saw what I was reaching for, but he didn't say a word.

"Do you think this will be the last night of our trip?" I asked quietly as a melancholy feeling surrounded us. Beck's frown deepened.

"We should probably head back to Dallas tomorrow. I'm not sure how long we can put off real life," he answered, staring at my scar peeking out from my dress. I swallowed and tried to push my fever aside. If we were going home tomorrow then I couldn't let our last night go to waste. The magic that clung to us on this road trip would be wiped clean the moment we stepped foot in Dallas. Home represented decisions. Decisions that weighed me down so much that I could hardly breathe. I wasn't ready to face them yet.

With small steps, I moved to Beck and wrapped my hands around his neck.

"Then let's make it count," I whispered as my finger trailed along the back of his hair. Before he could answer, I pulled two towels off a shelf and tugged Beck out of the teepee and over to the outdoor showers. There was a chance that people were still awake in the camp, but we'd be quiet. I looked back to see the sinful grin spread across Beck's lips.

"Are you leading me where I think you're leading me?" he asked.

I shrugged and threw him a smug smile.

The showers were empty when we walked inside. The rock wall was more than enough privacy from the rest of the world. Without a word, I stepped into one of the big stalls and started to unzip the back of my dress.

I turned to see Beck watching me as he pulled his shirt off over his head. He dropped it on a bench beside him and I let myself marvel at the sharp contours of his chest longer than usual. I didn't want to rush, not when we'd never get this night back.

The night we saw the Marfa lights.

The night I told him I loved him as he stepped closer and helped me unzip my dress.

"I know, Abby," he answered with a whisper, and then tugged my dress over my head. "I love you, too." We stood there, taking each other in, and then Beck reached behind me to twist the shower head to warm. Icy cold water shot out onto my back and I squealed, throwing myself into Beck's arms.

"Sorry," Beck smiled into my hair, holding me against his warm body. I closed my eyes and inhaled his scent. I wished I could have bottled it up; Beck mixed with the campground and fresh air.

When he reached down to kiss me, it didn't feel rushed. It was slow and intimate. And when he pressed me back against the stone wall, he held my weight so that the rocks didn't scrape my back. We murmured I love you under the stars, and the water dripped down around us as he thrust into me with such sweetness that I couldn't hold the weight of my body up any longer. I let Beck lead us, and when I had that blissful orgasm in the shower of El Cosmico, I cried because I thought it might be the very last time.

I didn't wake up that next morning.

CHAPTER TWENTY-FIVE

My worst fear, and yet the one thing I'd spent the least amount of time worrying about over the past few months, had been realized. My body was rejecting my heart transplant. The moment my fever spiked in the hotel room, I knew in the back of my mind that something was wrong, but I didn't let the idea fester. I pushed it aside and hoped for the best. And instead of turning to head home and getting treatment when I should have, I'd put my entire life in jeopardy and now faced an unknown fate.

There were voices talking, I could hear them through my haze, and yet they still seemed so far away.

"I can't believe you two went all the way to Marfa. What were you thinking? There's not a proper medical facility for miles. What if the ambulance hadn't gotten there in time?" my mother asked. Who was she talking to? I tried to pry my eyelids open, but they felt like lead weights. I could feel my fingers moving and I wiggled my toes so that the soft hospital sheet tickled the tips of them.

"Oh! She's awake! Nurse!" my mother called, and I tried to pry my eyes open again. This time a thin shaft of light appeared through my lids. I heard hurried footsteps as what I assumed to be the nurse ran into the room. The power controls of my bed cranked to life and my upper body began tilting upward. When was the last time I'd sat up?

Finally, I could blink my eyes open. It seemed like gravity had less of a hold on them now that I was sitting up.

I kept blinking, trying to adjust to the bright light of the room.

He was the first thing I saw.

Beck.

Sitting at the foot of my bed with crazy hair and bags under his eyes. He looked like he'd survived the zombie apocalypse. When our eyes met, he visibly sighed and ran a hand through his hair. I wanted him to move closer.

"Abby, I'm so happy you're awake, honey. How do you feel?" my mom asked, filling my vision with her brown curly hair.

"She's probably not feeling too well," the nurse answered for me. I cast her an appreciative glance. She was older than my mom, with a no-nonsense ponytail and kind eyes. "I've put you on quite a heavy cocktail, Abby, so please try to relax. If you need anything, just press the call button for me, sweetie."

I nodded gently and tried to clear my throat. It was dry and crackly.

"I'll go get you some water, hold on," my mom called as she dashed out of the room. The second she was gone, I shifted toward Beck and expected him to jump up to kiss me, but he was keeping his distance. Why was he keeping his distance?

"Beck," I croaked. My voice sounded like I'd been smoking three packs a day for fifty years. But it worked; Beck hopped up and came toward me. He sat next to my body and laid his hand over mine. I couldn't discern his expression, and for some reason that seemed more troubling than my failing heart.

"I'm so…" he paused, looking down to our hands, "so sorry."

His guilt was written across every single feature. His eyebrows sagged, his mouth frowned, and his hazel eyes held angry tears that he fought to contain.

"No, no, Beck," I started to argue, but then my mom came back with some ice chips and water. Her eyes landed on us sitting on the bed and her brows furrowed. I guess her opinion of Beck had changed since they'd last met. Did she blame him? He hadn't done anything wrong. It was my fault that I didn't take better care of my health.

"I've got to run home and shower." Beck peeled his hands away from mine and stood off the bed. I didn't have time to protest. "And my dad wants to see me, so…"

I followed his body as he walked around my bed, past my mom, and through the hospital room door. My hand lay bereft on the sterile sheet.

"You need to rest. Drink some water and try to sleep," my mom said as she hushed me against my pillows.

Sleep. Sleep sounded heavenly. Sleep meant I didn't have to worry about life or the fact that my hero had just walked out of mine.

I slept off and on over the next two days, and when I woke up, Beck wasn't there. My mom was doing a crossword puzzle in the corner and the second my eyes opened, she hopped up off the chair and came over to sit with me.

To her credit, she asked me all of the necessary questions before laying into me about my carelessness and lack of responsibility concerning my health. I listened to her and nodded, agreeing with her completely. She was right after all. I couldn't rely on my mother to take notes for me any longer. I wanted to know everything about my illness. There was always the possibility that my body could reject Colby's heart, but I couldn't skip appointments anymore. My life would just have to fit around them.

The rest of my day was a blur of various doctors running tests and discussing my treatment plans.

"We've adjusted your medications and your body is no longer attacking your heart. However, we need you to stay for an extended period so that we can take routine biopsies," my cardiologist explained when I asked how much longer I needed to be hospitalized. It was a vague answer and I had no way to gauge my plans for the future.

I kept expecting Beck to visit that day, but the later it became, the more I realized he probably wasn't going to show. My phone sat on the bedside table, blank and foreboding.

"Mom, do you think you could bring me a journal when you come back tomorrow?" I asked as she packed her stuff to head home to be with my father. I didn't mind having to stay in the hospital by myself at night; it felt good to have a little privacy.

"Sure thing. I'll bring it with me in the morning."

She kissed my forehead and stroked my hair back

away from my face.

"I'm really sorry about everything," I told her, trying to erase some of the anger she was harboring toward Beck and I.

• • •

The next morning, my mother brought me a journal and I spent the first half of the morning writing down every detail of my trip with Beck. There were so many details that I didn't want to forget about. I wanted to record each event so they would always be vivid memories I could flip back to and read again and again.

When I paused around lunch time to shake out my hand, my mom looked up from her crossword. "How about we try to head down to the cafeteria for lunch? I think it would be good for you to stretch your legs and we can take it slow."

A part of me wanted to say no in case Beck stopped by and found my room empty, but she was right. I needed to get out of this hospital room and move my achy bones. We took the wheelchair just in case, but I didn't end up needing it until the return trip. I'd almost made it back when a wave of fatigue hit me all at once.

"Sit down, sit down. There's no rush," My mom insisted. I sank into the chair gently and she patted my shoulder as she rolled me down the hallway. When we approached my room, I saw Beck standing outside of my door. He looked painfully handsome leaning against the wall with his baseball cap on. His lips were a rosy red and a tan still lingered on his skin, making his greenish hazel eyes look even more mesmerizing. But there was something off about him, less life behind his expression. The Beck that I'd seen on the road trip was long gone. He'd been replaced by the shadow of that person and I couldn't figure out why.

Was it guilt that ate away at him?

"Hi," I smiled meekly as my mom rolled me closer. All of sudden I felt self-conscious about sitting in the chair. I crossed my hands over my lap and adjusted my hospital gown so that it covered more of my legs.

"Hey, Abby Mae," he answered with a ghost of his usual tone. My mom stopped pushing me forward when we reached my door, but before she could sneak around, Beck started to help me stand up.

His touch sent tingles down my arm and I looked down to study his hands on me. It was my favorite sight in the world and I knew I'd taken it for granted before.

My mom cleared her throat behind us, "I'm going to run down to get some coffee. I'll be back in a little while." We nodded and then Beck led me into the room and helped me back onto my bed. Once I was tucked under the covers and there were no other distractions to bother with, I finally looked up to meet his eyes.

There were so many emotions sparking through the air between us and I didn't even realize I was crying until a tear dropped down my cheek.

"Abby-"

"No," I cut him off, needing to get his guilt off my chest. "This isn't your fault. I don't know what you're thinking right now, but my heart was rejected because of the medication dosage they had me on. You didn't cause it. Our trip didn't cause it. Yes, I should have been more careful, and I will be in the future, but there was nothing you could have done." I thought my speech would clear the air between us, but his gaze was focused on my hands. In that moment, I realized his distance ran deeper than what I'd predicted.

"Abby, I know that, but it was still so dumb to go way out to Marfa. When I was waiting for that ambulance to arrive and you were unconscious in my arms, I thought you were dying. I thought I was watching you take your last breaths, and I can't describe that feeling to you. It ripped my heart in two." He pushed off the bed and started pacing back and forth in my hospital room. "Your parents trusted me to take care of you and instead I drove you out into the middle of fucking nowhere. For what? Lights? Was that worth your life? Fuck no!" He ripped the baseball cap off his head and slapped it against his thigh, making me jump from the sound.

"Beck!" I protested, wishing desperately that my body was strong enough to stand up and fight for him to see logic.

"MIT approved my transfer into their journalism program," he muttered, and I felt the contents of my lunch rising in my stomach.

What?

I don't know how long I sat there before answering, "Wow. That's amazing, Beck."

He finally stopped pacing and turned toward me. "I'm not going to do it, though. I can't be in Boston when you're in Dallas."

What? He'd give all that up for me? His future? What future would he have without a degree? Surely his father would be even more livid than he already was.

"Beck. You can't do that," I answered, ignoring my own protests even though I wanted to scream for him to stay. The heart monitor started to spike, but I hardly registered the noise. Every fiber of my being was focused on the fact that I was losing Beck whether I wanted to or not. I wasn't going to be the source of his regret in life. I heard the nurse enter my room, but I couldn't peel my gaze from Beck.

"Is everything okay in here? You need to be resting, Abby." The nurse glared from Beck back to me. Her recommendation was clear: no lover's quarrels when you have a failing heart.

We nodded and when she turned to leave, Beck came to my side. "I won't leave you. Let's not talk about it anymore today. I don't have to make the decision for another week or so. Let's just hangout. I just want to be with you." His arms enveloped me in a hug. He was careful not to pull any of my IV's or bump my nasal cannula. I tugged his shirt and scooted over onto the bed so that we could both fit. The tiny hospital bed dipped with his weight and I naturally rolled toward him like he was my center of gravity.

I'm not sure if my mom ever came back to check on us, but we turned on the TV and I fell asleep as we watched an old rerun of *Friends*. My arm was wrapped tightly around Beck's waist and I was trying my hardest to breathe in the scent of him rather than the sterile smell of the hospital.

CHAPTER TWENTY-SIX

My decision to push Beck away wasn't made on a whim. That last week we had together, I contemplated our relationship and what was best for him. It didn't escape my notice that I was being slightly hypocritical. I'd been so angry with Caroline for telling me to leave when she was at her lowest. Except, Caroline passed away quickly. I wasn't going to pass away. I didn't know what my life would look like for the next few weeks, the next few months, or years. I couldn't put Beck through that. I reasoned with myself that if I knew I was going to die soon, then I would let Beck stay. Instead, I was most likely going to live a mundane existence for a while. And that's why I chose the path I did.

Please don't judge my actions. I tried to take the noble path, not the path that would make me the happiest.

I gave Beck up the only way I knew how: cold turkey.

It was the last day he had before he was supposed to head back to MIT and get everything situated for the semester. I knew his father had booked a ticket for him, but he still insisted he was going to let it go to waste.

I wasn't going to let that happen.

It was early morning in the hospital. The nurse had opened my blinds so that I could see the playground outside. There were children running around, sliding down the slide, and chasing one another. Their carefree playing distracted me for a few minutes, but the hospital's windows blocked out their laughter so that I was left with a silent movie of sorts. When I heard a tap on the door, I quickly closed my journal, shielding it in my two hands on my lap.

My mother hopped up from her seat and gave me a nod. She knew to stay outside in case I needed any help. She'd told me the night before that it should be Beck's decision whether he stays or goes, but she respected my choice. I gave her a wistful smile before she opened the door and let Beck inside.

He smiled wide and strolled into the room, filling my life with his presence.

"You'll be happy to know that I've now been a vegetarian for four days!" He turned in a circle as if showing off his makeover.

I couldn't bring myself to laugh, but I mustered a smile. "That's awesome, Beck. Has it been hard?"

I didn't see the harm in attempting to have one last normal conversation before my life became post-Beck.

"Impossible. But I'm starting to like tofu, so that's good. And peanut butter has become a staple in most of my meals," he answered, coming to sit next to me on the bed. He was so warm and full of life, whereas I'd become ten shades paler since coming into the hospital. I wanted to soak up his heat.

I didn't trust my vocal cords, so I just nodded and pressed my lips together.

He was more than happy to lead the conversation. "I brought some books and I thought we could go outside if you're feeling up for it? The nurse said if I brought your wheelchair it would be okay. You just have to wear a mask and we can't stay out too long." He seemed so excited about his plan that I almost agreed. But then I thought about what he'd said. I had to wear a mask. A mask to prevent me from catching anything. My heart couldn't handle anymore obstacles thrown at it. I was a shell of existence. I couldn't stand, I couldn't walk, I couldn't breathe fresh air. And for that reason, my fingers tightened around the journal and I resolved to stick with the plan.

"Um, actually, let's stay here. I'm feeling tired," I lied, feeling my hands start to shake around my journal.

His brow dipped forward in concern, the dimples disappearing as his mouth turned into a frown.

"What's up, Abby?" he asked, scooting back an inch so that he could turn completely toward me. His hazel eyes weren't going to let me off easy, so I looked down at the journal.

"You have to go to Boston," I whispered.

I could feel his body stiffen on the bed. His hand clasped into a tight ball. "This again? Seriously, Abby?"

He was so angry, angrier than I'd seen him at the bar in Marfa. All because I was doing the one thing that needed to be done.

"Beck-" I started to push the journal toward him and he bristled away from it.

"Don't do this, Abby," he argued with his jaw

clenched tightly. "I mean it. Don't do this to us. I've told you every day this week that I don't want to leave you." His eyes held fire and I was completely helpless against them.

I shook my head, trying to speak past the emotion lodged in my throat.

"I don't care. It's already done. I'm not letting you stay. I'm breaking up with you." My voice held conviction I hadn't known existed. I sounded stubborn and confident in my decision.

"Abby, please," he begged, and my stomach clenched into a fist of pain and regret.

"I don't want you to stay. I have to focus on my health and you have to go to school," I answered with a dead tone. It was the truth muddled with lies. I'd been a burden to people my entire life. Beck deserved more.

"I could help you get better," he murmured. His fists clenched on top of the sheet and I wanted so badly to lean forward and comfort him. But who would comfort me?

I shook my head infinitesimally.

"I'll go if you ask me to, but I'm not coming back," he threatened. "If this is what you want, then I'll do it, but we're over." I knew he was being harsh so that I'd see reason and change my mind. But still, his words were venom. They cut right to the core of my happiness. But it was *exactly* what I wanted. I didn't want him tied down to me when he went back to Boston. I loved Beck because he was the epitome of what life should be, and I'd never forgive myself if I took that away from him.

When I didn't respond to his ultimatum, he pushed off the bed and stood facing the wall for a moment. His hands cradled the back of his head and I could see his back muscles shifting beneath his shirt.

"I'm so sorry," I whispered, trying to reach out for him and causing my cannula to slip out of my nose. It only took a few seconds before I felt light headed, but I had to push through it.

"Please understand. Please," I begged, needing him to turn toward me. I didn't want us to end like this. I needed him to tell me it was okay. That he agreed with me.

When he turned to face me, his chiseled features were sharp as stone.

"No, actually I don't understand," he snapped, and I cringed back against the bed as if he'd hit me. "Don't do this, Abby." A second later, the door knob clicked open and my mom peeked in, most likely to make sure everything was okay. As soon as I saw her face, she moved away to give us privacy. But, the noise of the door snapped Beck out of his death stare. He shook his head and turned to leave.

"Wait!" I yelled, grasping the journal and jumping out of my bed. My head spun and I fell forward, catching myself on the nightstand. My body protested and my heart pumped overtime as it tried to send out enough oxygenated blood to keep me standing.

He didn't turn around.

"Beck! This is for you." I held the journal out in a desperate plea for him to take it. I didn't want to move away from the nightstand for fear that I'd face plant into the tile. The heart monitor was beeping wildly behind me and I knew we only had seconds before my nurse rushed in. It didn't bother me that everyone in the ward could hear me yelling. I just couldn't let him leave without reading everything in the journal. He had to know how much he meant to me.

But nothing in life is perfect. I got what I wanted:

Beck was going to live his life. It just wasn't going to be on my terms.

I tried gulping in breaths of air and slowing my heart, but nothing helped. I needed to sit back down, but I couldn't yet. He was leaving me. His hand grasped the door knob and my lip quivered as tears streamed down my cheeks.

He pulled his hand away and was swiveling on his feet back toward me. He was about to turn around, I *know* he was, but then the nurse and my mom rushed past him to get to me.

"You need to leave now, young man!" the nurse barked, her voice much too harsh. "You've done enough!"

"Beck!" I screamed, trying in vain to get him to turn around and take the journal. But the nurses and doctor blocked his path. I chucked it across the room so that it hit the door with a loud thud. The world spun around me, but I tried to hold onto consciousness. I needed one more glimpse of him to tide me over, but instead I was met with a black ring impinging on my vision as the nurse lifted me back onto the bed.

I felt my mom's hand rub my hair back as she leaned down to hold me.

"He's gone. Sweetie, just rest. Just rest."

She kept repeating those words as she rocked me against the hospital bed. I clung to her shirt with a vice-like grip, wishing she could erase every cruel moment in my life.

I'd done the right thing and I knew it, yet the doubt that seeped into my thoughts was enough to cause nightmares anytime I shut my eyes. My brain had a way of finding the most gut-wrenching ideas and replaying them in my mind over and over again.

Beck at parties. Beck with girls. Beck sleeping with a new girlfriend. I squeezed my eyes shut and told myself it was for the best. But it wasn't enough. I reached for the pail next to my bed and threw-up the contents of my stomach until I was left dry-heaving and praying for the pain and sadness to go away.

• • •

Beck called everyday for a month and I didn't answer once. I had to fight myself about it every single time, but I knew if I heard his voice, I'd cave and beg him to come back. So instead, I'd watch the phone vibrate on the hospital's night stand, jarring the silence from the room and reminding me of how much I'd been forced to give up in my life.

ONE YEAR LATER

CHAPTER TWENTY-SEVEN

I sat in Dr. Lucas' office just as I had twice a month for the past year. Her stylish glasses were sitting on the brim of her nose as she ran through everything on her checklist one last time. My eyes scanned down her burgundy cardigan and I smiled thinking of how different our relationship used to be.

"You've got your schedule in order. I think it's wise that you're taking basics the first year. That way if you change your major, it won't be a problem," she chimed in as her finger dragged down the list. We'd already gone through everything ten times, and I knew my session was almost over. I think she was dragging it out because she knew it was the last time I'd be visiting her. My life no longer required a life coach. I smiled at the silly thought and stuffed my papers into my purse.

"I don't think I'll be changing my major, but I agree," I said, leaning back and eying her.

She met my eyes and nodded. We'd finally come to understand one another and I'd truly appreciated her help throughout the last year.

"You should be proud of yourself, Abby. You did it. You got into college and you're leaving tomorrow. Are you nervous?" she asked, her tone shifting into friend-mode.

Her question was one I'd been asked quite a few times over the past few days. I'd visited Caroline's parents the day before so I could say goodbye. We had dinner and they asked about college, if I was nervous to move, if I was anxious to start classes. I knew they were truly happy for me. Just as I was leaving, her parents had surprised me with a going away present. They'd put away some money for Caroline to go to school and instead of using it for themselves, they wanted to give me a scholarship. They knew I was paying for college on my own, much to my parent's disapproval. So they bequeathed upon me a "Caroline College Fund" of sorts. I'd cried when they'd handed me the check, and I'd vowed to make it count for her. Even in death, my friend was always watching out for me.

That money would help me get through the first year of college along with the savings I'd built over the past year working in a coffee shop. After all the medical expenses that had come about after my most recent stint in the hospital, I couldn't ask my parents for help with college. Even if they could afford it, it felt like I should do it on my own.

Dr. Lucas cleared her throat and I shook my head. "I'm just ready to get up there, I think," I answered, pulling myself out of my reverie.

She nodded with a tight-lipped smile and I knew she was getting as worked up as I was. Did she realize how much I'd changed in the past year? How much she'd helped me?

"It's funny that the assessment test was accurate," I mentioned, thinking about the silly options it had provided me with a year earlier: park ranger, writer, accountant, biomedical engineer.

She smiled wide and wrapped me into a hug. "I'm glad it all worked out. Although, I still think you would have made a good park ranger," she laughed, pulling away to hold me at arm's length.

I rolled my eyes at her playfully.

"Make sure I get an acknowledgment in your first novel, okay?" She gripped my shoulders and I mashed my lips together so that I wouldn't cry.

"Of course," I winked.

In the past year, I had stuck to a routine: working at the coffee shop during the day and heading home to write non-stop at night. It all started with the journal my mom brought me at the hospital. I'd filled it cover to cover. Then I filled journal after journal, no longer recanting stories from our trip, but writing down stories that had lived in my head for the past nineteen years. When my hands ached from writing with a pen, I switched to creating stories on my laptop. It became my thrill in waking up each morning. I wanted to be a writer and I'd worked hard to make it happen. I'd been accepted to a well-known creative writing program so that I could hone my skills. There was nothing holding me back now.

"I hope you like Boston, Abby," she said, wrapping me in a final hug.

• • •

There are almost sixty colleges in Boston, but only two of them mattered to me: Boston University, where I was enrolled, and MIT. It didn't take me long to get settled. I was living in a small dorm just off campus with a roommate that hadn't moved in yet. My dorm was built in the seventies and all of the furniture and appliances looked like they were on the brink of collapse. I picked the side of the room that had the most sunlight, and then I set up my writing space so that my desk faced the window.

I couldn't see MIT from my room, but I knew it was there. Boston University and MIT were separated by the Charles River. I could literally walk to MIT in a matter of minutes. That first night in my new dorm, I sat at my desk, staring at my reflection in the glass, and contemplated the fact that I didn't know a single person in the entire city except for one. And he didn't know I'd left Dallas.

The next morning, I rolled out of bed and sifted through the new pieces of my wardrobe. Even in early autumn, it was chilly in Boston. My jean shorts were packed far, far away and I quickly grew to love the art of layering. Once I had my jacket zipped up, I locked my apartment and headed out to explore the city.

It was starkly different than Dallas. The buildings were older. They had character that came with being built hundreds of years ago. Brownstones spanned city streets and I let them lead me toward the Charles River. I wanted to inspect the MIT campus. I knew the chances of running into Beck were beyond minimal, but that was okay. I wanted to get a feel for where he spent his time; where he'd spent the past year without me.

I trekked over the Harvard Bridge and paused in the middle to watch a group of rowers pass underneath me. Their synchronized strokes were mesmerizing to watch and I snapped a picture to send to my mom. She hadn't loved the idea of me traveling to Boston for school, but she couldn't argue with my reasoning. It had taken a little convincing and quite a few tears at the airport, but I promised to talk to her every day and visit home as often as I could.

Abby: I'm officially a Bostonian. This picture is on the Harvard Bridge.

Mom: Don't fall over! You look like you're right on the edge...

I smiled and pocketed my phone. Some things would never change and that was okay. She'd worked hard to keep me alive. She didn't need the fruits of her labor falling off a bridge by accident. After walking for a few more minutes, I reached the epicenter of the MIT campus. The buildings were stoic. Tall stairs led up to an imposing building that reminded me of the Pantheon in Rome. But that wasn't what held my attention.

There was a statue just off the sidewalk that looked at once solid and transparent. It was a stainless steel shell of mathematical symbols in the shape of a giant human form. The plaque at the base titled it "The Alchemist".

It stood almost three times my height, and the front of the sculpture, where the man's legs should have been, was cut out so that you could stand inside of it. I peered in, unsure of how claustrophobic the space would make me feel, but the way they layered the symbols made it feel like you were at once inside and out. The blue sky streamed in through the holes in each symbol and I took my time walking in and out, inspecting it from all sides.

Students walked around me, shuffling to their dorms or to buildings on campus, but no one bothered me as I stood and inspected the sculpture for the rest of the afternoon. It gave me an idea of how to reach Beck, and I sat there piecing it together in the Boston sunlight until I felt a buzzing in my pocket.

I looked down at my screen and smiled before pushing back onto my feet.

"Hi, Mom," I answered, waiting for a break in pedestrian traffic so I could start to head back to my dorm. It was early afternoon and I'd skipped lunch. She could probably sense that. Moms are superheroes, I swear.

She sighed into the phone, almost inaudibly. "I won't bother you this much all the time. Just cut me slack for the first week, okay?" I could tell she'd been crying and I'd be lying if I said I didn't miss her just as terribly.

"I'm glad you called, Mom," I told her, trying to keep my emotions at bay. "I miss you, too. Want to talk to me while I walk home?" I offered, sticking my free hand in my coat pocket and heading back to the bridge.

"You're still out walking?" she asked. I could hear her shuffling around the house in the background. Maybe she was preparing dinner for her and Dad.

I looked back and forth, making sure no one was around to hear me. "I was formulating a plan to reach Beck."

"Oh, I want to hear about it!" she sang into the phone. "But wait, you have his number and everyone's on Facebook nowadays. Couldn't you just do it that way?"

"Mom. Where's the romance in that?" I joked.

"I'm just saying it might be a little easier. Maybe it could be a backup plan," she added, and I scrunched my nose. I didn't want a backup plan. I didn't want to text or call Beck. He deserved more than that. He deserved a grand gesture.

That night when I got back to my dorm, I sat at my desk facing the city lights and started on my plan. I had no clue if Beck was still in Boston or at MIT, but I would just have to assume that he was. I tapped away on my keyboard— creating, erasing, and rethinking my ideas until I had it complete. It was almost impossible to condense my feelings into a page. But I did it. One single page with a bold title that would hopefully catch people's attention. I planned on waking up early and taking it to a printer to get as many copies as I could on my measly budget.

When I tried to sleep that night, I tossed and turned, thinking over the memories of our road trip. I slid open the journal that I kept on my nightstand and read over my favorite parts. The pages were worn and stained. A few of the edges were curling in on themselves. The journal had been my crutch the past year. In a strange turn of events, Beck had actually done me a favor when he walked out without taking it, but I wasn't going to let him walk away again.

CHAPTER TWENTY-EIGHT

I walked through the MIT campus with a stack of papers in hand. The campus was still mostly empty. I'd woken up at the crack of dawn to be sure I could do my dirty work when there weren't thousands of students in the way.

MIT's campus is enormous, but I looked up where the journalism classes usually were held and hit that area especially hard. There wasn't a safe surface in sight. I pasted pages up on the buildings, on telephone poles, and bulletin boards.

I pasted sheet after sheet in the student union until the walls were almost completely covered in flapping pages. I kept moving toward the center of the campus where I'd seen the statue yesterday. I pasted as I went, trying to move quickly, but just when I thought I was in the clear, I felt a looming presence behind me.

"Ma'am, do you realize that you're vandalizing school property?" A stern voice questioned behind me. I turned slowly to look into the eyes of a distinguished man. He had thick white hair, cut short and styled nicely. Horn-rimmed glasses perched on his thin nose. A navy sport coat rested on top of his crisp white shirt.

"I…I," I couldn't formulate a response. He was about to ruin my plan or yell at me. I didn't do well with confrontation and I was seconds away from breaking down in embarrassing, ugly tears.

"We have janitors that are hardworking individuals. They have enough on their plate without having to clean up after vandals. Do you understand that?" His tone was harsh and his sharp stare made me feel like a juvenile delinquent.

"I'm sorry," I murmured lamely, glancing down at my stack of unused papers. My plan felt foolish now. Why had I thought this would work?

"May I at least see what you're posting?" he asked. I fumbled quickly to pass a sheet over to him, unable to meet his gaze. My cheeks reddened beyond what I thought possible. If he hadn't thought I was foolish before then he definitely would after reading my plea to get Beck back.

His eyes glanced down at the sheet and I watched him scan the page, his expression imperceptible. His thick white eyebrows shot up in surprise and then the edge of his mouth curled up into a hint of a smile.

"Is this true?" he asked, and I gulped down a swallow.

My head nodded before my vocal cords could catch up. "Yes, sir."

I stood frozen, waiting for him to call campus authorities or threaten me somehow. I imagined the campus police hauling me off in handcuffs at the precise moment Beck walked onto campus. Instead, the distinguished man stretched out his hand.

"Give me a few so that I can put them over in the Architecture school. I'm a professor over there." My eyes practically bulged out of my head at his words. Could he truly be serious? He was going to help me?

I grabbed a dozen and handed them over to him with shaky hands. I couldn't believe the turn of events. Before he turned to walk away, he looked up at me and narrowed his eyes.

"I met a girl when I was studying abroad in Italy. We walked the same path to college every day and I never worked up the courage to stop and talk to her. I'd hate for you to have the same regret." He nodded to himself, the hint of a smile still playing on his lips before he turned and walked off with a confident stride. I felt like I'd stepped into the twilight zone. A laugh escaped my lips as I stood there, completely dumbfounded, watching him disappear around the corner.

When he was gone, I glanced down at the sheet of paper, trying to read it from his perspective.

Distressed Damsel Seeks Brawny Hero

If you're reading this right now, chances are you're an extra in my love story. But I need your help. You play a vital role in how my story ends.

My name is Abby Mae, and one year ago, I gave up a part of my life that I thought I'd be able to live without. I knew I was doing the right thing, but now I'm left wondering what could have been.

If you've ever had a missed chance at finding love, or if you've ever locked eyes with a girl across a coffee shop, or a guy next to you on the bus, this is that moment for me. I'm making my move and I'm throwing myself at fate in hopes that the boy I'm seeking will find this note.

I can't divulge his name, but our story is short and sweet, and I think you deserve to hear it:

He was a handsome guy in a baseball cap and I was a cynical girl picking out an urn.

He was a stubborn boy who weaseled his way into my road trip and I was a girl who learned that you can never have enough s'mores.

Caroline was my friend that cut our trip in half and we were the ones to appreciate the indefinity of our timelines.

He was a boy that watched me sing karaoke and I was the girl who almost got us kicked out of the bar.

John Denver was our road trip muse and I learned to trust the power of his songs.

I was a girl who chose to Dare and not Drink and he was a boy that screamed he liked me into the ocean.

He left because I forced his hand, but now I'm begging him to understand my reasons.

If you're that guy, meet me in The Alchemist statue tomorrow at six pm. If none of that story rings a bell, please help me and pass this note along so that I can find him.

I chuckled under my breath at the fact that the distinguished professor wanted to play a part in my story. If he believed in the note, then maybe Beck would as well.

The sound of a skateboard slamming up onto the curb pulled me out of the moment and I glanced up. In a matter of minutes, the campus had transitioned from a ghost town into a bustling zoo. I frowned and took in the people swarming around me, trying to spy a pair of familiar hazel eyes or brown hair hidden beneath a baseball cap. Instead, I found a rather diversified mix of students that looked nothing like Beck.

I still had a pile of papers in my arms, but students were stopping to check out the ones I'd already posted and there was no way I could continue posting more without them noticing me. In a rush, I gathered up all of my supplies and started heading back toward the Harvard Bridge.

CHAPTER TWENTY-NINE

The next day dragged by at a snail's pace. I craned my neck off my pillow to see that it was eight in the morning. The next time I checked it was eight fifteen.

"Motherf-" I groaned into my pillow, allowing it to drown out the end of my curse.

I hadn't been able to fall asleep until around two am the night before. Then, when I did finally sleep, visions of Beck laughing while I stood inside the statue crying had circled in my head until I'd bolted awake in a cold sweat. I should mention that I was dressed up as a T-Rex in the dream, so I'm not sure what my brain was trying to tell me other than that I shouldn't dress up as a dinosaur if I wanted to win Beck back. Maybe I should steer clear of costumes all together.

I rolled myself off my bed and went to my closet to

pick out the clothes I would wear later. Jeans and a long-sleeved striped fitted shirt. Not too shabby, but it didn't look like I was trying too hard either. Once my clothes were lying on my bed, I sunk down to the floor.

If Beck wasn't at MIT, I would survive and laugh off the experience. Maybe. But, if Beck had a girlfriend, I didn't know what I would do. A year is a really long time and we hadn't spoken once. Not once after his month of calls. I'd be lying if I hadn't secretly wished that it had been a situation like The Notebook. I'd even asked my mom if she was hiding away all of the love letters that he'd sent me. She just rolled her eyes and told me to get out of my apartment and take a walk. Still, it was nice to think that maybe Beck hadn't moved on from me with the snap of a finger. I mean, the idea of someone writing you a letter everyday for a year *is* pretty romantic, but also unrealistic. That's a lot of paper and a lot of postage.

Suddenly a knock on my dorm's door rattled me from my thoughts and I looked up just in time to see the door pop open. I held my breath as a girl with long brown hair and a slew of freckles walked into the room, rolling a suitcase behind her. Her eyes scanned from the empty bed, to our desks against the windows, and then down to the floor where I was sitting with my legs pulled up to my chest.

What a great first impression. I looked like an escaped mental patient.

I saw her swallow and then a tiny smile spread across her lips. She was just as nervous as I was.

"Hi," I offered, confused about which social skills I was meant to employ in this situation. For the past year, my closest friends were my life coach, Danny the Drag Queen, my gay neighbors, and my parents. I hadn't made a real friend since Caroline's death, and now that I was staring at someone my age, I felt my lungs constrict in fear of what she thought of me.

I hopped up to my feet and realized we were practically the same height.

"I'm Abby," I offered gently.

"Hi." She smiled timidly. "I'm Sammy."

We stood silently, soaking in the awkwardness of our introductions, and then I finally spoke up. "I picked this side because of the sunlight, but if you want to swap, we definitely can. I just wanted to face the window when I wrote," I kept rambling, pointing to various things in the room as I went.

She interrupted me mid sentence. "Oh, no. No, that's perfect. I don't mind." Her voice was small, like a mouse.

I exhaled, trying to calm my nerves. Then I laughed, a tiny giggle that turned into a belly-aching laugh. Sammy looked at me like I'd just stepped off Pluto, but then I think the situation sank in for her and she started laughing as well.

"I was really nervous about having a potluck roommate. None of my friends from home got into this school," Sammy explained as she sat back on her bed, finally relaxing.

I shrugged and sat back on my bed as well. "I think we'll be okay." And I meant it. It felt good to know that I'd have a friend soon. That even if things with Beck didn't work out later, I'd still have Sammy. "I can help you grab your stuff, if you have more?"

Her face lit up, "That'd be great. And then," she paused, fidgeting with her stuff on her bed, "we could get lunch if you want? There's this sandwich shop down the street that looked like it had vegetarian options."

"You're a vegetarian!? So am I!" I smiled wide, holding the door open so we could head down to grab her luggage.

I ended up spilling my plan to Sammy after we'd returned from lunch and exploring around the city. Not so much because I wanted to divulge secrets with her, but more so as a public service announcement. She had the right to know that I could be potentially wallowing on the floor of our dorm unable to muster the energy for any human contact for the next few days. Yes, that was the worst case scenario, but still feasible.

"Wow… that's really brave," she commented as I laced up my Keds.

"It doesn't feel brave. It feels reckless, like I'm throwing myself into oncoming traffic," I laughed, wondering if we were to the point where I could divulge my true sense of humor. Her laughter put my mind at ease.

"Do you want me to walk over with you? I won't stay if you don't want me to." Her tone sounded so sincere that I could almost hear Caroline cheering from wherever she stood watching that moment.

"That'd actually be great. I feel like I might chicken out." I stood and took a deep breath, wondering what else I would need. I caught my reflection in the mirror. My jade green eyes popped against my fair skin. My strawberry blonde hair framed my face in natural waves. No makeup, just me. The me that Beck hopefully still loved.

"You look great," Sammy offered, tugging her purse over her shoulder. I met her gaze in the mirror and gave her a silly smile before we locked up and headed toward the statue.

CHAPTER THIRTY

Love will make you reckless. It can drag out parts of you that common sense and fear usually keep hidden away. Because love is selfless and selfish. Heading toward that statue proved just how selfless I was going to have to be if I wanted to win Beck back. When I walked onto the MIT campus and stumbled upon a sight that made my heart stop, I didn't turn around even though my feet didn't want to keep carrying me forward. I had to be brave for Beck.

I kept pushing past people, contemplating the fact that there was a crowd waiting around the statue that could have rivaled the attendance of a rock concert. Everyone was milling about, holding my flyers and talking animatedly. The closer I attempted to get to the statue, the more condensed the crowd became.

Sammy's wide eyes confirmed my fears. My heart hammered against my chest, deafening the sounds of the crowd. Whatever was about to happen wouldn't be private. There were cell phones, cameras, and one thousand memories that would forever capture my inevitable heartache.

"Are all these people here because of the letter you put up yesterday?" Sammy asked, clutching onto my elbow so we wouldn't get pulled apart in the crowd.

"I have no clue," I answered in a daze. But the closer to the statue we pushed, the more I realized that whatever bravery I thought I needed would have to be doubled.

"I'm not sure I can do this." I shook out my hands, feeling a panic starting to rise. I didn't think people would care. I was scared no one would even read the letter. But this? The fact that so many people were curious about the outcome made my stomach twist into a tight pretzel.

"Abby," Sammy looked down at her watch. "You've still got fifteen minutes. Let's just walk closer to the statue and you can decide when we get up there." Her suggestion seemed reasonable enough. No one knew I was the girl from the flyer yet, they just thought we wanted front row seats. We kept pushing, getting some angry stares from people who'd clearly been waiting for quite some time. I didn't know what to say. I tried to hide my blushing cheeks and keep my head down until we finally pushed our way through to the other side.

The statue was an island stuck smack-dab in the center of no man's land. No one wanted to get too close. I peered toward Sammy wearily, but her eyes were wide and she kept shaking her head in disbelief. I wondered if she thought her first day at college would be quite so interesting.

Why had all these people come? Maybe since classes hadn't started yet, no one had anything better to do? I should have planned better. Maybe my mom was right about calling him instead. I pulled my phone out of my purse and looked down to see a blank screen. If he'd seen the flyer, would he have called me already?

"Abby, you only have five minutes now, do you think you should…?" Her eyes darted from me to the statue, then back again. She couldn't finish the sentence because she knew how insane it was.

I pocketed my phone and puffed out a breath. My hands felt clammy. Sammy nudged my arm and I realized I was still standing there, not deciding what to do. I either had to move forward, or leave and try something else.

I didn't think I'd be able to do it.

But then I locked eyes with the distinguished professor from the day before, the one who could have turned me into the authorities. He was across the circle, watching me with a half smile and I couldn't help but gape. It may seem strange considering I barely knew him, and I hardly knew Sammy, but having them both there made me feel like I wasn't so alone. Maybe they'd have my back if people started throwing rotten tomatoes or something at me.

You know that feeling when you're about to jump into a cold pool? You realize that it will be freezing and that you just have to hold your breath and get it over with. There's a moment when you're on the ledge and your heart leaps in your chest and then before you realize it, you're bending your knees and jumping whether you consciously decided to or not? That's what happened when I took my first step into the circle. It was a baby step, but my body took it as an approval on my part, and before I knew it, I was halfway to the statue. My body was proceeding as planned and my brain was screaming for me to retreat, to get out while I still could.

The crowd erupted into whispers and shouts, but the conversations were nothing more than background noise. Everyone's faces blurred into nothingness as I walked toward the statue. It greeted me with silence, and I stepped inside, just past the entrance.

I peered over to see Sammy give me a thumbs up before I squeezed my eyes shut. When I pried them open again, I stared into the crowd without seeing anyone. They were all a blur of skin tones and clothing. My fingers darted up to the tiny locket lying on top of my shirt. I fingered the gold heart, thinking of the flea market and the old ladies that condemned our kissing.

I could feel my heart beating in my throat. Each beat felt like it was another step closer to my impending doom. Thump. He's not coming. Thump. He's probably not even at MIT. Thump. What if he has a girlfriend? Thump.

"I think I'm the person you wrote about in your note," I heard a voice mutter confidently. My stomach dropped and I whipped my head around to see a stranger standing a few feet in front of me. He was tall and lanky; he wore Converse and a trendy pair of glasses. But he was definitely not Beck.

"Um," I muttered awkwardly. I hadn't considered what would happen if someone *other* than Beck came forward. "Are you joking?"

His face split into a smile. "All I'm saying is that if your guy doesn't show up, I'd be more than happy to fill his shoes."

Wow. I couldn't even process his request because in a matter of seconds a bevy of guys stepped forward to offer their proverbial glass slippers as well. They each wanted a piece of the limelight. It would have been beyond flattering to assume they meant their proclamations, but I knew it had more to do with their twenty-year-old brains. Their need for attention and approval from the female population meant that they were willing to step forward so that they could brag about it over dinner in the dorm cafeterias later.

I tried to smile at them, but I was too nervous. The attention was too much and I balled my fists next to my legs to keep from running.

"You can't give up. I'll be the guy," one shouted from the crowd.

They meant well, but their sweet jokes told me one thing. It was past six pm and Beck hadn't showed up. That's why they stepped forward. They were trying to help me in a pitiful way. I ran the heel of my palm against my chest, trying to break the tightness that had suddenly formed there. I felt like my heart was constricting and I blinked my eyes in quick succession. My hands fell limp to my side and I took a small step out of the statue.

He hadn't seen the note. Or if he had, he wasn't going to come. Everyone was watching me with piteous faces. I didn't want their pity. I wanted Beck to be at MIT still. I wanted fate to be on my side for once. I wanted to be able to erase the pain from last year. But I couldn't have my cake and eat it too. I gave Beck up so that he could follow his dream, and that's the way it had to end.

It was over.

I raised my gaze, trying to find the distinguished man in the crowd. It only took a moment; he was the only person there beyond the age of twenty-five. His eyes locked with mine and he shrugged his shoulders, as if to tell me that it would be okay. I bit down on my lip, trying not to cry. It felt like I'd let him and Sammy down somehow.

Seconds turned into minutes and people began to realize the show was over. Some of them looked disappointed, but most of the people didn't care all that much. It was like watching a reality show to them. The fair-weather guys in the center patted my shoulder and turned back to find their friends. Each one of them leaving me as quickly as they'd stepped forward. Converse guy didn't turn right away. I think out of everyone, he might have been serious about his proposition, and for that I was grateful. Without him, I would be crawling along rock bottom, but instead I was dangling by a limb just a few feet away from it. That counted for something.

"Thank you," I muttered toward him with a tight smile. It felt forced and I knew he could tell.

"Yeah, I really meant—"

His voice faded out as my gaze drifted to where his Converse rested on the concrete. Directly beneath his left foot there was a small white arrow chalked onto the sidewalk. A few feet in front of that one, I noticed another. They were leading away from the statue.

No *freaking* way.

I didn't pause to let the moment sink in; I followed the arrows and pushed my way through the crowd. Most of them followed after me, but I picked up my pace, keeping my nose to the ground. The arrows led me around the back of the statue and passed the campus library. Some of the arrows were rubbed almost completely clean from foot traffic, but I kept connecting the dots until I turned a corner and arrived in front of an expansive field. The field was in the center of the undergrad dorms, but at that moment there was only a single person occupying the sprawling space.

The first thing I saw was that brown hair glistening in

the sun and curling right around his ears like always. My hands shot to my mouth and the world slowed to a crawl. For a moment we stood there, frozen, but then someone gently pushed me from behind and I realized I had to keep going. I took a deep breath and stepped up onto the grass. We were yards away from each other, but he started walking to meet me half way.

My breath hitched when we were close enough for me to see his hazel eyes brimmed with dark lashes and swirling with green madness. His flawless features, confident air, dimpled smile. Everything was there, just like I'd imagined every night for the past year. A spontaneous laugh escaped my lips as we stopped a foot away from each other.

He nodded, as if convincing himself that it was really me.

It was my Beck. My Beck, just as I'd left him.

His gaze held utter amazement and I couldn't temper the tears running down my cheeks. To see him, smiling and present. To know that in the middle of a thousand people, he was still the one person who could turn my world into a splash of color.

When he spoke, I could tell he was flustered. His voice hung on a nervous tone and his gaze teetered between my features, as if he wasn't sure where to concentrate.

"I was the guy who should have never left and you were the girl who should have found me earlier." My hands gripped my mouth as I started to cry harder. They weren't even cute tears; just ugly, uncontrollably happy tears. I couldn't pull myself together no matter how much I tried.

His hands reached out to capture the back of my neck, hitting the spot that made goose bumps bloom down my body. I took a step forward, placing my hands against his hard chest. He pressed closer to me.

"Do you want to know why I followed you into that funeral parlor?"

I titled my head, recalling our first encounter like it was yesterday. "You said you followed me on a whim," I answered with a small smile.

"That's the truth, but there's more to it." He ran his hands down my arms to entwine them with mine. "I was parking at the gas station across the street and I saw you get out of your car. I didn't think much of it until you paused on your way inside the shop. You tilted your head toward the sun and closed your eyes, like a prisoner stepping outside after years of being locked away. It seemed so odd. No one just stops and appreciates life like that— but you did. I could see your smile from across the street and I couldn't look away. I knew in that moment that I was completely uninterested in pursuing a life in which I didn't cross that street and meet you."

I wiped my tears from my cheek and furrowed my brow in recollection. He was referring to the moment I felt truly free for the first time in my life. The first time I took a step toward beginning my little adventure.

His words made my apology lodge in my throat.

"I'm sorry I made you leave," I sputtered.

"Abby— "

"I had to get healthy for you. For me." I stared at my hands resting against the cotton of his shirt. I liked feeling his heart thumping against his chest at the exact rhythm as mine. "I had to figure out what I wanted to do with my life." I had so much to catch him up on.

He nodded, and the movement brought my gaze back toward his eyes. When he finally spoke, the edge of his mouth quirked up. "I liked your headline."

I laughed; pressing my face to his chest and inhaling

the scent that I'd wanted to bottle up months and months ago. "Good enough to be on your UIL team?" I smiled into his chest.

He shifted his hands to push my hair away from my face, and then he left his hands on either side of my temples. He gently tilted my head back so that I had to look up at him.

"Are you making a joke right now because you're too chicken to tell me you love me in front of all these people?" he asked, his confident grin as smooth as honey.

I wanted to tell him. But I had things that were on the tip of my tongue and I couldn't wait another moment to share them. "I want to be a writer. I got accepted into BU."

His mouth dropped open. He scrunched his eyebrows together, a disbelieving smile halting his confidence. His head tilted to the side and he huffed out a breath, trying to catch up. "You're staying in Boston? You're staying here?" He pointed to the ground and I laughed at his amazement. But I guess that's exactly how I felt as well.

"I came for you." I paused, sucking in a shaky breath. "I love you, Beck…I needed you to follow your dreams so that I could follow mine alongside you."

He clenched his jaw and I could tell he was trying to keep it together. His hand trembled in my hair and I reached up to lace my fingers around his forearm.

"I love you, too."

And then, like always, he kissed me when I least expected. He bent forward and pressed his lips to mine. He stole my breath with a kiss that held everything we'd buried deep within us for so long. My arms wrapped around his neck, and his arms tightened around my back so that we were pressed together. We would have stayed there all day, wrapped up in each other, but I heard the students erupt with applause and cheers.

Beck pulled away from me laughing, then looked around us and lifted my hand into the air like I was a fighter who'd won a match. He fell forward into a little bow and everyone started cheering more. I was laughing and crying. My face was splotchy and I tried to fan away my emotions, though it was impossible.

"Let's get out of here," Beck whispered in my ear, and I looked up into his eyes. The gravity of the situation hadn't sunk in yet. It felt like a lucid dream. I had to know that he was real, that I wouldn't wake up.

I looked over to find Sammy. "My roommate is here. She just got to Boston today so I don't want to leave without her. " She was standing off to the side of the field by herself, smiling at me, but obviously a little out of her element. I didn't want to abandon her. There was something in her that spoke so close to my soul. Maybe we were both just shy vegetarians, but it felt like I should take care of her like Caroline would have taken care of me.

Beck followed my line of sight and nodded. "That's okay. We can walk back with her to your dorm and then maybe go somewhere, just you and me?"

A shiver ran down my spine at the idea of being alone with him again.

He reached for my hand, but just before we left, I twisted around to look for the professor one last time. I'd lost track of him when I'd followed the arrows, but I felt like I owed him a thank you. Most of the crowd had dispersed by then, but I found him leaning against an oak tree a few yards away from the field.

I smiled and gave him a little wave. He bent his head in a small nod and turned in the opposite direction.

CHAPTER THIRTY-ONE

"So this is what you call home?" I asked, stepping past the threshold into his one bedroom studio apartment.

He ran a hand through his unruly hair and nodded. The space was intimate with just the right mix of Beck's eclectic taste. A vintage Texas flag hung above a painted brick fireplace. It reminded me of the flag that was in that teepee in Marfa. I glanced over my shoulder and pointed to it. Beck nodded and stuffed his hands into his back pockets, but didn't offer any explanation. I wondered if he got it after our trip.

His apartment wasn't spotless, he was in college after all, but his bed was made and there weren't any dishes in the sink, so he got a few points for that.

"Does it pass inspection?" he asked, stepping up behind me to wrap his arms around my waist.

My eyes fluttered closed and my head fell back against his chest. I murmured some sort of "yes" and didn't care to elaborate.

"I can't believe you're really here," he spoke, spinning me around to face him. Having Sammy with us until a few minutes ago had provided us with a buffer. We couldn't attack each other when she was there, but now? Now, all bets were off.

"Have you slept with anyone else? Dated anyone else?" Beck asked quietly.

What a strange concept. As if anyone other than Beck could have occupied my thoughts for the past year. There was no room for anyone else.

"No," I shook my head.

I heard him sigh, but now I was curious. "Have you?" I asked.

I told myself that if he had, it would be okay. I wouldn't let it be our Ross and Rachel moment. We weren't together and I'd deal with the jealousy later.

"I almost did," he answered. "It was right when I got back to Boston and I was so pissed off at you for pushing me away. I went to a party and got drunk. I made out with a girl and we went upstairs—"

"Stop," I said, pressing my hands to his chest. "I don't need the details if you guys didn't have sex. God, I was so scared you would have a girlfriend. When I posted those flyers yesterday, all I could think about was how I would deal with the outcome if you had a girlfriend you were in love with."

He laughed and shook his head. "Impossible."

My cheeks flushed and I turned to inspect the kitchen. He kept his distance, watching me move around. I fingered his coffee maker and towel. The zombie salt and pepper shakers sat on top of his stove. I was soaking up details of his life. I wanted to know how many cups of coffee he drank a day. I wanted to know what he preferred to eat for breakfast. Maybe now we'd finally get the chance to figure those details out.

I turned to face him and then propped myself up to sit on the counter.

"When did you see my note?" I asked, anxious to know how my plan ended up working.

His eyes danced with the memory of it. "I saw them all over campus yesterday when I was going to pick up some school supplies. But it wasn't until I was sitting at a table in the union eating lunch earlier today that I actually read it. I guess someone had dropped a few on the tables because I was taking a bite of my sandwich and then I looked down to see that headline. I didn't believe it at first; I thought my eyes were playing a trick on me."

I felt weightless sitting on top of his kitchen counter. His voice carried hints of surprise, elation, *love*.

Then he swapped the topic on me in a flash. "How's your health? Is your heart okay?" he asked, crossing his arms and studying me intently.

"It's finally good, Beck. I've been on the same medication and dosage for eleven months. My immune system is as good as it can be while I take the medication. It won't be easy, but I already have a cardiologist up here and it's my top priority. I have an appointment with him tomorrow actually."

He nodded and closed his eyes as he inhaled deeply. Had he been worried about my health over the past year?

"Now it's my top priority, too. I'll drive you to your appointment tomorrow if you'll let me." His eyes flickered open again. They were a darker shade of hazel than usual.

He stared right at me as he crossed the kitchen and came to stand in front of me. His hands drifted up my knees and over my thighs. His thumb ran along the inseam of my jeans.

I mashed my lips together, unable to look away from his exploring fingers. With a gentle tug, he pulled my thighs apart so that he could step in between them. My hips were right on the edge of the counter, so when he stepped forward our bodies pressed together.

"I'd like that. Then maybe we can see if Sammy wants to get lunch or something," I asked, hopeful.

"Sounds good. My friend, James, just got back into town for classes, so I could invite him, too," he answered. He was still running his fingers along the inseam of my jeans, making it more and more impossible to concentrate on the here and now. His hands trailed up my jeans and traced along the bare skin that touched the hem. My stomach flip flopped and I felt my skin flush in response. His touch flooded me with warmth I hadn't felt since he left.

"Stay the night with me," he murmured, gently unbuttoning my jeans. By that point, I was beyond comprehension of things that didn't entail his touch on my skin. I'd sleep on the ground outside if it meant he wouldn't stop.

"Okay, but no sleeping," I grinned.

He chuckled and then grasped either side of my cheeks to tilt my mouth toward his. "Okay, no sleeping, Abby Mae."

I closed my eyes and pressed my lips to his. A glimpse of the old Abby, the pre-Beck Abby, flashed before my eyes and deep awareness spun through my mind.

My life had taken quite a few sharp turns in the past

few years. I'd prepared myself for the end and had come to terms with the abrupt conclusion life seemed determined to provide for me.

And then my beeper went off.

That archaic piece of technology vibrated on my night stand, telling me that I had a donor.

Suddenly, I had an abundance of life and no idea what I wanted to do with it. Being in Boston, in college, was a surreal feeling. I'd been given a second chance. A chance to make dreams and see them through. A chance to make mistakes and fight to make them right.

But it didn't always feel that way. When I first had the transplant, there was this immense pressure weighing me down at every turn. To prove I was worthy of receiving the heart, I felt like I had to live every single moment to the fullest. If I wasn't being the best, living the most, screaming the loudest, then I wasn't doing Colby's heart justice.

I was living for everyone around me. Caroline, Colby, my parents. I couldn't breathe for fear that the decisions I was making weren't the right ones.

I couldn't ignore the nagging questions in the back of my mind:

Are the lives of some people more valuable than those of others? Had the world lost more from Colby's death than it had gained from my life?

Is value based simply on one person's impact on the world around them? How many friends we leave behind in death?

A year ago I thought I knew the answer to those questions. But now I realize that no one has the capacity to judge the value of a human life.

We all value different things and life left out a

conversion chart *on purpose.*

We aren't supposed to know the answer.

I couldn't live for Colby or Caroline any longer.

The fact is, I was given a heart. I was given this gift of life that few receive and I had to decide how *I* wanted to use it. Not how others would deem noble.

So I finally stripped away the fear and anxiety, and suddenly life became crystal clear. I wanted to write. I wanted to create stories like the ones I'd written in my journal. I wanted to be with Beck, and I wanted to wake up each morning and appreciate the feeling of my heart beating beneath my scarred chest.

CHAPTER THIRTY-TWO

BECK

I couldn't believe she was finally back. The awkward, beautiful, unathletic girl that stole my heart when I was trying to steal hers. She looked so innocent perched up on my kitchen counter. I couldn't keep my distance from her. On some level I thought I should play it cool, but I wasn't fooling anyone. She'd kicked my ass last year when she told me to leave. I'd fought with her about it for a week, and when she brought it up again the day before I was scheduled to leave, I couldn't handle it. There's only so much a guy's ego can handle, and she crushed mine under her tiny frame as if I was wearing my heart on my sleeve.

Who knows, maybe I was.

I can't help it around her.

Her jade green eyes swam with desire as my hands drifted up over her slim stomach. I tugged her shirt over her head and tossed it onto the kitchen floor behind me. The sexy moan she didn't think I could hear told me how much she approved of each action.

"Abby…"

I stood back and stared at her for a moment, taking in her breasts hidden beneath a pink bra. I bent low and scooped her golden hair behind her shoulders so that I'd have better access to her chest. Her beautifully imperfect scar sat just where it had the last time I'd had a chance to be with her. I traced my fingers and lips along her collarbone, down the center of her ribcage, and around her scar in a testament to her innocent sexiness. That was the thing about Abby. She had no fucking clue what she did to me. She thought her Keds and girl-next-door style kept her safe, but in reality it just begged me to tease her more.

It drove me wild to see a side of her that no one else had the chance to witness.

"I've missed you so much," she murmured as my lips pressed against the small swell of her breast, just beneath her scar. Her words could undo me like no one else's. To know that she was here, healthy, and happy…I shoved the thought away and pulled her close to me. My hands wrapped around her hair as I forced her lips to mine. There were too many layers left between us. She was clinging to my shirt as my hands unclasped her bra. I needed her here and now. Our movements were urgent and hurried. Nails on skin, hands tugging off clothing. She was breathing hard and I could see her chest rising and falling in a quick rhythm.

With one hand I pulled my shirt off as my other wrapped around her as soon as the shirt was gone. She was so small in my arms, but she felt exactly like I'd remembered.

"Beck, not on the counter," she murmured, her lips dancing across my ear when she moved her mouth. "I feel like a knife is going to stab me in the butt or something." Her sentence started out lusty, but by the end I couldn't help but laugh. We both fell into hysterics and I lifted her up and away from any sharp utensils.

"Your choice: the bed or the futon." Our lips were pressed together and I could feel her smile against my mouth.

"You would have a futon."

My head tilted back far enough that I could look down at her.

Her smile was still there, just like mine had been since I saw that sign on the table in the union. I'd resigned myself to the fact that we were over. I thought she saw me as a summer fling, a guy to take her mind off the sadness surrounding those few weeks.

"How about against the wall?" she asked, pulling me out of my reverie. Her words were quiet and unsure, adding to her allure.

My feet started shuffling us backwards. "Like we almost did that first time?" I asked. I pressed her back against the wall and angled her so that our bodies met perfectly with her legs straddled around me. She was warmth, the type of warmth you had to earn. The type of warmth that sears your skin so that for as long as you live, your body remembers what it was like to be close to her, to be buried inside of her.

"Or the time in Marfa," she mentioned, her jade green

eyes clouding over with lust. I peeled my eyes down her pearly white skin. She was so soft and flushed with arousal, it was hard to decide if the appeal of making love to her against the wall was better than taking our time on my bed. Maybe we'd do that afterward.

"Tell me you love me, Abby," I demanded, kissing under her chin and down her neck. She arched away from the wall, pressing her skin against my lips for more. My mouth pressed against the chain of her locket and I smiled at the memory of the flea market.

"Beck," she began to answer, but I pulled one of my hands away from her hip to open the locket. I wanted to see if she'd replaced the old couple inside. The tiny hinge was hard to open, but she didn't rush me. The rising and falling of her chest pressed against my hand as I pulled the tinted metal open.

My body stilled.

Tucked inside were two pieces of paper; one on either side. The first had my name, written small and in cursive. The other held a small outline of Texas with tiny hearts over specific areas. She'd drawn a thin red line to connect the hearts. It was hard to see when it was drawn so small, but I tugged it closer to my face and then grinned when I realized what I was looking at.

Each heart was drawn over a city we'd visited a year ago.

She'd mapped out our trip and kept it in the locket over her heart.

Her hand wrapped around my fingers, tightening my hold on the tarnished locket. "I love you with this heart." She tipped her head forward and pressed a kiss to my lips. Then she moved her hand and pointed to her scar, to the beating heart that lay beneath, "and *with this heart*."

ACKNOWLEDGEMENTS

To my family for all of their unconditional support.

Mom, you are my first round beta reader and my books would never feel complete without your stamp of approval. You believed in Abby and Beck's story before anyone else.

Lance, thank you for all of your support. Thank you for reading and tweaking this book. You helped bring these characters to life, and there is quite a bit of your personality within Beck.

Thank you to all my beta readers: TK Rapp, Stacey Lynn, Brittainy C. Cherry, Jennifer Beach, and Cassidy Cayman. Your feedback was wonderful and truly, truly appreciated!

Thank you to my amazing editor over at Taylor K.'s Editing Services. This book might have never been published without your prodding, ha-ha.

Thank you to all of my fellow indie authors (within Author Support 101 & Write Club). I don't think I'd have the energy to write without the help from all of you ladies. Thank you for providing support and a sense of community within a crazy world!

Thank you to Gabby for your proofreading magic.

Thank you to everyone who accepted an ARC edition of this book and for giving Abby & Beck a chance.

Thank you to every awesome blogger that has pushed to get this story into the hands of readers. I couldn't do it without you guys.

Other Books by R.S. Grey:

Behind His Lens

Twenty-three year old model Charley Whitlock built a quiet life for herself after disaster struck four years ago. She hides beneath her beautiful mask, never revealing her true self to the world... until she comes face-to-face with her new photographer — sexy, possessive Jude Anderson. It's clear from the first time she meets him that she's playing by his rules. He says jump, she asks how high. He tells her to unzip her cream Dior gown; she knows she has to comply. But what if she wants him to take charge outside of the studio as well?

Jude Anderson has a strict "no model" dating policy. But everything about Charley sets his body on fire.

When a tropical photo shoot in Hawaii forces the stubborn pair into sexually charged situations, their chemistry can no longer be ignored. They'll have to decide if they're willing to break their rules and leave the past behind or if they'll stay consumed by their demons forever.

Will Jude persuade Charley to give in to her deepest desires?

Recommended for ages 17+ due to language and sexual situations.

Available on: AMAZON

Scoring Wilder

What started out as a joke— seduce Coach Wilder—soon became a goal she had to score.

With Olympic tryouts on the horizon, the last thing nineteen-year-old Kinsley Bryant needs to add to her plate is Liam Wilder. He's a professional soccer player, America's favorite bad-boy, and has all the qualities of a skilled panty-dropper.

• A face that makes girls weep – check.

• Abs that can shred Parmesan cheese (the expensive kind) – check.

• Enough confidence to shift the earth's gravitational pull – double check.

Not to mention Liam is strictly off limits. Forbidden. Her coaches have made that perfectly clear. (i.e. "Score with Coach Wilder anywhere other than the field and you'll be cut from the team faster than you can count his tattoos.") But that just makes him all the more enticing…Besides, Kinsley's already counted the visible ones, and she is not one to leave a project unfinished.

Kinsley tries to resist Liam as they navigate through forbidden territory, but Liam is determined to teach her a whole new definition of the term "team bonding."

A fun & sexy New Adult Romance. Recommended for ages 17+ due to language and sexual situations.

Made in the USA
San Bernardino, CA
22 January 2016